THE PROMISE
OF EASTER

Center Point
Large Print

Also by Marta Perry and available from
Center Point Large Print:

A Christmas Home
A Harvest of Love
How Secrets Die
The Second Christmas
A Springtime Heart
When Secrets Strike

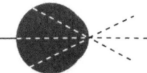

**This Large Print Book carries the
Seal of Approval of N.A.V.H.**

THE PROMISE OF EASTER

AN AMISH HOLIDAY NOVEL

Marta Perry

CENTER POINT LARGE PRINT
THORNDIKE, MAINE

This Center Point Large Print edition
is published in the year 2023 by arrangement with
Berkley, an imprint of Penguin Publishing Group, a
division of Penguin Random House LLC.

PUBLISHER'S NOTE: The recipes contained in this
book are to be followed exactly as written. The publisher
is not responsible for your specific health or allergy needs
that may require medical supervision. The publisher is
not responsible for any adverse reactions to the recipes
contained in this book.

The text of this Large Print edition is unabridged.
In other aspects, this book may vary
from the original edition.
Printed in the United States of America
on permanent paper sourced using
environmentally responsible foresting methods.
Set in 16-point Times New Roman type.

ISBN: 978-1-63808-656-7

The Library of Congress has cataloged this record
under Library of Congress Control Number: 2022949853

THE
PROMISE
OF EASTER

This book is dedicated to my granddaughter Estella Johnson in honor of her graduation and to my husband, for his unfailing support.

CHAPTER ONE

Matthew King took the first step on his long journey home and suddenly felt as if he'd walked into a wall of ice. The April day was sunny and warm, but Promise Glen itself was rejecting him. Even after nearly two years away, he still wasn't welcome.

"You sure about doing this?" The tart voice of his great-aunt echoed his thoughts. Aunt Ella stood in the doorway of her house, scanty white hair screwed back under a snowy kapp, her faded blue eyes as sharp as her voice.

"I have to." Matt didn't expect her to understand, but he knew he couldn't go on carrying his load of guilt. The need for relief pushed him into movement.

She sniffed. "No point in stirring up things to my mind, but you'll do what you want. You always did." The door closed with a snap, punctuating her words.

Aunt Ella's advice was typical of her. She had a sharp tongue, and she seemed to know everything that went on. No wonder most folks treated her with caution. Still, she was always fair. Whether she liked you or not, a person could count on her to be fair. Besides, she'd taken him in without question, and he owed her for that.

9

Once started, Matt kept on moving. It was less than two miles to the Stoltzfus farm—not much of a walk in Amish terms, but his years of living out in the Englisch world had changed a lot of things about him, including the fact that he drove a car, not a buggy.

He'd guess that nothing had changed here for his great-aunt or the rest of the Amish community. Mindful of Aunt Ella's feelings, he'd pulled his car into an unused corner of the barn and shoved bales of straw in front of it. He wouldn't care to offend the only person who'd shown any signs of welcoming his return.

The Amish clothes he'd once worn had been waiting for him, stored in a trunk in the attic, left here by his parents when they'd moved to upstate New York. Their rigid interpretation of Amish beliefs wouldn't allow them to destroy his clothes, but they didn't have any trouble cutting him off.

The clothes weren't a great fit. Two years of construction work had added both to his height and breadth. Still, he'd look Amish to strangers, and he'd still be recognized by the Amish community. They'd know him only too well. He was the man who'd let his best friend fall from Hawk Cliff to his death.

I shouldn't have come back. I had to come back.

The war raged in his mind as he strode along the lane bordered by the pale green growth of early spring. Given a few more days like this, the forsythia bushes would be covered with yellow blossoms. Too bad that the touch of spring didn't seem to bring any rebirth to him.

He hadn't come for that anyway, he supposed. He'd come to confess his guilt to those he'd hurt. He'd come to make whatever atonement he could. Then he'd leave again.

The lane into the Stoltzfus farm appeared on his left, and soon Matt was approaching the farmhouse. He couldn't help remembering how welcome he'd once been here. Filled with laughter, noise, warmth, and joy, it had been as different as could be from his own home.

Simon Stoltzfus had accepted his son's friend as an extra member of his own large family, doling out chores and advice impartially. His wife, Miriam, had dispensed hugs and food in equal measure, her love overflowing to everyone who entered her home.

They'd given all that to Matt, and he'd brought them the worst grief any parent could bear.

The lane curved as it approached the back of the house, and Matt cut through the windbreak of evergreens toward the barn. It was time for the afternoon milking, so he might catch Simon there alone.

As he neared the door, he caught the sound of voices—Simon and his father, the man Matt had always called Grossdaadi, were doing the work

11

together. Sucking in a deep breath, Matt stepped into the doorway.

The dimness inside contrasted with the bright afternoon sunshine, and he hesitated while his eyes adjusted.

"Who's there?" It was Simon's voice. To Simon, Matt would be a dark shadow against the sunlight.

"It's me." He stepped forward. "Matthew King." He stopped, holding himself rigid, waiting for the response.

"Matthew." Simon sounded choked. Then he stepped forward, his face working. "It is you. So you've come back." His arm moved, and before Matt could duck, it was warm around his shoulders. "Thank the gut Lord, you're back where you belong."

Unbelievably, Simon sounded glad to see him. Simon had never been demonstrative, not like Miriam, but here he was with his arm around Matt, holding him. "Look, Daad. Our Matthew has come home."

Matt's head was spinning. This wasn't going at all the way he'd imagined it. He struggled for words.

"Not home . . . I mean, I just came back to . . . to tell you how sorry I am . . . I should have been able . . ." His own voice choked now, and he couldn't get out the words he'd practiced.

"Ach, don't be so foolish." Simon grasped him

12

more tightly. "The past is over. You're here now, praise the gut Lord."

Matt sucked in a breath. "I came to tell you how sorry I am. I hoped maybe I could do something to help you . . . to make up for what James would have done."

Simon's hand, hard with years of physical work, pressed against his cheek for a moment. He didn't seem to know what to say.

"Help?" Grossdaadi's voice creaked, and as Matt's gaze focused on him, he saw the difference nearly two years of grief had made. The old man was as lean and weathered as his son, but his skin was crinkled as old leather, and he seemed in some way to have shrunk.

"You want to help, you can take over this milking stool for me, young Matt. My old bones don't get down so well anymore." He patted Matt's shoulder as he stepped away from the stool. "You haven't forgot how, have you?"

The familiar chuckle that seemed to underline everything the old man said warmed Matt. This was real. He'd come here to meet anger and blame and found only forgiveness. They had forgiven him, and all he could think was that he didn't deserve it.

Simon was chuckling, too, shoving him gently toward the waiting cow. "Course he hasn't forgotten. You taught him, remember? Show him you remember, Matthew."

13

He didn't seem to have a choice. He slid onto the stool, leaning against the cow's warm, smooth side, and hoped he wasn't going to make a fool of himself.

But apparently it would take more than two years to wipe away the familiar movements and the equally familiar gush of milk into the pail. The rhythm took over, and he began to relax for the first time since he'd left Aunt Ella's.

"You're staying over at Ella's, ain't so?" Grossdaadi's rumble of laughter sounded again. "You won't find her changed, that's certain sure. Ella just gets sharper with age. That's how it is. Us old folks get more of whatever we already are."

"Better not let Mammi hear you saying that." Simon winked at Matt. "She's still trying to reform you, ain't so?"

"That makes her happy, that's her way. My old woman is the sweetest thing that ever came out of Promise Glen. Did you know that every boy for miles around was after her, and she picked me? Still can't figure out why after all these years."

"Why don't you ask her?" Simon retorted.

Matt, listening to their familiar banter, found every muscle in his body had eased. He'd been geared up for a battle that hadn't come. Simon and his father were the same as they'd always been, still teasing each other about the same things, still working together with the pleasure that had been so missing between Matt and his father. Amid everything that had changed in his life, Matt was glad to find something the same.

"Matt, you'll stay for supper with us, yah?" Simon said. "Miriam and Grossmammi won't forgive us if we let you get away without seeing them . . . and the young ones, too. Ella will understand."

He opened his mouth to say he couldn't, and found instead that he was agreeing. It was too tempting to stay in this warmth a little longer. Besides, he hadn't really had a chance to say all he'd come to say.

The sound of a horse and buggy approaching the barn made Simon glance toward the door.

"That'll be Anna, coming home from school. You know she's the teacher at Orchard Hill now?"

"Yah, Aunt Ella told me." He shook his head. "Seems like little Anna can't be old enough to be the teacher."

"Don't let her hear you say that," Simon said. "She's a fine teacher, though I do say it myself, and she certain sure loves it."

Grossdaadi nodded in agreement. "How could the scholars help but learn when she gives them that sweet smile of hers? Like her grossmammi, she is."

The clink of harness told Matt that Anna was

unharnessing her horse. He lifted the full bucket, and Simon grasped it. "I'll do this. Go and greet Anna. It's been a long time."

Nodding, Matt stepped out of the barn and moved toward the buggy and the slim figure who was walking a bay mare from between the shafts.

"Anna?"

He watched her stiffen, spin, and fix an incredulous gaze on his face. She clearly couldn't believe what she was seeing.

And then she realized he was real, and he saw her heart-shaped face become rigid, as if carved out of ice. Only her deep blue eyes were alive.

Alive? They were on fire with fury at the sight of him. Now he'd found the reaction he'd expected all along.

Anna didn't know how long she'd been standing there, staring, until Daisy nudged her with that heavy head of hers, impatient to get into the pasture. Anna fought with the evidence of her own senses. Matthew King, here, in the place she'd thought he'd never have the nerve to come. How could he show up here, of all the places in the world?

The mare shoved her again, harder, pushing her forward a step. Once started, Anna kept on moving, aware only that the movement was taking her away from Matt.

16

As she fumbled with the gate into the pasture, he spoke, close behind her. "Sorry if I shocked you, Anna."

His familiar voice made the past rush in, flooding her mind with images. She could hear him and James laughing, teasing, sometimes fighting, but always together. Always together until that last night, when Matt wasn't where James needed him.

Why? the cry demanded. *Why didn't you save him?*

Her anger and grief welled, and she fought to contain her feelings, knowing what Daad's reaction would be if she burst out with all the anger and blame that filled her.

Daad didn't preach. He just lived his faith and expected his children to do the same. She struggled to say something that wouldn't offend.

"I didn't expect you to come back." She muttered the words, feeling as if pain crushed her chest. She stared at him, hardly seeing him for the haze of anger in front of her eyes. "Why? Why did you? Why are you here?"

Matt's face twisted. It was different from the face she remembered . . . leaner, with hollows under the cheekbones and a harsher look to the lines of his mouth and jaw.

"I had to." He seemed to force the words between firm lips.

Before she could repeat the question, Grossdaadi came out of the barn, gripping the door for a moment as he looked at them. His face broke into a wide smile.

"See, Anna. Isn't it wonderful gut that Matthew is back with his own people at last?"

She shouldn't say anything to upset her grandfather, but before Anna knew it, the words spilled out. "He doesn't have any people here anymore."

Her grandfather's expression showed disappointment as he moved toward them. "His parents may have moved away, but there's still his aunt Ella, don't forget. And more than a few cousins scattered around the county, I expect." He put one hand on her shoulder, and the other on Matt's, as if connecting them. "Besides, he's always been part of our family, ain't so?"

Anna stiffened. She glanced away with a gesture that might have meant anything. Grossdaadi's attitude didn't really surprise her. A devout man, he'd always put a high value on forgiveness, just as Daadi did.

They had never blamed Matt for what happened to James, but she did. Probably a lot of other people in the community felt the same way. Matt had better enjoy this welcome. He wouldn't get much from anyone else.

Daadi came out, wiping his feet as he always did when he left the animals, and smiled at them.

"You must be surprised at our Anna, yah, Matt? She's all grown up. How she makes boys bigger

18

than her behave is more than I can say, but she does."

Relieved at the change of subject, Anna answered at random, trying to think of something that would make Matthew go away. "Ach, I don't have any problem kids at Orchard Hill School. That would be silly. I know their parents too well." She took a step back, determined to end this conversation with Matt, even if she had to run for the house.

"Aunt Ella says there's a new family that bought the farm where we used to live," Matthew said, acting as if he had no plans except to stand here talking. "I guess you have their young ones, ain't so?"

She hadn't thought about the fact that the Burkhardt family lived next door to Ella. "Yah, two of them." Grudging the words, she added, "The boy is in eighth grade, and the little girl is our Micah's age." She hesitated. They were such recent arrivals that she hadn't gotten to know them yet. "They're just settling down," she said at last.

She turned toward the house. "I'd best help Mammi with supper. Goodbye, Matt." *Go away and stay away.*

Daadi spoke before she'd gotten more than three steps away. "Komm along in, Matthew. Miriam will be eager to see you, and supper will be ready in a few minutes."

Anna's throat tightened. So Matthew was going to be welcomed right into the house, despite the fact that just knowing he was breathing the same air made her feel sick. She bit her lip to keep from speaking and hurried inside.

The kitchen was as busy as always at this time of day. The Dutch oven on the back of the stove must contain pot roast, judging by the aroma. Mammi seemed to have one eye on it and the other on something she was stirring in the large saucepan.

As Anna came in, she turned toward her. "It's wonderful gut you're home." She gave Anna a quick hug that calmed Anna's stress. "You can finish the gravy for me in a minute."

Nodding, Anna tied a work apron over the dress she kept for teaching. "Did the kinder get home all right?" she asked, looking around for the three youngest of the family. Often they rode home with her in the buggy, but today had been such a warm afternoon that she'd sent them off with their classmates to walk home.

"Yah, they're here." Mammi wrinkled her nose and exchanged looks with Grossmammi, who was cutting fruit into a bowl.

"Betsy is unhappy with you," Grossmammi said, her keen blue eyes showing amusement. "Was ist letz?"

"She's fourteen, that's what's wrong." Anna resisted the temptation to say that her sister Betsy was unhappy with the world and everything in it. Today she'd started off irritating and progressed to obnoxious. "She didn't want to settle down when her grade was reading its assignment."

"Talking?" Mammi's eyebrows lifted. They all knew that Betsy had trouble keeping her opinions to herself, but by her age, a scholar should know how to behave.

"Don't say anything to her about it," Anna said quickly. "You only know because I'm her teacher, so . . ." She hesitated, sure there was something about the connection between sister and teacher that caused at least part of the problem.

Mammi, frowning, was opening her mouth as if to speak when the door opened, and there was Matt, coming in right behind Daadi, with Grossdaadi bringing up the rear.

"Matthew!" Mammi dropped the pot lid she was holding. It hit the floor with an echoing clang. Mammi nearly tripped on it rushing to grab Matthew in a strong embrace, hugging him close. "Thank the gut Lord. You're here."

"Let the lad breathe," Grossmammi said, but as Mammi drew back, Grossmammi clutched him just as hard.

Mammi wiped her eyes on a snowy dish towel. "Ach, you've surprised me so much I'm all befuddled."

"I'm sorry." Matt seemed to have trouble getting the words out. "James . . ."

21

Mammi was shaking her head already. "Foolish to cry, but I'm used to seeing the two of you together. I felt he should be here with you."

"He should be." His face was white. "I should have stopped him."

Anna had no space in her heart to be sorry for Matt. He *should* have stopped James.

"Now, stop that kind of talk." Grossdaadi looked as severe as Anna had ever seen him. "You aren't to blame for what happened. It was an accident."

If he said it was God's will, Anna thought she might scream.

But it was Grossmammi who had the final word. "James was in the Lord's hands, then and now." She reached up with a trembling hand to pat Matt's cheek. "And so are you."

Tears stung Anna's eyes, and she blinked them back furiously. Everything Grossmammi said was true, but her heart refused to be comforted. Whatever anyone said, James was gone. And Matthew, who should have helped him, was here in his place. It was too much to bear.

It wasn't long before Matt realized that the angry feelings Anna had toward him were obvious to everyone. He understood. While her elders were maybe too quick to forgive, Anna wasn't even trying. He didn't judge her. She was putting the blame on him, and she was right.

She'd been jealous of his close relationship

22

with James—the realization hit him like a blow to the chest. Why hadn't he seen it before this?

Anna and James had been only ten months or so apart in age, very alike with their thick blond hair and blue eyes. They'd been more like twins than ordinary siblings. But once there was another boy his age to play with, James had changed. She'd been left behind.

Not always, he told himself, struggling with looking at his past from this angle. But definitely when it was something James considered too dangerous for a girl.

As far as Anna had been concerned, nothing James could do had been too dangerous for her. She had been as daring as anyone, all the more surprising because she looked so sweet.

Did she feel differently about it now that she was a teacher? Having charge of a roomful of kids sounded scary to him, and Anna was responsible not just for teaching them but for keeping them safe. Safe. The very word made his heart wince.

He brushed those thoughts away. If he wanted to succeed in what he'd come here for, it would be better if Anna didn't vent her anger . . . at least not in front of her parents.

Fortunately supper seemed nearly ready, and the younger children began to troop into the kitchen, distracting everyone. They were accompanied by a stream of noise and laughter, which died away as they took in the fact that he was there. All those pairs of blue eyes focusing on him made him nervous, but at least they didn't look openly hostile, like Anna.

"Komm along to the table." Miriam clapped her hands. "Grace, set a place for Matthew between you and Betsy. Hurry up now."

Grace, who must be about ten now, managed to take her eyes off him long enough to fetch another plate and more silverware, obediently setting a place on the far side of the table. Then she resumed her careful study, as if weighing him in some balance of her own before making a decision about him. That almost made him more uncomfortable than Anna's reaction.

Betsy, a couple of years older than Grace, pulled a chair into place in front of the plate and silverware. She nodded to him, jerked out the chair to the right of his, and plopped down. Betsy must be nearing rumspringa age, but he didn't see any signs of it. She moved more like a boy than a girl, and her plain dress was the standard blue one mothers turned out almost automatically unless met by a demand for something pink or yellow or any color more feminine. Not that he knew a lot about it, but he remembered the array of colors on the girls in the classroom as they moved into seventh and eighth grades.

Just as they were about to sit down, the kitchen door opened again. This time it was a quiet entrance. Sally, who was the next daughter after

Anna, drifted in. Drifted, he decided, really was the right word. She looked around vaguely, as if not seeing anyone, and floated to the table.

Betsy, next to him, muttered something he didn't hear and then looked past him to Grace, on his left. "Look at her. What do you want to bet she's in love again?"

Grace rolled her eyes. "Who?" she whispered.

Betsy shrugged, looking disgusted. "Who knows?"

"Sally, you were nearly late for supper." Anna reached between him and Betsy to put a bowl of gravy on the table. "Did you need me to pick you up from work?"

"What? No, I had a ride." Sally pulled out her chair and glanced around the table, not seeming to notice that there was an extra person there. "Joseph Miller brought me home." She said his name reverently and then sighed.

"Why him?" Betsy muttered toward Matt, almost as if she were asking him. "Last week it was Adam Holst."

He shrugged, in case she was looking for a response, and cast his memory back a few years. That would be the Miller family that had a dairy operation, he supposed. He could barely picture a skinny, pimply kid, all arms and legs. Not someone you'd expect a girl like Sally to fall for.

Sally was pretty, with her rosy cheeks and the

eyes that seemed to smile at people. Prettier than Anna? He didn't doubt that most folks would say so. But Anna had something special, some quality that made a person look twice to notice the maturity in her eyes and the amazing sweetness of her smile.

Pushing away his impressions of a grown-up Anna, he reflected that Sally's boyfriend might have improved since Matthew had left. But judging by Anna's expression as she slid into a chair across from him, she didn't think much of her sister's choice.

Anna sat next to Micah, the baby of the family, and looking at him was the hardest thing yet. Micah looked exactly like James had at seven or eight. He had only to blink to see James sitting there, staring at him with those solemn blue eyes and that thick thatch of yellow hair.

Miriam put a basket of biscuits, warm from the oven, in front of him and took her seat. He started to reach for one, when he realized that everyone else around the table had closed eyes and bowed heads . . . everyone but Anna, that is. Her head was bowed, but she was watching him, and she gave him a disdainful stare as he snatched his hand back.

He'd been away too long. Imagine forgetting the silent prayer before meals. Matt shut his eyes and tried to wipe everything from his mind. It wasn't easy.

Finally he heard the rustle of movement that said Simon had finished. Platters and bowls began to sail around the table, and chatter broke out, relieving Matt of the need to say anything.

Too bad it was Anna who'd seen his error. She certainly had changed from the shy, sweet girl she'd once been. That girl would never have looked at him as if she challenged his right to breathe.

Well, he'd changed, too. What happened to James stood between them like an uncrossable chasm. It had changed Anna, and it had shattered everything he'd believed about himself.

"What have you been doing out there among the Englisch, Matthew?" Anna's grossdaadi looked as if he really wanted to know.

"Working construction, most of the time," Matt said, trying to make it sound normal. "I've been with a small family-owned operation near Baltimore for the past year."

"Why did you leave them?" Anna's voice had an edge that was just short of being an insult, as if implying he'd been fired.

Grossdaadi gave her a look that seemed to push her back in her chair. Isaac Stoltzfus was a kindly man, and everyone knew that, just like Simon, he expected the same standards from his family.

Matt spoke quickly, hoping to stave off any chiding the old man planned to give her. "I haven't left them, exactly. I took some time off after . . . after an accident."

It hadn't been his accident, but they didn't need to know that.

The image was never far from his mind, and it slid back now. Himself, high above the ground, seeing the panic in Kevin's face as Kevin clung desperately to the edge of a beam, fingers sliding . . .

It had been like James all over again until Matt had touched his hand, grabbing it.

"Whatever the reason, we're glad you came home." Miriam's voice was as gentle as her smile. "We hope you stay for a long time. At least you'll be here for Easter."

Anna clearly didn't wish any such thing, and the younger kinder looked either undecided, like Grace, or just uncaring, like Sally.

"What are your plans while you're here?" Simon asked, giving him the opening he'd been looking for.

"I was hoping to talk to you about that. I could use some advice." He waited, hoping that was the right approach to get the opportunity he needed.

"For sure. Once supper's over, we can have a talk."

Matt let go of the breath he was holding. That was one step forward. The next thing was to figure out what exactly he was going to say in that talk.

The meal ended with slabs of pumpkin pie topped with cream. He had to refuse more than once before he'd convinced Grossmammi that he didn't have room for more than the one huge slab she'd given him. She'd always been the one who'd pressed packets of brownies or cookies into his hands when he went home. Maybe his mother hadn't been much of a baker, but he hadn't been starving. Still, those brownies had a taste of love about them that had warmed his heart.

Another silent prayer announced that supper was over. This time he remembered to bow his head. Anna wasn't going to catch him again.

Chairs skidded against the wide oak floorboards, and plates rattled as everyone scraped and stacked. Grace had grabbed his plate, so he stood still and let them whirl around him. It had always been this way at James's house—noise and laughter and chattering. It carried him back to the days when he'd been a small boy, trying to figure out why this place was so different from his own home. He could recite the differences, but he could never figure out why.

Not then. Now he realized that his parents had been as disappointed with each other as they'd been with him. Not that they'd realized it. They'd had only one child, and he hadn't been able to fill what was missing in their lives. He hadn't even known what it was.

Matt made an effort to stay out of the way. Simon was giving some instructions to the younger ones, but he glanced across at Matt and pointed toward the door. "I'll meet you at the barn in a few minutes, yah?"

Matt nodded. He'd slip out now and have a moment to himself in the clear air. That should let him arrange his thoughts. He'd just . . .

He'd reached the mudroom between the kitchen and the back porch when someone grabbed his arm. Anna.

Frowning, he pulled his arm free. Or tried, but she didn't want to let go.

"What do you want to talk to Daadi about? Haven't you upset everyone enough already?"

He looked at her, knowing he couldn't find any way to express his agony of soul-searching, of trying to understand what had happened to him and finally to see what he had to do before he could go on.

He didn't even try. And she wouldn't understand or forgive no matter what he said. She'd already judged him and found him guilty. There was no way back with her.

CHAPTER TWO

Daad had called Matt away before Anna had a chance to push him into answering her question. She might not have succeeded anyway, she realized. Matt didn't look like he'd give in to pushing.

He had grown into a man while he'd been away from Promise Glen. Pushing him, with his broad shoulders and sturdy frame, would be like pushing a boulder, and she might not have gotten any better results.

Later. She'd watch for her chance to see him alone. He had to understand. It wasn't right for him to come back and reopen a wound that had barely begun to heal.

She kept an eye on the barn door from the kitchen window, but a half hour passed with no sign of him. Could she have missed seeing him leave?

Anna pulled on her thick black sweater against the evening chill and set off to find out for herself. If they were still talking, Daadi wouldn't welcome her butting in on a private conversation. Still, maybe there'd be a chance to catch Matt.

She spotted Betsy walking toward her from the chicken coop, striding along with a purposeful step. Betsy always looked full of energy when it was a question of the outside chores. She wasn't so enthusiastic about the chores Mammi planned for her inside.

For the past year, as Betsy neared the end of her school years and her own rumspringa began to loom ahead of her, she'd been trying to convince her family that when it came to farm work, she could do everything a boy could do.

Why? That was just one of the things Anna hadn't figured out about this sister of hers. Was it just that leaving the familiar world of school and childhood behind frightened her? She remembered that difficult period when a girl was bouncing between childhood and being a young adult.

At least Betsy didn't imagine she was in love with someone every other week, like Sally.

Betsy caught her eye. "If you're looking for Matt, he's gone," she announced as soon as they came within earshot of each other.

"Why would you think I was looking for him?" She plunged on, knowing she wasn't doing a very good job of covering up her feelings. "Gone? Gone home, you mean? Or doing something with Daad?"

Betsy shrugged. "Home, I guess. Anyway, I saw him walking away toward the road."

"It doesn't matter." Anna shrugged, trying to look as if she were totally unconcerned about what Matthew did or didn't do. "I need to talk to Daad, that's all."

"I wouldn't," Betsy said. "Not now. I tried to

tell him something, and he about bit my head off." She grimaced. "Not like Daad at all. So don't go making it worse, whatever it is."

If Daad was cross after his conversation with Matt, she wanted to know why. What right had Matt to come here and stir up people's feelings?

"I'll see what's wrong."

She headed for the open doors of the barn, trying to ignore the fact that Betsy was shaking her head behind her. Just because Daad wouldn't talk to Betsy, that didn't mean he wouldn't open up to her.

A few minutes later she was back again. Turned out she'd been wrong. Daadi, always so approachable, had no time for her. Or anyone, it seemed, right now.

"Told you so." Betsy was still standing where she'd been, apparently just for the purpose of annoying her big sister.

Anna glared at her. "Don't you have something useful to do? Like your homework, for instance?"

"You're not my teacher here, you know. So stop acting like it."

Pressing her lips together, Anna vowed not to let anything else critical come out. She'd just promised herself that she'd keep her roles as teacher and sister separate, and she'd broken that promise already.

Anna shoved her annoyance to the back of her mind. It wasn't Betsy's fault that Matt was causing problems. Or that Daadi was cross.

"Sorry, Betsy. You're right. I'll try to do better."

Betsy went from open-mouthed surprise to grudging acceptance. "Okay. Guess I shouldn't have . . . well, you know."

"Yah, I know." Anna managed a smile. "Ready to go in?"

Betsy nodded, and they walked to the back door together. "Seemed funny," Betsy said. "Matt being here, I mean. I thought maybe we'd never see him again after he jumped the fence."

Anna's stomach twisted at the words. "I was surprised, too."

Surprised? Surprised was too mild a word for her feelings, but she figured she should keep that to herself.

Mammi and Grossmammi were both in the kitchen, puzzling over a piece of paper Grossmammi held.

"Here, Anna, see if you can read this writing for us. It's too faded to make out." Grossmammi thrust the paper at her.

"What is it?" Anna slid out of her sweater and took the paper closer to the lamp. "Osterbrot," she said, making out the light pencil marks on a much-creased, yellowing paper. "It's your mammi's recipe for Easter bread, ain't so? Are we making it already?"

The Easter bread was a tradition in the family, not usually made this early, because they didn't eat it until Easter morning, when Lent was over. Grossmammi always insisted her mother's recipe was the only genuine one, and other people's versions were nothing to compare with it.

"I'm not making it for us yet," Mammi said. "But Grossmammi wants to make a loaf for Elmer Miller, since he's all alone this year."

Elmer Miller had plenty of family who could provide him with Easter bread, but Anna knew if Grossmammi thought they should do it, there'd be no argument about it.

"Why not for us?" Betsy leaned over her shoulder to glance at the recipe. "I love Easter bread. You'll put the almonds and apricot jam on it, won't you?"

She looked anxiously at Grossmammi, eager to be sure the Osterbrot would be as good as ever. After weeks of Lent, everyone loved the sweet Easter treat.

Grossmammi patted her hand. "Don't worry yourself, Betsy. When it's time, we'll make it for us, and you'll get plenty. You can brush the glaze on yourself. It's time you learned a bit more baking."

Anna's lips twitched. Betsy's eagerness to take over the farm work didn't include cooking and baking.

"What do you need done, Mammi? Do you want me to copy this out in ink for you so it won't fade?"

"Ach, denke, that's just what I want. In your gut teacher printing, too." Mammi's eyes twinkled. "I think we might have spilled milk on this too often."

"I want this paper kept, though," Grossmammi said, touching the paper lightly. "It's in my own mammi's hand."

"For sure," Mammi said quickly. "Just let Anna have it long enough to copy, and then you can put it away in the family Bible."

The family Bible not only held the complete genealogy of the family going back to the Swiss Germans who'd come to America in the 1700s, but it had become the repository for all sorts of letters and papers Grossmammi wanted to save.

Anna hurried to get pen and paper and settled down at the kitchen table with her grandmother there to fill in anything Anna couldn't read.

"Osterbrot is special, ain't so?" she said, to get her grandmother talking. She loved hearing Grossmammi's memories of how things used to be.

"Very special." Grossmammi pressed the paper flat with thin fingers that seemed to tremble a little. "Our family came to Philadelphia with the first few groups of Amish, and this tradition came with them."

"We do love it. Maybe we should make some extra loaves for the family, the way Betsy is eating these days."

"There will be enough for us and for all the neighbors." Grossmammi spoke placidly. She seemed to study Anna's face as the neat lettering appeared on the paper. "Now tell me what is troubling you."

Anna glanced at her in surprise. She hadn't shown a thing in her face, had she? But not only could her grandmother see what was behind her back, as the younger ones insisted, she could also see whatever you were hiding. She didn't always bring it out into the light, but she always saw.

"I guess it's no good saying there's nothing?" Anna ventured.

Grossmammi shook her head, her eyes amused. "No gut at all."

Anna frowned down at the paper as she completed the copy. "I wanted to know why Matthew was so eager to talk to Daadi. And what he's doing here."

"He told us why he's here. He had some time off his job. And as for what he had to say to your father . . . well, maybe you should ask him if you need to know what Matthew said."

Anna wrinkled her nose, suspecting Grossmammi of leading her right into how she had to answer. "I tried. Daadi said to leave him alone."

Her grandmother smiled. "Then you'd best do that. Whatever the problem is, your father is well able to deal with it without your help, ain't so?"

Anna felt her cheeks growing pink. "Yah, I know. It's just . . ."

"Just what?" Grossmammi put her hand over Anna's. "You don't want to be reminded of James, is that it?"

"Ach, no! I could never forget James. I wish I felt I could talk about him more, but I'm afraid of making Mammi sad."

Grossmammi considered, her wrinkled face carrying the weight of her years. She sighed and seemed to choose her words carefully. "It must always make us sad that James is not with us anymore. But when we tell stories about him and laugh at the funny things he said . . ." Grossmammi's eyes grew bright with tears. "It brings him back to us for a little while."

Nodding, Anna blinked back her own tears and wondered if her throat was too tight for speech.

But it seemed Grossmammi wasn't finished, because her hand tightened on Anna's. "You must search your heart, little Anna. You are holding a grudge against Matthew. Isn't it time you let it go?"

"I can't." She wanted to cry out the words, but she whispered them instead. She put her hands over her face for a moment. "He should have stopped James from doing something so foolish."

"Ach, now you are the one being foolish." Grossmammi's voice had become firm. "No one could have known what would happen to James that night—not you, not anyone. Each of us must wish we had done something to stop him from being there, but we didn't. The sooner you accept that, the better."

"Matthew could have . . ." she began, her voice stubborn.

"Stop that." Grossmammi took her hand away, making Anna feel cold and alone. "You must ask forgiveness, Anna. Stop and think. We are told that we must not come to the Lord's table if we have anything against a brother or sister in the faith. Think how you'll feel if you could not take part in the Spring Communion. Make yourself right with others so you can bring an open heart to the table."

The tears were coming down Anna's cheeks now. Grossmammi slipped a tissue into her hand, and Anna pressed it against her eyes and tried to straighten out her scrambled thoughts. Everything Grossmammi said was right. Anna should do it. But she couldn't suppress the stubborn anger inside that kept forgiveness far away.

Aunt Ella was fixing supper, and probably taking more trouble with it than she did when she was here by herself. Feeling he should make some return for her hospitality, Matt had found an old stepladder in the shed and set it up next to the back porch roof, where several shingles had blown off.

He took a deep breath, shook the stepladder

to be sure it was steady, and went up a step. He paused there, checking his reactions, needing to be sure panic wasn't going to swamp him.

Another step would put the low roof within reach. Not bad, he told himself, and went up another rung, gripping it firmly, and reminding himself that he was only a couple of feet from the ground. He could do this.

Funny. Under ordinary circumstances, a woman like Aunt Ella would have dozens of kinfolk in the valley, all lining up to help with her house repairs. But his own branch of the King family hadn't produced many offspring. With his parents moved away, there weren't many left. The least he could do was take care of a few repairs while he was here.

Besides, it kept his mind from going over and over his encounter with the Stoltzfus family. Their reactions had been mixed, but that was probably better than he'd had any right to expect.

Nothing mixed about Anna's opinion, though. She'd be glad to see the back of him.

As for the request he'd made of Simon once he'd gotten him alone . . . no answer, unless you could call his startled, almost appalled expression an answer. At least Simon had said he'd think it over. All he could do now was wait for an answer. If Simon rejected him . . .

He really didn't want to think about that possibility. He'd become convinced that the answer to his problem was here in Promise Glen, where it had started. He couldn't conceive of a solution that would take him anyplace else.

Reaching to put a new shingle in place, Matt managed to drop an entire handful of nails. Muttering to himself, he started to climb down only to find a hand reaching up, holding four or five of them.

Two kids, a boy and a girl. The boy was older, probably thirteen or fourteen, and he was the one holding up the nails while the little girl squatted, searching through the gravel for the rest.

Matt accepted a couple of nails. "Denke. You two are from next door, ain't so?"

The boy nodded. "I'm Thomas. This is Rebecca."

Thomas seemed sturdy for his age, with shoulders already broad and strong hands. His expression must put folks off, though. He looked sulky, as if he didn't see anything he liked in this new place.

Rebecca, the little one, didn't look up enough to give him an opportunity to see her face. Shy, probably.

Matt smiled down at them. "Gut to meet you. Did you come to see Ella?"

Thomas gave a quick shake of his head to the question. "We saw you working." He apparently considered that enough of an answer. Thomas didn't seem to waste any extra words. So far, little Rebecca hadn't said anything at all.

They'd seen him and come to watch him working. Well, that was fine with him. At least they didn't babble, like some kids.

After another five minutes he decided silence could be overdone. "I hear you just moved in a few weeks ago. How do you like it so far?"

To his astonishment, little Rebecca buried her face against her brother's arm. But not before he'd seen the tears.

He plunged into speech, embarrassed. "Sometimes it's hard to get used to a new place." He should know. "It'll be better after you get to know some more people. There must be kids your age at school."

"Yah." That was Thomas's answer, while Rebecca wiped her cheeks with her sleeve.

Matt's curiosity propelled the next question. "How do you like Teacher Anna?" Living where they did, they had to go to Orchard Hill School.

Thomas shrugged. "Okay, I guess." Rebecca pinched his arm. Thomas looked at her and then shrugged. "Rebecca says she's nice."

Matt gave a final tap to the last shingle and looked down at them. "Doesn't Rebecca . . . talk?"

The two exchanged glances, and Thomas answered for her. "Sometimes."

It might be interesting to hear what Teacher Anna thought about her new pupils. Not that she was likely to talk to him about it. Or anything else.

Gathering up his tools, he paused for a moment

before starting down, reminding himself of how close the ground was . . . He realized that Thomas had reached out to take the tools, and Matt handed them over gladly. At least that way he could keep both hands on the ladder as he stepped down.

Thomas hovered over Matt while he put the tools away in his toolbox, breathing down his neck.

"You're a carpenter? Was that what you did out there?" A jerk of the head seemed to indicate the world outside the valley.

"Construction work," he said shortly, beginning to wonder how he was going to get rid of them now that he'd finished his chore. It seemed rude just to put down his tools and walk away. "Not fine carpentry."

"It sounds like a gut job. You must have made a lot of money there among the Englisch."

Matt had to smile, remembering his reaction to his first paycheck. "Maybe, but it costs a lot more to live out there on your own."

The boy shrugged that off. "Yah, but you were free to do what you wanted, ain't so?"

An alert rang in his mind. It wouldn't do his stay here any good if folks started thinking he was encouraging kids to leave. "Not exactly. No matter where you are, there's going to be somebody telling you what to do . . . bosses, landlords, people like that."

"Might be better than . . ." Thomas stopped as the back door opened.

Aunt Ella appeared, holding a plastic bag containing cookies. "I saw you kinder were watching Matthew. I thought you might like to have a snack." She handed the bag to Thomas. "Share with your sister, now."

"Yah, I will." Thomas smiled.

Matt blinked. The smile made him look like a different kid, someone young and alive.

Just as quickly, his face slid back into sullen lines. He took his sister's hand. "Gotta get home for supper." He turned away, then glanced back at them. "Denke."

It wasn't clear which of them the thanks was aimed at.

Matt picked up his toolbox once they'd gone. "Funny kids."

That earned him a frown from his aunt. "Those kids have trouble. Anyone can tell that. If you weren't so set on your own problems, you might see other people's."

She stamped back into the house, leaving him alone and staring after her.

Anna liked to spend the trip home from school thinking back over the day, holding each of her scholars in her thoughts. Who had had a good day, who had seemed out of sorts or easily distracted or cross? Had each of them had his or her share of their teacher's attention?

Unfortunately, the next day her thoughts kept

bouncing from her scholars to Matthew and back again. She'd had no chance to speak to Daad alone yesterday, and this morning he had turned such a forbidding expression on her when she tried to bring up the subject that she'd backed away.

Scholars, she reminded herself. The school year was growing short, and she wanted to feel that she'd given her best to each child in her care. She couldn't do that if she was constantly distracted.

Take the two new children, now. They puzzled her by their withdrawn attitudes. She hoped it was just the inevitable need to adjust to a new place, but she couldn't be sure.

Look at Thomas, for instance. He was big and strong for his age, which would usually make him popular among the older boys for their daily baseball games. But his face seemed constantly set in sullen, sulky lines, and they tended to avoid him.

It would be easy to think Thomas a trouble-maker just because of the way he looked, but she couldn't let that make her feel negative toward the boy. She had to give him a chance to prove himself.

As for the little sister . . . well, she was quiet and well-behaved, but maybe too quiet. She'd answer a direct question in a whisper, but otherwise, Anna couldn't get a word out of her. Maybe if she asked them to stay and help her with something, she could get to know them better.

Daisy turned automatically into the lane, and Anna shook her head. She'd driven the last mile without paying attention to what she was doing. There were enough accidents on the roads without her contributing by her inattention, like those Englisch teenagers glued to their cell phones.

Right now she'd best focus on another try at talking to Daad. If she could only find him alone . . .

She was being guided, it seemed, because when she pulled up at the barn, Daadi walked toward her. He gave her a hand as she hopped down.

"Was it a gut day at school today? Or have the scholars all got spring fever on these nice days?" He smiled as if his earlier withdrawal had never been. Or maybe as if he wanted to make up for it.

"Plenty of spring fever going around among the older ones," she said lightly. "And I'm afraid Grossmammi's usual remedy of blackstrap molasses won't cure what ails them."

Daad chuckled. "Some things you can't prevent, and one of them is boys and girls noticing each other when they get to the right age. And after Easter passes, they'll all be so eager for the last day of school that you'll need to lasso them to get them to pay attention."

"That's for sure."

Anna hesitated, reluctant to break into the

46

friendly chatter with something that might upset him, but she had to speak while she had the chance. If she waited, someone was sure to interrupt.

"Daadi, I can't stop thinking about Matthew being here. Won't you tell me what he wants?" She tried not to let her own feelings toward Matt leak into her words.

Daad frowned, staring down at the harness buckle in his hand as if he didn't see it. When he finally spoke, it seemed he was talking to himself.

"Everyone will have to know sometime, I guess," he murmured. He seemed to make up his mind, and he looked steadily into her face. "Matthew came to ask me if he could help us on the farm this spring."

She froze. Matthew, helping with the farm work, here every day, probably even having meals with them. It couldn't be.

"Ach, Daadi, no. You can't. How could you even think of it?"

The lines of Daad's weathered face seemed to tighten. "Matthew has been as close to us as family for a long time. He was James's best friend. What is more natural than for him to help with the spring planting?"

"It's *not* natural." She forced the words out from a tight throat. "Not to have Matt here every day, reminding us that he is here and James isn't.

47

Reminding us that if he had done what he should, James wouldn't have died."

"Anna." His voice was sharp. "I won't have you talking that way. You've no reason to hold Matthew at fault in James's accident. We have told you that before."

She managed to swallow a tart retort. Yah, they had told her that, but she didn't believe it. James had always gone where ever Matthew led. And that night it had been fatal.

"I'm sorry, Daadi. I just don't feel that way."

He shook his head. "Then you must either change your feelings or refuse to be controlled by them. Set your mind on forgiveness, if you can't do anything else."

Anna had nothing more to say, and it seemed her father didn't, either. His face dark with disappointment, he turned away and walked toward the house.

Forgiveness. A keystone of Amish belief. Their history was filled with stories of forgiveness, even for those who persecuted them. She'd always imagined that she would act the same in the place of those martyrs of the faith.

Right up until she faced a loss so painful that it threatened to consume her. And then she couldn't forgive.

Maybe, in time, she would be able to master her feelings, but not now. It was too soon and the pain of losing James too sharp. To see Matthew every day, to see him working at the jobs James had once done . . . she couldn't bear it.

She stood where she was for a moment, and then she started to re-buckle the harness, settling it on the mare's back. There was one way to prevent it that she could see. Matthew himself must decide to give up this idea of his and go away. She'd have to make him see that . . . now, before it was too late.

CHAPTER THREE

When Anna headed back out onto the road again, Daisy turned her head as if to ask a question. This was clearly not what was supposed to happen after she had brought Anna home from school, as far as Daisy was concerned.

"Step up, Daisy." It was an impatient mutter, and the mare moved on. It seemed even Daisy didn't approve of her actions. At least the mare didn't know anything about her thoughts.

Forgiveness. She tried to push the word and all its connections out of her mind. She knew that everything Daad had said was true, and yet it didn't seem to make a dent in the coldness that gripped her heart when she thought about James's death.

She had to talk to Matthew—had to find out why he wanted to do this thing. Didn't he realize that it would be painful for all of them? Or didn't he care?

Anna's thoughts couldn't seem to get beyond that, revolving with the turn of the buggy wheels. Ahead of her she could see the gateposts that marked Ella's drive. Too soon. She hadn't figured out what to say. Maybe she should have walked. That would at least give her more time to think out her approach.

Ella would be there at this time of day, and Anna couldn't take her feelings about Matt out on his aunt. Ella wasn't to blame, although if she hadn't taken him in—

Anna stopped, aghast at her own thoughts. Despite what she thought of Matt's return, she had no right to blame Ella. Daad would say she should be ashamed of herself, and she'd have to agree.

Halfway to the hitching rail at the back door, Anna saw movement at the kitchen window. Not Matt . . . it was his aunt.

The buggy came to a stop at the hitching rail. As she slid down from the seat, Daisy gave a look at the daffodils along the porch, as if wondering whether they were edible or not. Anna fastened the line short enough to discourage any sampling. Or stepping on them before they'd had a chance to open.

Ella opened the door, nodding to her. "Good to see you, Anna."

"And you," she replied, her mind going blank. She glanced again at the flowers. "Looks as if your daffodils will be in full bloom by Easter, ain't so?"

"Maybe past it, if the days stay this warm." Ella didn't even glance at the flowers. She focused in on Anna, her eyes keen. "You didn't come here to talk about flowers. Matthew is in the barn."

Anna felt the color come up in her cheeks, and

she tried to find something to say. There wasn't anything. With an embarrassed nod, she headed for the barn.

Ella never changed . . . she just got a little sharper as she grew older. She always had come right to the point, and she had little patience with folks who didn't do the same.

Realizing that she was walking uncomfortably fast, Anna slowed a little. There was no point in racing as if running away from Ella. Or toward Matt.

She took a steadying breath as she stepped into the barn, standing still for a moment to allow her eyes to become accustomed to the dimness. As they did, she saw that the barn had only one stall in use. Ella wouldn't have need for more than the one buggy horse that took her to town for shopping and to worship. The elderly mare reached her head over the stall bar and breathed hopefully in Anna's direction.

Anna patted the mare, noticing the gray hairs on the muzzle. The horse was here, but Ella had said Matthew was, too, and she didn't see anyone. She was about to call out, when a noise above her head drew her attention. The sound of something sliding was capped by a hammer's tapping.

Moving back a few steps brought Matt into view. He hadn't seen her yet. On his hands and knees, he was nailing a board into place on the loft floor, his expression intent and his arm moving in smooth, even strokes.

He thought he was alone, she guessed, and his face had relaxed from the tense, almost angry expression he'd worn the last time she saw him. He looked younger . . . that was it. More like the boy he'd been than the man he was.

The horse whickered, and Matt looked down and saw her. Nothing moved . . . they looked at each other, that was all. But Anna felt some faint shift in the atmosphere in that moment.

She gave her head an impatient shake. "Can we talk?"

Matt's face, looking down at her from above, slowly tightened until all the youth was gone from it. He gave a short nod, ducking his head as he rose, and moved to the ladder.

He came down the first few steps of the ladder slowly, but when he reached the second one, he dropped lightly to the floor. When he faced her, his expression was carefully guarded.

"What is it?"

"I came . . ." She hesitated, because a change had come over him quite suddenly. His face lightened into eagerness.

Before she could finish, he took a long stride toward her. "Did your father send you with a message for me?"

Hope blossomed in his eyes. He didn't realize that Daad had not made a decision yet.

The craziest of ideas slid into her mind. She could tell him . . . tell him her father said no. Then he'd go away and leave them alone.

No, she couldn't. That would just compound her lack of forgiveness with falsehood. There seemed no end to the problems she could get into.

"Daad didn't make any decision yet, but he told me what you want."

Disappointment sucked the light from his face. "Then why are you here?"

"That's my question." The words burst out. "Why, Matt, why? Don't you realize how much it hurts to see you? To be reminded . . ." Her throat closed.

He didn't speak, but his golden-brown eyes darkened so that they were almost black, boring into her as if he'd see right through to her inner-most self.

"Don't you want to remember James?"

That brought her voice back in a hurry. "I want to remember him the way he was. You remind me of how he died."

He just stared for another moment, and she surged on, determined to get it out. "Why, Matt?" she cried again. "Why did you come back?"

The mask that hid his face seemed to crumble as he stared at her. "Because I couldn't do anything else. Because I had to. Because there's no place else for me to go."

• • •

Matt clamped his lips together. He'd already said more than he should. Fortunately Anna was so angry with him that she probably wasn't even listening.

Anna shook her head, more as if to clear it than to reject his words. "You couldn't think you'd be welcome here. This isn't your home any longer."

"No." He could feel cold envelop his heart. "Your parents are supposed to stand by you no matter what, aren't they? My father and mother started a new life for themselves, up among the Swartzentrubers in New York State. I'm certain sure not welcome there."

"I . . . I'm sorry about that." The genuine feeling in her voice disturbed him. Maybe it was possible for her to understand.

"Don't be. You know what my home life was like."

"That's why I'm sorry." She hesitated, and when she glanced up at him, she had a lost expression. "Your parents—"

"Yah." His mouth twisted. His quick comment had been accurate. Anna had known what his family was like. How could he forget the afternoon she'd stumbled on him hiding behind the barn, nursing his bruises?

He'd poured out everything to her unwilling ears, trying to make her see that the bruises on his body were the least of it. What a fool he'd been to say anything. She'd only been twelve or so then, certainly not old enough to understand. He'd only hurt her sensitive heart for no reason. She couldn't have helped him. No one could.

"They don't matter," he said quickly. "I didn't expect anything else from them."

She turned away, staring at the mare as if looking for an answer that didn't come.

There weren't any answers. His mouth tightened on the thought. They may as well focus on what she wanted, because nothing else mattered now.

"Look, Anna, you blame me for James's death. I understand. But you can't blame me any more than I blame myself."

Anna swung back to him, anger flaring in her eyes again. "James always followed you." She flung the words at him, and her meaning was clear. James followed him.

Not that night, he thought, but he didn't bother to say it. Whatever James had done fueled by his own daring and the alcohol that had flowed at that party, Matt still felt responsible.

"I should have saved him." He said the words out loud. That was always the bottom line, no matter what else was said.

"You should have." She said what he'd expected, but without the anger that had been there a moment ago. Her voice trembled. Her anger was swallowed up in sorrow. "He . . . he was gone so quickly. We didn't have a chance to . . ."

"No." He understood. No one had a chance to say goodbye. Not even him, and he'd been there. A sense of hopelessness swept over him. "What do you want from me, Anna? I can't bring him back."

"Just . . . just go away from here. We don't need you."

He sucked in a breath and tried to focus on what had seemed a clear leading to come back. "*You* don't, but can you speak for your father? Or your grandfather? Don't they need some help? That's all I've come for—to do what I can for them. Then I'll go away again."

"Back to your job?"

He managed a smile. "Yah, back there. Don't you believe I have one?"

Embarrassment tinged her cheeks. "I . . . I'm sorry if I acted as if you were lying about it. If it's any consolation, Grossmammi lectured me about it."

"It's okay." His tension eased as he saw the Anna he'd once known so well . . . the Anna whose sensitive heart always reached out to anyone who was hurting. "I came because I felt like . . ." He hesitated. "It seemed to me there was something I could do here."

"For us? Or for yourself?"

That showed a keener insight than he'd expect of Anna. "For your daad, mostly. You can't say he doesn't need it. Grossdaadi is getting older,

57

and he even said to me that he can't do what he used to. And Micah's only eight."

"You're forgetting the girls."

His lips twitched, but he controlled a smile. "You're teaching all day. And it looks like Sally has a lot of other things on her mind."

"You noticed." She couldn't stop a smile. "All right, granted, but the younger ones do help, and Daad never complains."

"Would you expect him to?" he countered.

"I guess not," she said, sounding reluctant. "But I don't want . . ."

"You don't want to see me. Fair enough. I'll try to stay out of your way. But if your father needs my help, I'm going to give it." He paused, struggling to be fair to her and not wanting to ruin this fragile understanding between them. "You were right about one thing, though. I am doing this for me, too. I can't go back without being sure I've done what I can here."

He couldn't go back until he'd gotten rid of the burden that had been riding him. At a practical level, he'd be no good to the construction company the way he was. Not unless he could figure out how to build a house without ever getting more than a few feet off the ground.

Anna couldn't know what he was thinking, of course, but she studied his face, frowning, for what seemed a long time.

"All right," she said finally. "If Daad really

wants this, I won't try to argue him out of it. Not that I could anyway. But don't expect any sympathy from me."

"I don't expect that from anyone. I know better." Life had taught him that, at least.

Anna glanced at the schoolroom clock. It was nearly noon, and a certain level of restlessness told her that her scholars were aware of the time. Lunchtime was always welcome, and especially so on Friday.

She glanced toward the window. None of the trees around Orchard Hill School were leafing out yet . . . it was too early for that. But off in the distance there was a pale green haze over the ground and the hedgerows. Spring would be here soon. And Easter, too—the first Sunday after the first full moon after the spring equinox. She'd used calculating the date of Easter as part of an arithmetic lesson for the middle grades, and the scholars had really gotten into that. Maybe it would help them remember what the vernal equinox actually was, but she didn't count on it.

"Let's start cleaning up for lunch now. Quietly, please," she added, knowing how quickly the children could react.

The murmur of voices and the clatter of desk-tops were expected, but the primary grades seemed to be carrying on a little more than usual.

"Ask her, Micah," someone said.

"Yah, ask her."

She pinpointed the two girls who were prompting her little brother.

"Ask me what?" she inquired.

Micah glanced at his classmates and cleared his throat. "Anna, could . . . I mean, Teacher Anna, could we have lunch outside today?"

Her lips twitching, Anna focused on the second graders. "Are you sure everyone wants to? Maybe they'd rather stay in."

A lot of heads shook at that. "Please, Teacher Anna," someone else said, and Anna looked around as if considering all the hopeful faces.

Her smile broke through. "All right, we'll have lunch outside, but not until everything is cleared up."

Judith, her assistant teacher, walked through the aisles, checking that schoolbooks were back inside the desks and pencils lay in their proper place. The younger scholars sat very still, probably trying to impress her with how obedient they were. Finally she nodded, satisfied.

"All right, take your lunch bags and file outside with your class. First ones out can help Teacher Judith to wipe off the picnic table."

With a bit of shuffling and chatter, her scholars started out, accompanied by Judith with the paper towel roll. Anna waited, as she always did, collecting her own lunch bag and thermos. As the last few scholars started out, she stepped forward and then slowed. Rebecca stood by her desk, looking a little lost. After a moment Micah came back and stood with her. He didn't seem to know what to do.

"What's wrong, Rebecca? Don't you want to go outside to eat?" She walked over to them.

There was no answer, but a tear glistened on the child's cheek. Her heart giving a sudden lurch, Anna knelt beside her.

"Komm now. Tell me what's wrong."

"She doesn't have her lunch bag," Micah said after a glance at Rebecca.

"She . . . we forgot our lunches today." Thomas stood just inside the classroom door, his face reddening.

"Ach, is that all?" Anna kept her tone light, even as she wondered. "That happens. I have more than I want today, so I'll share with you." She plopped her own bag on the desktop.

Micah hurriedly followed suit, dropping his next to her. "Yah, me, too."

Anna pulled two paper bags from the supply in her desk drawer. It wasn't unusual for children to come to school without lunch in public schools, she'd heard, but it was surprising here. If any family were in need, the rest of the community should already know about it and be taking steps.

This family was new, of course. And maybe the children had just overslept and rushed off without their lunches. She'd have to move carefully to keep from offending anyone.

"Here we go." She delved into her own bag. "I have egg salad sandwiches."

"I have baloney and pickles," Micah volunteered. "Which do you like, Rebecca?"

Anna's heart warmed at this sign of kindness from her little brother. Micah might not show it much to his older sisters, but he had a generous heart.

Rebecca, confronted with a choice, pointed a small finger toward the egg salad.

"Good enough," Anna said, putting it in a bag and adding an apple. "What about you, Thomas? Baloney okay for you?"

Thomas wore that sullen look she disliked, but his flush showed embarrassment. "I don't need any."

"Sure you do. You don't want your stomach to growl during your history lesson, ain't so?" She quickly assessed the contents of the bags, splitting the lunches Mammi had sent for two into a lunch for four. Because Mammi was always eager to feed the multitudes, that wasn't a problem. She handed a bag to each of them.

"We'd best go out now, before Teacher Judith comes looking for us." She took Rebecca's hand. "Thank you for helping me with your sister, Thomas."

She said the words loud enough to be heard

by the scholars closest to the door, just in case anyone was wondering why Thomas and Rebecca were still inside. It was amazing how quickly gossip could spread, with everyone adding on his or her share of speculation.

Once outside, the older boys scattered, most taking their lunches over near the ball field, while the girls headed for the benches under the trees. The younger ones gathered around the long picnic table. Experience had taught Anna that they weren't as messy and were more apt to finish their lunches that way.

Thomas headed off by himself, but Rebecca hung close to Anna, squeezing in next to her on the bench. Anna smiled at her, her heart contracting again. She'd have to pursue answers about these children. There could be lots of reasons why children might come without their lunches, but that didn't explain Thomas's sullen attitude, or Rebecca's shyness.

She looked across the table at Micah. He was quiet as he finished his lunch, but he was keeping an eye on Rebecca, as if to see that she had enough. Micah wasn't a chatterbox, although he certainly held his own when he was in school or on the playground. Come to think of it, he probably had trouble getting a word in at home, with all of his sisters talking at once.

As they were cleaning up from lunch, Judith stooped to pick up a straying bit of waxed paper before the wind could get it. She looked at the Burkhardt children and then gave Anna a questioning glance.

Anna shrugged. "I don't know," she said quietly. The scholars had scattered to play, so it was probably safe to talk. "Have you heard anything about the Burkhardt family?"

Judith shook her head. "Just that they bought the farm near Ella King—the one that used to belong to Matthew King's family." She flushed a little as she said his name, probably not sure how Anna would react.

Anna tried to keep her expression unmoved. After all, this wasn't about Matthew. It was a school problem.

She trusted Judith to be sensible and keep this sort of thing to herself. If she hadn't known how mature the girl was, she wouldn't have accepted her as an assistant teacher.

But trustworthy or not, she didn't want to discuss anything about Matthew.

"They'll be in church this Sunday," Anna said. "I'll find a chance to talk with the children's mother. If there are any problems, I'm sure folks are ready to help."

Judith nodded, her round face unusually serious. Even the dimples in her cheeks weren't showing. "I won't say anything."

"Gut." Anna patted her arm. "I know I can count on you."

Her thoughts skipped ahead to worship on Sunday. They were already into the series of services leading up to Easter, and this was Council Meeting Sunday.

She had been looking forward to it. She hadn't been a baptized member long enough to find it routine. It was a time to go over the Ordnung, the rules of the congregation, and also to discuss any problems between members so they could establish harmony before the Spring Communion.

That being so, the ministers would speak about the need to humble themselves as little children. They'd be sure to talk about forgiveness. There should be no quarrels or hard feelings among the brothers and sisters in faith.

And then each baptized member would be asked to declare his or her agreement with the rules of the church.

Ich bin einig. I am agreed.

Would she be able to say that, feeling as she did about Matthew? There was no getting around it. She had been trying to hide her lack of forgiveness, but it had to be dealt with.

Matthew might already be there at the farm, working with Daadi when she got home. What then? Panic seized her. How was she going to get through this if she had to see him every day?

CHAPTER FOUR

Anna sat quietly in her designated place in worship, wishing she could sit farther back a couple of rows. But here she was, between the single girls and the young married women, advertising her unmarried state. At least this put her next to Leah Stoltz, now Leah Burkhalter since she and Josiah had married.

Unfortunately, this seat also gave her a perfect view of Matthew King, who was sitting at the end of a bench in the last row of the men's side, opposite his aunt.

Admit it, she lectured herself. *You're bothered because Matthew King is here.*

Matt's unexpected presence, combined with the fact that Leah, next to her, could see her every glance, left her more than a little flustered.

The rustle of movement as they slid to their knees for prayer made a cover for Leah's whispered question. "Did you know he was going to be here?"

Soft as it was, the whisper had attracted a few glances. She gave Leah a warning look and shook her head slightly. No, she hadn't known. If she had . . .

It wouldn't have made any difference, Anna admitted to herself. She'd have had no choice but to do what she always did, which meant sit here and try not to catch his eye.

She closed her eyes, pressing her face into her hands, clasped on the bench. It wouldn't have made any difference if she had caught his eye, she told herself. Matt was wearing what she thought of as his stone face—as rigid and stern as a boulder.

As the face of Hawk Cliff. The image forced itself into her thoughts, and she winced. She hadn't been there since James's accident, but that didn't matter. She still saw it plainly. The face of the cliff looked as if a giant hand had brought a knife down through the ridge, exposing the rock face and leaving a rubble of boulders at the bottom like toys dropped by that hand.

They were rising again, sliding onto the benches for the last hymn and the final words of the service. Thank goodness Matt would leave after lunch, although he'd probably have to come back later to pick up his aunt Ella. He wouldn't be able to stay for Council Meeting, and Ella would never miss it. He might even skip out before lunch, she thought hopefully.

Leah nudged her as they made their way out of the barn where the Leit had met today. "I heard he's going to be helping out at the farm. Is that true?"

"Yah." She'd like to leave it at that, but Leah was her best friend, and she knew Anna's feelings better than anyone. "He seems to have some idea of making up for James's death, as if anything could." She glanced around as they were caught up in the crowd outside the barn. "We can't talk here. Later?"

Leah gave a quick nod, her bright eyes still showing concern. "I'm supposed to help cut sandwiches anyway. But you need to tell me about it. Soon." She scurried off in the direction of the kitchen.

Tell me about it, Anna mused as she sought out her mother and grandmother. Talking about it wouldn't change anything. But she had to admit she'd like to sort out the jumble of feelings that jostled around inside her. Telling everything to Leah might help her see things more clearly, if that were even possible.

By the time they'd all had lunch and were almost ready to head back into the barn for Council Meeting, Anna was completely frustrated. She'd been trying to talk with the parents of the Burkhardt children, but each time she got near them, they seemed to slip between her fingers. That was probably unfair, she told herself. Naturally everyone wanted to greet them, because they were newcomers.

"Anna." She could tell by her mother's expression that it wasn't the first time she'd said her name. "It's almost time. Please collect your sisters and brother and get them started for home. I want to know they're on their way before we go inside."

"Yah, I will."

It was easy enough to locate Sally—she was leaning on the pasture gate, looking dreamily into Joseph Miller's face. Anna couldn't help wondering what she saw there. It must be more than Anna did.

"Time to go." She caught Sally's hand, knowing if she didn't, Sally would linger over her good-byes for half an hour. The two of them rounded up the girls and then pulled Micah out of a game of tag. Given how red his face was, she'd probably shown up at the right time.

"Komm on now. Up you go." Anna ushered them into the buggy, aware the whole time that Matt was harnessing his buggy horse right next to them.

"Heading for home with them?" he asked, pausing with the headstall in his hands.

Anna shook her head, a bit startled. But of course he wouldn't know she'd joined the church in the fall.

"I'll be here for Council Meeting. That's why we brought two buggies today. Does your aunt need a ride home?"

"No, she's talked the Burkhardts into giving her a lift back after the meeting." He frowned, as if not happy about it. "I think if it had been anyone else, they'd have gotten out of it, but nobody ever succeeds in saying no to Aunt Ella."

69

"Good for her." Anna's own concerns about the family came back in force. "They don't seem very friendly, do they? I was trying to have a word with them about the children, but I didn't have a chance."

"I noticed," he said, making her sorry she'd mentioned it. Had he been watching her?

"It doesn't matter." She waved it away with a quick gesture. "Just school stuff anyway."

"And you don't want to talk to me about it," he said, finishing her thought.

Her lips pressed together for a moment, and then she tried for a noncommittal smile. "I'll make arrangements to stop over one day and talk with them about where the kinder were in school before they came here."

"Maybe you can find out what's wrong with them," he muttered.

She glanced up, surprise widening her eyes. "What do you know about it?"

"Only what anyone can see."

"No, I mean . . . well, why are you interested? Has Ella said anything about them?"

Matt shrugged, looking as if he regretted mentioning it. "Not much. Only that anyone can see that those kids have troubles." His lips twisted in a wry smile. "And she said I should know that if I paid attention to anyone's problems but my own."

Anna made an effort to fit that into her thoughts

about the Burkhardt family. Ella had a sharp tongue, but she wasn't one to say anything that wasn't true. Maybe it was Ella she should talk to first.

"I'm giving the kids a ride home since they're right next door. Aunt Ella arranged that, too. If I hear anything helpful, I'll tell you tomorrow." He hesitated. "You do know that I . . ."

"Yah, Daad told me that you were going to be helping him this spring. I suppose you think I tried to talk him out of it, but I didn't."

For just an instant, his face softened. "Don't worry, Anna. I know one thing for sure. If you make a promise, you keep it." He turned. "I'd better tell them I'm ready," he said, and walked off.

Her siblings were ready to leave, too, and she waved to them automatically, hardly hearing their goodbyes as the buggy moved out.

Matt had shown a surprising amount of understanding. She should appreciate that, but she didn't. She didn't want him understanding anything about her.

By Monday afternoon, Matt was beginning to think his immediate goal—being accepted by James's family—was in sight. He'd been nervous when he arrived at the Stoltzfus farm this morning, but his immediate welcome by Simon and Miriam had been echoed by the grandparents.

71

Anna, Betsy, Grace, and Micah were at school, and he'd only seen Sally at lunch, when she was so busy dreaming that she didn't seem to notice who was at the table.

No one brought up the subject of his attendance at worship, but they seemed to skirt around it. In other words, people were wondering what his intentions were.

He didn't want to give anyone the idea that he'd come back to stay, but Aunt Ella had expected him to go to worship with her. Trying to come back and be Amish for a short time was a balancing act, and he wasn't sure he was succeeding.

The job for the afternoon was mending the roof of the brooder coop, which had lost some shingles over the winter. Matt spared a moment to be grateful it wasn't the high barn roof that was in question. The coop roof was only about six feet off the ground. That shouldn't bother him.

He and Simon worked together, with Simon standing on a stepladder while he stepped up on the low roof of the adjoining woodshed.

"Bishop Paul mentioned he was going to stop by and see you," Simon commented, carefully not asking a question.

Still, it was the sort of comment a person had to answer, Matt thought, smiling a little at Simon's air of cautious indifference.

"Yah, he came over yesterday evening to talk. Said he was glad to see me back."

Maybe there was something doubting in his tone, because Simon gave him a look. "I'm sure he is. We all are."

"That's gut of you to say."

No doubt Simon meant it as far as he was concerned, but Matt had had the feeling at worship that more than a few people had doubts about him. Not just Anna.

If he wasn't going to stay, that didn't matter, he guessed. They'd be able to say they'd known it all along.

"Bishop Paul is a fine man," Simon observed, punctuating his words by tapping at a shingle that had blown loose. "There's no one better to confide in, should you be wanting to talk."

Matt nodded, wondering how hard it would be to change the subject. "You know, I missed a lot while I was gone. I hadn't even realized that Anna would have been baptized into the church by now."

"She wanted it." Simon stopped, frowning down at the shingles as if he didn't see them. "We were a bit worried that she rushed into it because of James. But Bishop Paul and the ministers talked to her, and they felt she was sure of what she wanted."

What could he say to that? If he had stayed, if James hadn't died, would they both have made the decision, too? He'd missed the time when most folks his age were courting, settling into a job they wanted, planning for the future. For most of them, that included making their lifetime commitment to live Amish.

"It was probably a comfort to her," he said awkwardly. His change of subject wasn't going very well. "She and James were always so close . . ."

He let that trail off. What was there to say? Simon knew it as well as anyone. With less than a year between them, they'd been like twins.

"Yah, I guess. It was a peaceful Council Sunday." Simon's lips twitched. "Nobody had any quarrel about whether we should use batteries, or whether it was right to have a cell phone if your business needed it, or how many teenagers did have them, or any of the other things that often come up."

Matt might not have been to a Council Meeting, but he remembered some of the debates that had swept through the community over any little step toward something modern. His daad had always been firmly opposed no matter what it was, and Mamm went along with what he said. He'd wondered sometimes if she'd ever had an idea of her own.

Fortunately he'd known people like the Stoltzfus family, who talked things over, even letting the youngsters have an opinion. Otherwise he might have thought all Amish families were like his.

He started to say something to Simon but saw that he was craning to look over the roof of the brooder coop. "The young ones are home from school already."

Matt took a look, realizing that Anna wasn't with them. They'd probably walked down the dirt road that wound behind several farms to the schoolhouse. At least he wouldn't have to dodge Anna, who'd made it clear she didn't want to see him. Maybe he'd be gone by the time she came.

So why was he feeling somehow disappointed that she wasn't here?

Simon was getting down. "I'll send Micah over to help you once he has a snack. Don't worry if we don't finish today. There's always tomorrow."

"I can work on it by myself . . ." he began, but Simon wasn't paying attention.

No doubt Simon wanted Micah to work along-side him. That was how the boy would learn. He was only eight, so Matt would have to find something suitable for his age. He tried to remember what his father had taught him at that age.

His jaw tightened. Too many of those experiences had ended badly, with his father berating him for clumsiness and inattention. Matt pushed the memories away. He wasn't his father, and Micah . . . Micah was James's brother.

Sure enough, a few minutes later, a small figure came running across from the back door. Micah carried an apple in his hand, and he was trying to eat and run at the same time. Matt dropped down to the ground to meet him.

With his black pants, blue shirt, and straw hat, Micah looked like any other Amish boy in the community. Then he came closer, and Matt saw James looking at him from Micah's blue eyes, James smiling in Micah's smile.

"You really look like your bruder did at your age." The words were out before he had time to wonder if it was a good idea to remind the boy.

But Micah nodded. "Yah, Mammi says so. She says I'm like him."

"You couldn't find anyone better to be like," Matt said, his throat tightening.

He hoped the boy had good memories of his big brother. How much was he likely to hold on to after two years had gone by? Would Micah remember the time Matt and James had taken him clear up to the top of the ridge to look for wild blackberries? Matt would have to ask after he and Micah got to know each other.

Micah was gazing up at the roof. "I'll work on that." He started up the ladder.

Matt snatched him off the ladder in a quick, unthinking movement, his heart pounding. The low roof of the brooder coop became the rocky face of Hawk Cliff for a split second.

76

"Hey! What'd you do that for?" Micah's face reddened. "I'm not a baby."

Hanging on to the ladder, Matt fought to compose himself. His hoped-for friendship with Micah could be gone in an instant if he didn't control himself.

"No, you're not. Did your daad teach you anything about climbing a ladder?"

Micah's flush faded as he studied the ground. "To always check if it's steady first."

Matt managed a smile. "It's gut advice. You know what? He taught me that, too, and I still remember."

"Honest?" Micah's eyes widened. "Didn't your daad do that?"

That wasn't a subject he wanted to bring up with a kid. "He was busy with lots of other things, so your daad taught me alongside of James." He caught hold of the ladder, shook it, and checked that the feet were firmly planted.

"So what do you think?" he asked, looking at Micah.

Micah gave that grin that looked so much like James. "Seems okay to me."

"Right. Up you go."

He stood close to the ladder, just in case, until the boy was settled. Then he stepped up the few feet to his own perch, taking a hammer for Micah.

"Your daad and I already replaced the ones that blew off, so we just have to check these bottom rows to see if they need another nail or two to keep them secure."

"Best to make sure," Micah said, obviously trying to sound mature. Hammer at the ready, he picked up a roofing nail.

Matt watched to be sure Micah knew what he was doing first, and then he turned back to work in the other direction. He glanced over, probably more than was necessary, at the boy working.

Micah *was* very like James in looks, he thought again. Time would tell if he was like James in personality. He'd grow into whoever he was meant to be.

Matt had a momentary wish that he could be around to see that happen, and he dismissed it just as quickly. This place wasn't for him. At least, not for good. But if his work could help the family, that should be enough.

Enough? He tested the next shingle and found it tight. What would ever be enough to make up for failing James? He glanced at Micah and then looked down at the ground as if to assure himself it wasn't far away.

In that moment the ground receded, and once again he was on the face of Hawk Cliff. Or was he on the fourth floor of the building he'd been working on with the construction gang? His fingers closed on the edge of the coop roof, holding tightly as the images flooded over him, almost smothering him.

Unable to control himself, he looked down, and vertigo sent the world turning around him. It was Kevin Walker, the boss's son, slipping from the beam, clinging desperately as Matt reached out— or was it James, in trouble, flown and careless with beer, trying to climb the cliff?

"Are you okay?" Micah's voice cut through the nightmare around him, and the world stopped spinning.

Matt forced himself to focus on the boy's face. "Yah, fine. Looks like we'll have this done in no time, ain't so?"

"Sure thing." Micah looked proudly at the shingles he'd given extra nails to. "I have to learn to do everything on the farm, 'cause when I know enough, I'll take James's place. That's my job."

Not yours. He heard the words in his head, but knew it was his own conscience that said them. The guilt was his. He'd saved Kevin, but he'd lost James, and one life didn't make up for the other.

Anna had intended to go straight to the Burkhardt place when she left school, but some impulse made her stop at home on the way. She couldn't deny that she felt a certain amount of curiosity about how Matt was working out. Searching her own heart during Council Meeting, she'd promised anew that she would do her best to practice forgiveness. That meant starting with her attitude toward Matt.

Daad and Mammi could do it. Why couldn't she?

But all the good resolutions in the world weren't enough to stop the flare of resentment when she pulled into the farmyard and saw Micah and Matt working side by side on the brooder coop.

She stopped at the hitching rail, slid down, and popped into the kitchen to let her mother know where she was going. Then she came back outside, paused for a moment, and walked quickly toward the coop.

She hadn't bargained for this in all her worries about having Matt actually working here. She'd pictured him with Daad, with Grossdaadi, even talking to Mammi, but never thought about his possible effect on her little brother.

They were talking together as they worked, and she could see the relaxed smile on Micah's face. Her heart twisted. It should be James working with Micah—James who was showing him how to do any of the hundreds of jobs involved in running the farm. Not Matt.

They hadn't noticed her approach. With an instinctive need to draw Micah's attention away from Matt, she called out. "Looks like you're busy."

Micah swung toward her, the movement over-balancing him. She gasped, rushing forward, but Matt had seized the back of Micah's shirt in an instant, steadying him.

She opened her mouth, ready to snatch him off the stepladder and scold him for carelessness, but Matt caught her eye. Ever so slightly he shook his head.

She knew what he was saying—*don't make too much of it, don't make him afraid or put ideas in his head.*

What's more, he was right. That didn't make her like him any better.

Micah grinned at Matt. "Yah, I know. Daadi told me. Don't bounce around when I'm on a ladder, yah?"

"Right." Matt patted his back. "Better answer your sister."

He nodded, turning back to Anna but without letting go of the ladder this time. "Look what we did. Daadi said I could help with the roof repair. Me and Matt got it all done."

"Matt and I," she corrected automatically. "That's gut. Are you coming down now?"

After a glance at Matt, he nodded. "We're done. We just have to clean the tools and put them away. Matt says Daadi taught him to do that every time you work."

"I'm sure."

Her glance at Matt was probably unfriendly, but it didn't seem to faze him. He was gathering up nails and hammers and handing them down to Micah before hopping down himself.

"All finished?" Daad's voice from behind her

startled Anna. "If so, you'd better let Anna drop you at home on her way over to the Burkhardts' place."

"Not necessary," Matt said cheerfully. "I'll walk."

"No point in walking when Anna's going right past your aunt Ella's house." Daad's tone was final.

Anna put a fixed smile on her face and turned back to Matt. "Yah. Whenever you're ready."

Matt looked from one to the other of them. "Okay, denke. Just as soon as my partner and I get the tools put away."

"I'll wait for you in the buggy." There was no reason that she could see for standing here watching him acting like part of the family. She started back to the buggy.

Did Daad think he was helping along the process of forgiveness by pushing her together with Matt? It would be like him, but she didn't think it would help.

Act as if you have forgiven someone, and true forgiveness will follow. The words spoken by the bishop in Sunday's service came back to her.

She'd thought it a strange concept to begin with. How could pretending help? Wasn't that just covering up? Or lying?

"What are you thinking about so deeply?" Matt dropped his small toolbox behind the seat, grabbed hold to pull himself up, and then hesitated, looking at her quizzically. "You want me to make up some reason I can't ride with you?"

"Get up here and don't be ridiculous." She wasn't sure whether she wanted to snarl or laugh. "Besides, what could you say?"

He shrugged, giving her a sideways glance. "Well, I could say that I had to go the other way, but then I'd really have to do it. Or I could say I promised my aunt never to ride alone in a buggy with a young woman. Or that—"

Suppressing the desire to laugh, Anna clucked to the buggy horse and they moved off down the lane. If Matt was trying to charm her, he wouldn't succeed. But it was the first time she'd seen that straight-faced humor of his since he'd come back, and it had disarmed her.

One of the things that attracted people was the way Matt could say the most outrageous things so seriously that one almost thought they were the truth.

"I see you still have a sense of humor in spite of living among the Englisch for so long."

"Nothing surprising about that, is there?" That spark of laughter in his eyes made him look younger. "The Englisch do a lot of joking. Well, I don't know about everybody, but guys working in construction do. Just like any group of Amish guys that work together."

Construction must have suited him fine. He'd

always been good at that sort of thing. Probably if he'd had his way, he'd have apprenticed with one of the Amish builders or carpenters in the area. But his father had been determined that he'd follow his footsteps and become a farrier.

"You enjoyed it." It wasn't really a question. She could see the truth of it in his face when he wasn't busy guarding his thoughts from her.

"Yah, I did. Walker Construction, that's the name of the outfit. A family business. Phil Walker was a fine man to work for. Honest."

She nodded, trying to think of something that would keep him talking and make the minutes they were together pass more quickly. "You said it was a family business?"

"That's so. His nephew works for him part-time, and a couple of men full-time, and there's his son, Kevin."

Was it her imagination, or did his voice change when he mentioned the son? She looked at him, trying to convey interest.

"How old is he?"

Matt shrugged. "About eighteen, I guess. Nice kid, but a little . . ." He hesitated, seeming to look for the word. "Well, not serious about the work. His dad was teaching him, since he'd take it over one day, but Kevin was more interested in motorbikes and girls."

"He's young, it sounds like."

"Yah."

There was still something there, in his voice and in his expression, that was off-kilter. None of her business, of course. She could have done the whole trip in silence, but . . .

She remembered the bishop's words. If she were to act as if she'd forgiven him, she'd show interest in his troubles, just as she always had.

But they were turning into the drive at the Burkhardt place, and there was no time for more. "Where do you want me to let you off?"

Matt gestured, pointing toward the side door of the farmhouse. "Just drop me there, and I'll cut across the lower field to Aunt Ella's."

Just like he always had when this had been his family's place. If it bothered him to be here, it didn't show in his face or his voice.

Anna pulled up at the hitching rail. By the time she got down, Matt was already there, clicking the lead rope onto the harness.

"Denke." Because she was nervous, she moved quickly to the door, eager to get this interview over with. She rapped.

Silence. No one seemed to be moving anywhere about the farm. She could see the barn and the other outbuildings from here. Empty, it seemed.

"I wonder if they've gone somewhere—" But even as she spoke, she saw the curtain move in the kitchen window and glimpsed someone behind it. She knocked again, louder.

Matt reached around her to pound on the door himself. "Miz Burkhardt! It's Matt King from next door, and the teacher from the school. Can we see you for a minute?"

His raised voice must have reached whoever was in the kitchen, but there was no answering sound. She looked at Matt, seeing him as baffled as she was. "What . . ."

At that instant there was a crash and a tinkle of broken glass. And then a woman screamed, loud and piercing and terrifying.

CHAPTER FIVE

Anna froze, unable to move for a moment. Even before her mind started working, she and Matt were both pounding on the door.

"Mrs. Burkhardt . . . Elizabeth . . . are you all right? Was ist letz? What's wrong?"

No sound answered her cry. Anna exchanged looks with Matt, realizing that he was just as baffled as she was. "Elizabeth, it's Anna Stoltzfus, the children's teacher. Please open the door."

She glanced at Matt again. "Do you think your aunt could do anything? She probably knows them better than anyone."

"Maybe." He was frowning. "You go. I'd best stay here."

"I'm capable of dealing with this. If she's hurt, she'd probably rather have a woman here."

"And what if it's more than that? I don't want you—"

The door swung open so abruptly that it must have shocked Matt into silence. Carl Burkhardt stood there, glowering at them, blocking the way in.

Matt went back a step, drawing Anna with him.

Anna had seen Burkhardt at worship from a distance, but she hadn't realized how big he was. He filled the doorway with his height and breadth, his heavy shoulders hunched forward.

She knew, suddenly, whom he reminded her of. Matt's father, with his powerful arms and lowering brow. Did Matt see that, too? She felt as if she couldn't look away from the man, glaring as he was.

"Well? What do you want?"

Anna found her voice. "I'm Teacher Anna, from the school. I hoped to talk to you and your wife about the kinder."

Before she could go on, Burkhardt was shaking his head. "Not a good time. Some other day."

She had the feeling that he regretted every word he had to spend on them, as if reluctant to say anything at all.

"We can set up another time," she said, endeavoring to sound as if this were any ordinary conversation with a parent. "But we heard a crash and a cry. If your wife is hurt, I'd be glad to come in and tend to her. Or Ella King, from next door, would come if you'd rather."

"Yah." Matt found his tongue. "My aunt would be glad to be of help."

Burkhardt's jaw moved, as if he fought with the words he wanted to say. Maybe guessing they weren't going to go away easily, he seemed to give in. "Wait here," he growled, and he shut the door in their faces.

Anna looked at Matt, and he shrugged, lifting his hands in a helpless gesture. "If he doesn't want to let us in, there's nothing we can do."

"But what if she's hurt? What if she needs help?" She murmured the words, not wanting anyone in the house to hear.

"Listen." Matt gestured her to silence, nodding at the window of the kitchen. There was a murmur of voices there. And then once a distinct word.

"No."

It was Elizabeth Burkhardt's voice, no doubt about that. A wave of helplessness swept over Anna. Maybe Matt was right. If he didn't want to let them in and she didn't want their help, they could do nothing.

Heavy footsteps sounded, and then the door opened. Burkhardt made a grimace that might have been intended for a smile.

"Denke. She's fine. Just dropped a pitcher that was her mother's. Upsetting, that's all."

He started to close the door again, and Anna held out her hand, not content to leave it at that, but not seeing any other choice.

"Please tell her that I'll hope to see her at the schoolhouse after school tomorrow. We can have a nice chat."

Burkhardt made a sound that might have been affirmative. Then the door shut with a final thud. It was unlikely that he'd open it again no matter what they might say.

She stood looking at the door, not satisfied but

not knowing what else to do. Matt tugged at her arm.

"Komm. We'll go over to Aunt Ella's and talk to her about it. She might have an idea."

Reluctantly, she nodded. There seemed no other possibility.

They were both silent as she turned the buggy, went back to the road, and pulled in at Ella King's house. By the time they had tied up the buggy horse, Ella was gesturing at them to come in.

Anna was glad to enter Ella's toasty kitchen. The day had turned chilly and damp after the warm sunshine that had brightened the scholars' recess. Now she was happy to move closer to the stove.

"I saw you from the window," Ella said, seizing the coffeepot automatically. "What was going on over there?" She was eyeing Anna with a curiosity that wasn't very well hidden. She probably couldn't figure out why Anna was willingly spending time with her great-nephew.

It wasn't willing, Anna protested in her thoughts. *It just happened.*

Matt pushed a mug of coffee over to Anna and then added the sugar to it without asking. She thought of protesting, but it seemed foolish. When you'd grown up as close with someone as her and Matt, of course you knew the normal little details about the other. That didn't mean you were friends.

Before she could gather her thoughts, Matt had plunged into speech, telling his aunt about what they'd seen and heard at the neighboring house.

"Anna made it clear she expects to see Elizabeth Burkhardt after school tomorrow, but whether she'll show up or not is anyone's guess."

"We shouldn't have left." Anna burst out with the words. "What if she was hurt? We don't know that he was telling the truth with that story about the pitcher."

"We did hear something break in the kitchen," Matt pointed out.

"If that's all it was, why didn't he let me come in and help?" Anna protested. "It doesn't seem right to me."

She stopped and took a breath before saying the words she didn't want to say, not in front of Matthew anyway.

"You're thinking he might have hit her." Matt said it before she had to. "We didn't hear anything that would prove it. And she could have come to the door if she'd wanted to."

"Could she?" She wanted to snap the words at him but couldn't, because she knew what was happening to Matt. He was thinking that this was too much like the situation with his father. Matt's daad had been another big man with bulky shoulders and muscles of iron after struggling with horses and hammering horseshoes for years.

"Maybe not," he admitted. "But we didn't really

91

see anything that would support your version of things. Maybe she really did break a pitcher. Maybe it really had belonged to her mother, and she was upset over dropping it."

Ella rapped on the table with her spoon. "If you two would stop arguing, maybe I could get a word in."

"I'm sorry." Anna felt her cheeks flush with embarrassment. "That's why I came over. I wanted your opinion of them. You've probably seen more than anyone else."

"True, I have." Ella's thin lips set, and she glared at them as if it were their fault. "But I don't know for sure what's going on over there. They keep themselves to themselves. She doesn't come out of the house much."

"That's not natural in itself," Anna protested.

"No." Ella frowned. "The few times I talked to her, she seemed sort of changeable. Like one time she was happy, looking forward to meeting everyone at worship. And the next time she dodged back in the house when she saw me coming."

"I guess you could have caught her at a bad time," Anna said, unconvinced. "Usually somebody moving into a new Amish community has relatives or someone who knows about them. Nobody seems to know anything. And everyone has been eager to welcome them, but they haven't been very receptive, have they?"

"Maybe not, but like Aunt Ella says, they keep themselves to themselves. That doesn't mean anything bad, does it? Maybe Elizabeth is shy, like the little girl is."

Matt seemed eager to deny the conclusions she'd jumped to. Was it because he thought the same thing, and didn't want to face it?

"I'm not sure what's happening," Ella said. "But something is wrong. You just have to talk to those kinder to know it."

Anna nodded. "That's what I've sensed with them. I hope she does come to the school tomorrow. After all, it's a neutral place, not like their own home. We have to know what's wrong before we can help them."

We. Had she really said that? It was as if she were allying herself with Matt, of all people. That wouldn't do.

Matt had been walking quickly the next morning, his steps moving as fast as his thoughts. Each time he remembered what had happened the previous day, his muscles tightened until his jaw hurt from the tension.

He knew what was causing it. The crash, the cry, the looming figure . . . those were the nightmares of his childhood. He didn't have to be a genius to figure out why that troubled him.

Anna had seen it, too. He'd known by the way she looked at him that she was remembering and hurting for him. He didn't want anyone's pity, but it wasn't pity with Anna. It never had been. She'd always given him the sense that she was on his side, standing with him in trouble. Even with everything that separated them, he could sense that hadn't changed.

Shaking that thought off, he tried to be reasonable about the situation. Just because of the way the man was built and the expression on his face, it didn't mean that he'd hit his wife.

Matt had no reason to imagine that the Burkhardt family was anything like his own. No reason at all.

He'd been denying it to himself ever since it happened. Sometimes he even believed himself, at least for a little while.

And then the image came back of the bull-necked, solid figure looming in the doorway. He knew that if he blinked, he could see his father's face instead of Carl Burkhardt's.

Matt turned in to the lane and realized just how early he was this morning. He must have been racing along the road to get here before Anna and the young ones left for school.

Anna was harnessing the mare. He jogged the rest of the way, intending to help her, if she'd let him. He found he was wondering what her first words would be. Would she greet him or snap at him?

He didn't care, he told himself, whichever it

was. Nothing had changed between them. Anna had every reason to resent his presence.

Still, in those moments when they'd been confronting Burkhardt, she seemed glad of his presence. Afterward, as they'd talked with Aunt Ella about the situation next door, she'd welcomed him into the discussion, even when she disagreed with him.

Why had he been so reluctant to see her get involved with those people? She was the children's teacher, after all. She'd say it was her job. She'd say she didn't need or want his protection.

So the emotional weather might be chilly or calm today. The only way to find out was to speak to her.

He caught hold of the harness strap when she tossed it over the mare's back and began to work on the buckles.

"Denke." She wasn't smiling, but her voice sounded calm enough. "The young ones are supposed to help with the harnessing when they ride with me, but you don't see them, do you?"

"Were they snatching some extra minutes of sleep?"

She smiled now. "Dawdling, more likely. It's a bit nippy this morning, so Mammi thought they should ride. Sally is in there telling Mamm about how she always had to walk when she was their age."

"I'm sure your mamm knows how to deal with that." Miriam had always been firm, but pleasant. She wasn't one to lose her temper when one of the kinder asked a question or complained.

"Yah." Anna pulled out a lap robe from the back and tossed it onto the seat. "Have you and your aunt come up with any new thoughts since yesterday?"

He shook his head, feeling the familiar tension at remembering. "You know Aunt Ella. She doesn't mind telling people outright what she thinks, but she's not one to interfere with their business."

"I wondered if we should speak to the bishop." Her tone made it a question, and he noticed that she said *we* again.

"*You* could speak to the bishop. I'm an outsider now, remember?"

She should remember. She'd done everything she could to point that out to him.

Anna flushed, the rosy color coming up in her cheeks. "I just don't know if I'd be justified in going that far. We don't actually know anything."

"We know that Carl didn't want to let us in yesterday. We know that it was his wife who cried out." He stopped to think. "We do know that, don't we? You don't think it could have been one of the kinder?"

"No, no. I'm sure it was Elizabeth." She countered that immediately. "Thomas has a bass voice already, and as for Rebecca, I can't imagine her making that amount of noise, no matter what."

"So that brings us to the really worrying thing—the way little Rebecca behaves. And Thomas, I suppose."

He wasn't sure about the boy. He'd seemed normal enough when Matt had talked to him, but he didn't know what he was like in school. Anna would have a better feel for that.

"I've been trying to think of something to account for it." Anna had picked up the lap robe again, smoothing it with her palm as if she needed something to do with her hands. "Maybe Rebecca had some frightening experience where they lived before. Or there might be some medical reason for her withdrawal. I just can't think of any."

"Aunt Ella says she'll keep an eye on things as much as she can from next door. And I'll talk to them whenever I see them out." He met her gaze. "But you have the best chance at getting to know what's wrong, yah?"

She nodded reluctantly, just as the back door opened and Micah and Grace spurted out, closely followed by Betsy. For a few moments all was confusion as they tried to climb up at once and then began a scuffle over the lap robe.

"Settle down or you can walk." Anna's tone was mild, but it was obvious she meant it. The two younger ones squeezed into the seat with the lap robe, and Betsy climbed into the front and left room for her sister.

"That your teacher's voice, ain't so?" Matt said, teasing.

Her smile was absentminded. "I suppose so." She started to step up to the buggy seat, and he took her elbow and steadied her.

"Denke," she said, her mind obviously on other things. "Maybe things will be clearer when I talk to Elizabeth after school. If she comes."

He nodded, stepping back as she picked up the lines. "Hope it goes well."

Whether she heard him or not, he didn't know. Her thoughts were clearly reaching ahead. He stood where he was and watched the buggy drive away.

As he turned back, the door opened and Anna's grandfather emerged, letting out a sound of female voices behind him and then cutting them off with a thud of the door.

Shrugging his jacket on, he nodded to Matt. "You're early today."

"So are you." Matt straightened the old man's jacket where it was rucked up in the back. He nodded toward the kitchen. "Something going on?"

"Females." Grossdaadi said the word with a wealth of feeling. "Get upset about the most foolish things." Then he shook his head, eyes crinkling in a smile. "They most likely think the same about us, yah?"

"I guess so." Matt started toward the barn, and Isaac fell into step with him.

"Seems like you and Anna have more to talk about now." Isaac made the observation and let it lie between them. It was an old habit of his to get you to tell him things.

Matt guessed it still worked, because he felt compelled to respond.

"Talk, yah. We're both a bit worried about the Burkhardt kids. But she's not happy I'm here, if that's what you mean."

"Ach, give it time," he said easily. "You used to be friends. You will again."

"I'd like to think so—"

The farmhouse door slamming had both of them turning to look. Somewhat to Matt's surprise, it was Sally who stomped out of the house and stalked off down the lane.

He raised an eyebrow. "Something gone wrong with Sally's romance?" He hadn't seen her in a temper before. She'd been too busy mooning around over Joseph.

Isaac shook his head. "Kids—always wanting what they don't have. Sally's trying to grow up too soon. And Betsy doesn't want to grow up at all. Both of them wanting what they can't have or to be what they aren't."

Matt had always found the old man's opinion

well worth listening to, and he considered that. He'd certainly always wanted to be someone else's son, that was for sure. And James . . . who had he been trying to be that night when he'd taken his life in his hands?

Matt didn't know, but now that he'd thought about it, he didn't like it. He'd come back to try to make what amends he could to James's family. To face what he had to in order to heal.

But maybe what he needed to face was worse than he'd counted on. What did he do then?

Anna was doing something a little different at the end of the school day today. Something that might, she hoped, give her a little more insight into the Burkhardt family, at least from the children's point of view.

She glanced up from the chapter of *Little House in the Big Woods* that she was reading aloud. Every head was bent, and fingers were busy with pencils and crayons. She'd announced that today they were to create a picture of their family, just as Laura might have done one of hers. They'd talked first about what little Laura might have drawn and what her house would have looked like with the big trees around it, and now they were making pictures of their own families.

No, everyone wasn't working—she noticed a little wiggling among the older boys and a certain amount of staring at the clock. They probably considered themselves too old for picture drawing.

She fixed a stern eye on the person she suspected was the ringleader of the bunch. For a moment he stared back at her, and then his eyes dropped and he flushed.

Satisfied, she checked the clock, saw that she had a few more minutes, and read to the end of the chapter. Her students knew better than to stop work before they were told, clock or no clock.

"That's all we have time for today." She closed the book. "Be sure your name is on your picture and pass it forward. Then tidy your desk."

At a glance from her, her assistant teacher began gathering up the pictures, and Anna dismissed the class row by row as she saw that they were ready. Even as she did so, she caught sight of a buggy pulling up outside. She'd half expected Elizabeth Burkhardt to skip this session, but it looked as if she had taken her appointment seriously.

Anna went to the door as the last row of scholars was dismissed, to see them out and make sure nothing had been left in the cloakroom. When she stepped out on the small porch, her stomach tightened.

Elizabeth Burkhardt hadn't come alone. She'd brought her husband with her.

Maybe that was for the best, but Anna wasn't convinced. She'd hoped to have Elizabeth alone, feeling that she might get more honest answers to questions that way. But Carl was walking beside his wife to the entrance, clearly intending to be a part of the conversation.

Was he truly interested in his children's schooling? Or was he concerned about what his wife might say if she came to the conference alone?

Anna tried to tell herself that she was being unfair. Just because the man didn't make a good first impression, that didn't give her any right to judge him. It was the same thing she'd felt about his son, but so far, Thomas had been, if not pleasant, at least cooperative.

Elizabeth Burkhardt came hurrying toward Anna, while her husband stopped to say a few words to the children. Thomas nodded, taking Rebecca's hand and tugging her toward the swings. For a moment Rebecca looked over her shoulder at Anna, and it almost looked like tears welled in her eyes. But then she went along with her brother.

Confusion and more confusion, Anna thought, and smiled a welcome at Elizabeth.

"Ach, Teacher Anna, I'm so sorry not to invite you in yesterday. I don't know what you must have thought of me."

By this time Carl stood in the doorway behind her, watching her with an expression Anna couldn't decipher.

"Here, come and sit down with me." She led

them toward the table along the side of the room, gesturing to the chairs. Her scholars' pictures were stacked at one end, and she quickly set them aside to look at when she had time.

"I understand why you wouldn't want to have anyone extra around when you had had an accident. I'm sorry that we pounded so hard on the door, but we were afraid you might be alone and hurt."

"Ach, no. I had my Carl with me." Carl stood behind her, a hand on her shoulder, and she reached up to pat it, giving him a loving look.

They were the image of a loving couple, but Anna couldn't rid her mind of the scream she'd heard.

"I'm so sorry. I hope you weren't badly hurt." Anna gave the obvious comment, wishing she could have seen what really happened in that kitchen.

Elizabeth put her left hand on the table. It was swathed with bandages, just leaving her fingers free.

"Ach, it's not so bad as it looks with the bandages. I was mostly upset because I broke a slipware pitcher that belonged to my mother. It just slid out of my hand, and then I cut myself when I tried to pick it up. I just can't stand the sight of blood. That's why I screamed."

She was talking so fast that it nearly made Anna dizzy trying to follow her. "I'm so sorry," she said, feeling that was the appropriate thing to say.

Elizabeth gave her a brilliant smile. "It's all right. Carl thinks he'll be able to mend it." Again she reached back to pat his hand.

Was all this demonstration of affection a little overdone? She couldn't imagine her own parents doing that in front of anyone. But if Rebecca was afraid of her husband, it certain sure didn't show.

"You wanted to see us about the kinder." Carl's tone was little better than a growl.

"Yah, that's so." Anna's mind scrambled for the right words. She'd been so engrossed in Elizabeth's reactions that she'd forgotten what she'd intended to say. "It can be hard on the scholars to switch to a new school, especially at this time of the school year. Were they at another Amish school here in central Pennsylvania?"

It was the best way she could think of to ask about where they'd lived before. Knowing that could fill in some of the gaps in the community's knowledge of them.

"Indiana," Carl said, and closed his lips on the word.

"Whereabouts in Indiana? I have a friend who went to Johnson County out there."

"Not near there." He'd managed to bring the questions to a dead stop.

"They've always liked school," Elizabeth said.

"And they're so happy here." She glanced at her husband. "Aren't they, Carl?"

Anna blinked. That wasn't the impression she got at all. And Elizabeth sounded as if she asked for assurance.

"Rebecca seems very shy." When Carl didn't speak, Anna forged onward, hoping to connect with the woman at some point. "I hope she'll feel more comfortable after a time. Is there anything I can do to encourage her to talk more?"

"No." Carl's answer came quickly.

Elizabeth laughed a little. "Now, I wouldn't say that. You'll give Teacher Anna the wrong idea," she chided. "She is very shy, as you've seen, but I'm sure she'll settle down and talk more as she gets to know you. Just let her move at her own pace. It never works to try to push her to talk."

"I would never do that." Anna had stiffened. Did the woman think Anna was that unfeeling?

"Gut." Carl filled in the silence. "That's settled then."

Before she had time to think that remark rather odd, Elizabeth had fluttered into speech. "We must thank you for taking care of the children's lunches. I'm afraid we were all behind schedule that day, and they hurried off without them."

"I'm sure it happens." She tried to make it sound as if it were not unusual. "I had a few things here, and we all shared. We made a picnic out of it."

"How sweet you are," Elizabeth exclaimed. "Don't you think she's sweet, Carl?"

Carl looked as if he'd been struck dumb at the question, and Anna hurried into speech. What was behind the almost artificial tone of Elizabeth's words?

"We all want the children to be happy here," she said carefully. "By the way, for the end of the school year, we usually have a picnic and invite the parents. It's a little celebration for the eighth graders, who won't be back next year. If you'd care to help . . ."

She left it open-ended. Parents, mothers especially, usually jumped at the idea.

But Elizabeth looked as if her mind were a million miles away all of a sudden.

"Mrs. Burkhardt?" Anna didn't know what to say. Nothing about this conversation was going as expected.

Carl seized his wife's arm. "Yah, I'm sure we will help."

"If we're here," Elizabeth said. "Who knows?"

You should know what your plans are. Anna wanted to pursue the subject, but Carl was already steering his wife toward the door.

"My wife is tired. I'll take her home so she can rest."

Anna hurried after them trying to think of something to say. "I'm sorry. If you need any help while your hand is healing, I'd be glad to stop over. And I'm sure Ella King is ready to do anything she can."

But he was already lifting Elizabeth into the buggy and motioning to the children. In another moment, they were pulling out of the schoolyard.

Anna stared after the retreating buggy, realizing she had even more questions than before. And almost no answers.

CHAPTER SIX

Anna sat at the desk in her bedroom that evening, still puzzling over the experiences of the day. Since she'd begun teaching, she'd had a room of her own, with a desk, bookshelves, and the ability to close the door to outside noise. She didn't, most of the time, because the room felt lonely without the usual buzz of a big, busy family.

It wasn't any outside noise that kept her from coming to a conclusion about the Burkhardt family. Maybe it was the noise in her head, instead. She kept going over their conversation, trying to glean the least spark of insight. She knew there was something there that would give her a clue; she sensed it.

But that was all. She couldn't put it together. If she had more experience . . . Teacher Dorcas, she felt, would have known how to handle something like this, but Dorcas had turned the school over to Anna, and it was her job to deal with it now.

Dorcas would have certain sure been more confident than Anna was. When Anna had been her assistant, she had been in awe of the way Dorcas could grasp any situation. Anna had thought that she had grown ready to handle anything that came along, as well, but this one had her baffled.

Anna stared down at the calendar on her

desk. The month was flying by. She ought to be working out the class schedule for the rest of the year. It would soon be Easter, and then the children would be thinking about summer.

She really did need to have covered all the proposed material before the end of the school year in May. The scholars would forget enough over the summer without the added stress of failing to complete the materials. Some of the children were fascinated by learning, and they were the ones who would make the most use of the library during the summer. At least she'd know they were reading.

As for the rest . . . there'd be work to do helping at home or in the businesses that their parents ran, to say nothing of trips to visit relatives and family reunions.

Thinking of families brought her right back to the problem. Elizabeth Burkhardt's face imposed itself on the squares of the calendar, one fleeting expression after another. The woman had skipped from topic to topic so quickly that Anna had struggled to keep up, even without analyzing the woman's attitude. Was she always like that, or was it some sort of act put on for the benefit of the children's teacher?

Anna rubbed her forehead. What she needed to do was talk this over with someone, but who? Mammi or even Grossmammi would have insights, she felt sure, but Dorcas had pounded into her the concept of privacy where the school was concerned. She couldn't discuss one parent with another—that was unthinkable. What happened in school was off-limits to anyone outside, unless it was something that should go to the school board. And she couldn't imagine talking to the three solemn board members about something like this.

Someone came stamping up the stairs, and she was startled to see that it was Sally. What had happened to the bright cloud of first love that Sally had been floating on all week?

Sally started past her door, then seemed to change her mind. She came in and flung herself on Anna's bed, making the springs creak in protest.

"Take it easy," Anna said automatically. "If you want to flop around, do it on your own bed."

Ignoring her comment, Sally rolled onto her back, threw her arms over her head, and sighed loudly. Then, seeming pleased with the sound, she did it again.

Anna put down her pen. Did Sally even realize how annoying she was being?

"I'm trying to get some schoolwork done here," she pointed out.

Sally sighed again. Even more loudly.

Anna felt like sighing herself. Obviously she wasn't going to get anything else done until she'd dealt with Sally.

She turned in her chair to study her sister's face. There was no doubt that Sally was appealing, with those huge blue eyes and the lightest of blond hair. Anna had expected boys to fall for her sister, but she'd never considered what that would do to Sally.

Anna planted her hands on her knees. "What happened to the girl who has been floating around the house in love? Did you and Joseph break up already?"

Sally had been in love three times since she started rumspringa, and Anna suspected she had a couple more to go before she actually settled. But at her question, Sally sat bolt upright, outraged.

"No! How can you say such a thing? Joseph and I love each other."

"Well, then, if there's nothing wrong with Joseph, what is it? And don't start sighing again or I'll throw a pillow at you. Or maybe something harder."

Sally leaned on her elbows. "You wouldn't say that if you knew how unhappy I am." Her big blue eyes welled with tears, something they seemed to do at the slightest provocation. She'd sometimes thought Sally did it deliberately. But no, she really was unhappy.

Anna felt a moment of sympathy, and a desire to wrap her arms around her little sister. But she held back, knowing that Sally could create a drama out of almost anything.

"Komm, now. Tell me what's making you so unhappy. If you and Joseph really like each other—"

"We *love* each other," she cried. "And Mamm and Daad are trying to part us. Just because they think we're too young."

"I doubt that Mammi and Daad are trying to make you break up. But you are young. You're only sixteen."

"Almost seventeen," she snapped. "And I'm mature for my age. Everyone says that."

Anna had never heard anyone say that. In fact, they were more likely to wish Sally would grow up a little. But Anna decided it wouldn't be tactful to point that out now.

"It's really up to Mammi and Daadi, you know. I can't do anything. If you just talk quietly to Mammi, I'm sure she'll listen."

"I've tried!" She grabbed Anna's pillow, as if looking for something to throw, but with a quick look at Anna, she put it back and smoothed the pillowcase. "Please, Anna." Eyes pleading, she clasped her hands together. "Please. You know Mammi listens to you. Just because you're the oldest, she thinks you're mature. But you've never even been in love."

Anna could only stare, feeling as if she'd been smacked in the face. "If it's being in love to walk around all moony and then snap at people who try to talk to you, I'm just as glad." She stalked

112

across to the door. "If you're not leaving, I will."

Fuming, she went down the stairs, careful not to indulge in stamping her way down. Nobody would appreciate that. At least Sally had distracted her from the very real problem of the Burkhardt family. Maybe she should be glad of that.

When Anna reached the kitchen, she found her mother and her grandmother having a cup of tea. They were so quiet that she knew they'd heard.

"Is there another cup in that teapot?" She got a cup from the cupboard.

"Always," Mammi said, pouring while Anna slipped onto a chair. "I take it your sister was telling you all her troubles."

"The only trouble I could see is that she's making too much of this relationship with Joseph. Chances are she'll be out of love with him and in love with someone else by Easter."

"I wouldn't be surprised," Mammi said.

"That child is looking for trouble. Imagine wanting you to let her go out alone with Joseph. And at night! Anna would never have done that."

Mammi smiled. "I think Anna spoiled us by being such a good girl. Not that Sally isn't good," she added hastily. "But goodness, she takes everything to heart."

"I certainly hope I never talked like that when I was Sally's age. You'd have sent her to bed if she were a little younger."

"Yah, I know the temptation. But she's a few

years too old for sending her to bed or making her sit in the corner." Mammi shook her head. "I suppose she'll get over it."

Grossmammi patted her hand. "She will. Don't you worry about that. You raised her right. She'll grow out of this stage."

Anna's thoughts had been going in another direction. "I don't know Joseph very well. Is there anything wrong with him?"

"Nothing except that he lets Sally talk him into things," Mammi said. "I'm sure this idea of going on a date was hers, and he's not strong enough to stand up to her."

Anna couldn't help smiling. "She told me I don't know anything about it because I've never been in love. Judging by Sally, it's a very uncomfortable thing to be."

It was Mammi's turn to smile. "You're a different kind of person."

"That's right. Falling in love is different for everyone." Grossmammi seemed to look back into the past. "I'd seen your grandfather every day for years. I'd have said we were friends, that's all. And one day I looked at him, and then I knew. He was the only man for me." She clasped Anna's hand. "You'll be like that."

Touched, Anna's eyes swam with tears.

Grossmammi went on. "We always thought one day you'd—" She stopped, and Anna looked at her curiously.

"You thought I'd what?"

Mammi shrugged. "We thought it would be Matthew for you. But then he went away."

Anna opened her lips, found she had nothing to say, and closed them again. Was that what her parents had believed? It was obvious that Grossmammi thought so, too.

She took a large gulp of her tea and discovered that it was still very hot. Hot enough to jar her into reacting to her mother's words.

Maybe, at one point, she'd thought of Matt that way. But if anyone still believed that, they were doomed to disappointment. She'd begun to think she'd never be married. But if she were, it certain sure wouldn't be to Matthew.

Matt was getting frustrated. As far as he knew, Anna had met with the Burkhardt parents after school on Tuesday, but by Friday he hadn't had a chance to talk to her alone. On Friday afternoon he decided that he would stick around the Stoltzfus farm until he'd managed to get some answers, no matter how obvious it was.

He'd watched the Burkhardts get home on Tuesday. They'd all marched into the house, and the door slammed behind them. Other than seeing Carl working outside, he hadn't gotten another glimpse of them, and Aunt Ella said she didn't think Elizabeth had been outside the house at all.

Leading one of the draft horses, he headed for the barn. If the gelding wasn't stopped, he'd munch the fresh sprouts of green grass to the ground and go down with colic as a result. Matt had already brought Belle in, and she was the more difficult one to deal with. Stubborn, that's what she was, but a fine animal regardless, with her wide, strong chest and intelligent eyes.

She and Beau were a good matched pair. Simon wouldn't admit to being proud of them, but Matt had seen him smiling as he watched them out in the pasture.

"I thought you'd be bringing them in," Isaac said, moving from the straw bale where he'd been sitting to open the stall door for him. He patted the animal as Beau moved past him. "About time for them to do some work. If this weather holds, we'll get the plowing done soon."

"Sure will. April weather can fool you, though." Matt latched the door.

"That it can." Isaac seemed to limp a little when he moved, but Matt stilled the question in his mind. The old man didn't like any hint that he was slowing down. It was all right if he said it, but no one else could.

Matt suddenly realized that Isaac was reaching for the ladder up to the loft. Moving quickly, Matt swung his foot onto the first rung. "Time for me to throw down the hay."

"Are you thinking I'm too old to climb in the

loft?" Isaac was frowning, but as usual there was a slight twinkle in his eyes.

"I'm thinking that if you do my work, Simon won't need me anymore. You don't want to put me out of work, ain't so?"

Isaac chuckled, the lines crinkling in his leathery face. "I know when you're trying to smooth talk me, young Matt. Well, I'll go along and see if the kinder are coming from school yet."

Matt moved carefully up the ladder. He'd grown used to the short distance to the loft, but he still had no desire to bring on that awful dizziness. His feet firm, he hauled the hay bales over to the edge. He found Anna's father standing at the foot of the ladder, looking up at him. Matt hesitated.

"Something wrong?"

Simon shook his head. "Toss those down, and I'll start filling the mangers."

Matt nodded, and by the time he'd finished and climbed down, Simon was tossing the last flakes of hay in, and the horses were munching contentedly.

"I heard what you and Grossdaadi were saying. You managed that pretty gut."

Matt knew Simon well enough to interpret that as a compliment. "I didn't want to hurt his feelings. But I didn't want him climbing up to the loft when his leg was bothering him, either."

Simon clapped him on the shoulder. "Yah."

He seemed to struggle with his own feelings. "Nobody wants to admit they can't do what they've always done."

"I guess not."

Matt tried to imagine himself in that place. Well, he was, in a way. He couldn't manage heights anymore—but that wasn't permanent, he told himself. He'd get over that, just like he'd gotten over other bad things.

"Life keeps changing." Simon glanced around at the animals, and Matt had the feeling he was drinking in the peaceful atmosphere. "But some things stay the same, yah? Animals still have to be fed, fields have to be planted. If the weather holds, we'll start on the west field on Monday."

Matt nodded agreement. "Want me to check over the plows and the harness?"

"You don't need to do it now. You can go ahead and knock off if you want."

But he didn't want, not until he'd had a chance to talk to Anna. "That's okay. I'll get started on it anyway."

Matt hadn't gotten far along before he spotted Anna's buggy coming in the drive. When she'd reached the side of the barn where she normally kept it, he was there to catch Micah when he hurtled himself out of his seat.

"I went higher than anybody on the swings today, Matt." He seemed eager to share his triumph with someone. Anyone would do, he guessed.

"Great." He sent a cautious look at Anna, but she nodded. Apparently Micah hadn't broken the rules about going so high that the seat snapped back.

"I asked Rebecca if I could push her, but she didn't want to." He turned to his sister. "Why doesn't she want to go on the swings? I wouldn't let her get hurt." He sounded a bit hurt himself that his friend wouldn't cooperate.

Betsy ran to the house as soon as she got down, but Grace lingered, helping to unload. Anna was handing her canvas bag to Grace to carry into the house, but she focused on Micah at once. "I'm sure she knows that, Micah. Maybe she doesn't like swinging."

"She should try it first to see if she likes it." Grace, the logical one, always had an answer.

"If you're afraid of something, you might not want to try," Anna said. "Remember when Betsy tried to get you to climb the apple tree?"

That seemed to strike a chord with Grace, as she looked a little embarrassed. "But I did try it later."

Anna nodded. "When you were a bit older, it didn't seem scary at all, did it?"

"Maybe Rebecca will want to swing when she's older," Micah said. "She'll be older by Monday. Will that be enough time?"

Matt smothered a laugh. "It might take a bit longer than that, Micah." His mind shifted to his own problem. "Some things take longer to get brave about."

"Go on, you two," Anna said, gesturing them toward the house. "Mind you take everything in from the buggy. We don't need any lunch crumbs to attract the mice."

She shared a smile with him when they'd run off to the house. "That was our ride home today. One question after another from the two of them. And after teaching all day, I'd just like to be quiet for a while and not say one thing."

Matt caught hold of the harness and started to unbuckle it. "I guess I'm going to be unpopular then, because I've got a question, too."

She blinked as if she had to readjust her thinking, and a faint blush touched her cheek. "Yah?"

"The Burkhardts," he reminded her. "You didn't tell me what happened."

"I'm sorry. My thoughts were in such a jumble. Besides, it didn't seem as if there was a chance to talk about it."

"I know. I'm beginning to see one of the drawbacks about having a big family." He slid the harness off, and the horse stepped free. "Did you know I always wished I had a family like yours?"

Anna picked up a brush and tossed him another one. They started currying on either side. "It is hard to be alone with so many people in the house, there is that." She looked as if she had something specific in mind. "But I wouldn't trade them for anything."

"No, I'm sure you wouldn't." He watched her face as she worked on the mare. She hadn't answered his question. Did she know how fortunate she was? Something about her expression said she was considering just that.

She must. Anna had always been the one to look out for the younger children, taking the time to listen to them. And listening to her grandparents' stories, as well. He'd say she was well aware of how blessed she was.

And whether she answered him about his own longing to be part of hers . . . well, Anna had known too much about his family to have any doubts about what it was like.

Families were challenging, and sometimes there didn't seem to be any reason why you were born into one or another. He wished . . . well, he didn't know what he wished. That things had turned out differently, that was certain sure.

Anna went on brushing down the pony, but her mind was caught up in what Matt had said about families. She had been fortunate, all of them had, until they lost James. That had ruptured the familiar family unit.

Still, they were solid, despite the fact that the gap where James had been would never be filled. Maybe that was the way it should be. Sensing the empty space that James used to fill kept him present in their lives.

The mare turned her head and nudged Anna. Enough of this, she seemed to say. She had her eyes on the paddock, where the grass was showing green beneath the brown carpet of last year's growth.

Anna roused herself. "I'll just put Daisy in the paddock, and then I can give you the story, such as it is. I haven't figured out what to think about it myself."

Matt walked alongside her, and once they'd turned the mare in, he closed the gate and leaned on it. She found a spot on the fence not far from him.

She frowned, arranging her thoughts. "I hope maybe you can make sense of it. First off, Carl came with Elizabeth, and I didn't expect that."

"Threw a damper on the woman-to-woman chat, did he?"

"That's certain sure," she said emphatically. "The funny thing was how . . . well, loving they were with each other."

Matt turned a little so that he was facing her, his elbow on the top rail of the gate. "Well, they are married, aren't they?"

"I know that." Was he laughing at her for being naive? "But Amish couples, especially when they've been married for a few years, don't generally show affection in public. I mean, Daadi might give Mamm a special smile, but he wouldn't go holding on to her in public."

He nodded a little doubtfully. "You don't think it was what it seemed?"

"That's what I don't know. I got the feeling he was concerned about what she was going to say. Like maybe he put his hand on her shoulder to remind her or stop her—oh, I give up. I don't know exactly what seemed wrong to me, but something did."

"Between them?"

Matt looked as if he was trying to understand her explanation. She couldn't blame him for struggling. The fact was that she didn't understand herself.

"Yah, I guess that's it. He seemed worried, and she was chattering away like we were old friends. She didn't even ask me about the children that I can remember. Usually that's the first thing parents say when they come in. 'How are the kids doing?' "

"From the little I've seen of them," Matt said slowly, "she doesn't seem like she's as connected with them. I mean, he's the one to call them in to supper and that sort of thing."

"That's odd, isn't it?"

"It definitely is." He frowned, his hands grasping the fence rail. "Well, what else did they say? Did she talk about why she screamed?"

Anna shrugged. "Same story as he told us. Her

mother's pitcher, and how it slipped out of her hand. She put her hand out like this . . ." She laid her hand, palm up, on the fence between them. "It was all bandaged."

"Cut across the palm, I guess." He touched her palm lightly, sketching an injury. "Does that seem as odd to you as it does to me? If you drop something on the floor, it's going to break, but why would it cut your hand? I mean, there wouldn't be a sharp edge until after it had broken."

Anna closed her hand, pulling it back to her side. There hadn't been any need for him to touch her. She thought she should be annoyed by it, but didn't find any such feeling in herself. Just a momentary warmth, that was all.

She forced herself to focus. "I guess she could have grabbed it to pick it up and cut her hand then. Anyway, it all seemed odd. And I asked her to help with the end-of-the-year picnic, and she said, 'if they were still here.' "

"They surely aren't thinking of leaving, are they? They just bought the place, and they're hardly finished moving in."

Matt looked as baffled as she felt.

"I know. I tried to find out what she meant, but she was . . . well, funny. Like she wasn't paying attention or hearing me, sort of. And then all of a sudden he said they had to go, and they hurried out, got the kinder, and rushed off."

He leaned on the gate, gazing at Daisy cropping

the grass. Finally he shook his head. "Nothing makes any sense. How do the kids seem?"

"About the same. Well, you heard what Micah said. Rebecca seems to be afraid of just about everything. And I still haven't gotten her to say more than a couple of words to me. If you ask Thomas, he just says she's shy." She gave a helpless gesture, palms up. "I'm trying. And at least Micah is making an effort. The other scholars just don't try anymore."

"Isn't there anything you can do to get one of the other girls to make friends?"

"I'll try, but if someone doesn't respond . . ."

"You don't suppose she's deaf, do you?" he asked suddenly. "That might account for it."

"It might." She was embarrassed that he was the one who thought of it. "But she must hear what I say. She follows instructions all right. Still, it could be worth checking. There are a few simple tests I can do. Even a slight hearing loss might make her feel isolated."

"But you don't think that's it." He seemed to read her thoughts, just as he always had when they were young.

"I'd appreciate it if you didn't tell me what I'm thinking."

"I wouldn't do it if it weren't written all over your face." He touched her cheek lightly. "You have a very expressive face, Anna. When you're happy, those dimples come out. And when you're angry, James always said that your eyes changed color like a stormy sky."

"James talked a lot of nonsense," she snapped. She stepped back so that his hand fell from her face.

"He did, didn't he?" A faint smile lingered on his lips. "You never knew what he was going to say next."

"No." She softened suddenly, remembering. "We had a second cousin visiting us once who was really a tartar. James, all innocence, asked why she didn't get rid of her mustache. Amish weren't supposed to wear them, he explained, because they were too military."

Matt's lips twitched. "Did she ever come back?"

"I don't think so." She chuckled. "Ach, it's not fair to make fun of the woman, but she was an absolute pickle. She told Mammi that her children were badly brought up—"

"I'm not surprised after James said that." He was laughing, too, and looked surprised at himself.

"No, she told Mamm that first. I think James was trying to pay her back. Daad punished him, of course, but James told me afterward that it was worth it to see her face."

"Yah, that sounds like James." His face changed suddenly, his skin seeming to draw tight against the bones. "I miss him so much."

Instinctively, without thinking, she put her hands in his. "I know. I do, too."

CHAPTER SEVEN

Anna took a deep breath and wondered how long it had been since she'd breathed. It seemed like forever that she'd been standing here with her hands clasped in Matt's.

She pulled away, and he let go at once. Then she didn't seem to know what to do with her hands, so she busied herself pulling her sweater closer around her.

"I . . . I'd best get in. Mamm will need my help with supper."

"Yah. Me, too. Getting home, I mean. I'll push the buggy into the shed." He cast a weather-wise gaze at the sky. "Looks like we'll be getting rain before long." He hesitated. "Good night, then."

"Good night." Anna hurried toward the house, trying to get her thoughts to stop spinning around so recklessly.

She'd actually talked to Matt about James. They'd laughed at a memory together. That wasn't right, was it? Not with Matt.

She'd tried to adapt to having him here. She'd been grateful for his help with the Burkhardt children. But that didn't mean she'd forgiven him. She didn't intend to do more than go through the outward motions. And she certainly shouldn't have let him touch her.

She scurried up the back steps and inside the mudroom, pausing to take off her sweater. She pressed her hands against her cheeks, hoping they weren't as red as they felt. Control, that's what she needed. She sucked in another deep breath, lifting her rib cage and consciously trying to slow down her racing pulse.

Another minute or two, and she felt able to face the inquisitive eyes of her family. She opened the door and stepped into the kitchen.

"There you are," Mamm said. "I wondered why you didn't come right in. Don't forget we have to get everything ready to take to the mud sale early tomorrow."

"The mud sale," she repeated. "Yah, of course. Sorry. I forgot for a moment."

Mammi and Grossmammi both seemed to be looking at her.

"You ought to remember, much as we've been talking about it," Grossmammi said. "The money is for the fire company."

"Yah, for sure. I hadn't really forgotten." James had been a member of the volunteer fire company, along with Matt. Serving the community had been important to him. "I'll help you pack things up to take." She glanced out the window. As Matt had suggested, the western sky was darkening. "We might have to wait until morning to load up, though. It looks as if we'll be getting rain."

"It can't rain." Sally came into the kitchen in time to hear her, and her voice rose in a wail. "I can't believe it will rain for the mud sale. Not for that, of all things."

Grossmammi, who seemed to have less patience with Sally's drama than Mamm, gave her a sharp look. "Don't be ferhoodled, child. The rain doesn't know or care that it's mud sale weekend."

Sally sniffled, but at least she seemed to make an effort to behave herself. "I know. Sorry." She stared out the window for a moment. "It'll spoil everything," she muttered, and then whirled and hurried back upstairs.

"What on earth is that all about?" Anna was beginning to think Grossmammi had the right of it. Sally had been acting like a three-year-old who'd lost her cookie.

"I wouldn't be a bit surprised if she planned to spend the whole day tomorrow with that Joseph." Mammi's mouth firmed in a thin line. "She has a surprise coming if she thinks I'll let her do that. She's too young to be getting so serious."

Anna took the glass of milk her mother held out and helped herself to a shortbread cookie. "Denke, Mammi." She considered. "I'm not sure that she is serious, despite all the fussing she does. Don't you think this romance will go the way the rest of them have?"

"I wish I knew." Mammi checked a kettle on

the stove and turned the flame down a bit. "Well, let's not worry about her right now. You look as if you had a hard week."

"Not really." At least, not a hard week at school, and that was what Mammi meant, wasn't it? "I'm just still worried about the Burkhardt children."

"Has anything else happened?" Grossmammi settled herself in her favorite rocking chair and took out her knitting.

Anna thought about the picture Rebecca had drawn. If only she could show it to Mammi and ask her advice. She didn't think she was knowledgeable enough to deal with this.

Rebecca had made a picture of her house. It was the same sort of picture most children would draw: a rectangle for the house, a chimney on top with smoke coming out, a door, and four windows.

But in each of the four windows there was a figure. Mother and father in the two downstairs windows, children in the upstairs ones. Each figure stood alone. They were hardly more than stick figures, but somehow, Rebecca had contrived to reveal a sense of loneliness in each one.

Anna's throat tightened, and she struggled to rationalize the feelings away. She was reading too much into it. She—

"Anna?" Mammi and Grossmammi were both staring at her.

"Sorry. I was just trying to come up with some way of getting through to those children."

Mammi reached across the table to pat her cheek with a gentle hand. "If anyone can do it, you can."

For an instant she remembered Matt's hand on her cheek. She pushed the thought away.

"What if I don't know enough?" Doubting herself came more quickly all the time.

She sensed Mamm and Grossmammi exchange glances.

"The school board is there to help with whatever is needed, ain't so?" But Mammi sounded doubtful even as she said the words.

"If it was a question of a leaking roof or a broken shutter. Not this." She couldn't imagine discussing it with the three men who made up the school board.

"Then you might have no choice but to speak to the bishop, dear Anna," Grossmammi said. "It sounds like it's too much to deal with yourself."

Anna nodded, but she wasn't convinced in her own mind. What if she was imagining things? What if they'd already spoken to the bishop about their problems? Then she'd look like a nosy neighbor building up trouble for no good reason.

"I . . . I'm not really sure. I think maybe I should wait a little longer before doing that."

"Didn't you say that Matthew and Ella wanted

to help? Maybe they will have some ideas." Mammi hesitated. "Was that what you and Matt were talking about?"

Anna should have known that nothing that happened to her children escaped Mamm's notice. Not that there was anything wrong with her talking to him, but perhaps her mother thought it strange after all she'd said.

"Matt says they really do want to help," Mammi said, "and living right next door, and if you can work with him, it might help."

Anna couldn't miss the twinkle in her mother's eye, and she spoke quickly. "You know how I feel about Matthew. About his part in James's accident."

Her mother looked dismayed. "Ach, Anna, we've talked about that. It was an accident. We might all think we could have done something to prevent it, but that's foolishness."

"I'm trying to forgive." Her voice trembled as she thought of the Spring Communion, fast approaching. "Really trying."

Mammi put her arm around Anna's waist and held her tight. "I know it's not easy," she said softly. "But it will come. And if Matthew can help with those kinder, it wouldn't be right not to use that help. Ain't so?"

Anna didn't trust her voice to speak. All she could do was try to still her hurting heart and to nod her agreement.

Matthew had had no intention of going to the community mud sale on Saturday, but Aunt Ella had other ideas.

"You'll enjoy it once you get there," she said briskly, settling next to him on the buggy seat. "Besides, I might need you to load what I buy."

They reached the road, and he turned in the direction of the fire hall. The rain had stopped overnight but left the ground sodden, and the clouds still lingered.

"Mud sale will live up to its name, ain't so?"

Aunt Ella lifted one foot, showing him the rubber boots she wore. "It always does."

He returned to her comment about needing him to tote something for her. "You looking for something big and heavy today, are you?"

"Never can tell until you see it, ain't so?" Aunt Ella drew her sweater tighter against the morning chill. "I'm looking out for a small harrow to use for the garden. The one I have is rusting out."

"Yah, I saw."

He'd felt a bit guilty when he'd seen it lying in the grass behind the barn. If she'd put it up in the barn . . . but that was the point, wasn't it? He'd done that sort of thing when he'd lived next door, but he hadn't given it a thought when he'd left.

He could get the place into good condition while he was here, but what about when he'd left again?

"You know, if you need any work done around the place when I'm not here, Thomas next door might be someone to ask. He'd probably like to make a little money."

"Yah, he might. And it's certain sure he'd like an excuse to get away from home sometimes."

Matt glanced at her, remembering some of her earlier comments about those children. She was looking straight ahead at the curving road, her lips set in a way that accentuated her wrinkles.

"Teacher Anna is worried about the kinder. Not so much Thomas but the little girl." He hesitated. How much to say? "Anna said Rebecca's so shy, she doesn't say a word in school. And even when the parents came to talk to Anna, it seems they weren't helpful."

His aunt nodded, her frown deepening. "There's something wrong over there, that's certain sure."

"Do you have any reason to think he knocks his wife around?" he asked bluntly. "Or the kinder?"

She was silent for a time, still frowning. "I just don't know. Once or twice I've seen her outside and thought she looked like she'd been crying. But the truth is, she seems to stick in the house mostly." Aunt Ella put her hand on his arm. "If we could do something to help . . . well, maybe I can talk to Anna today."

"Gut," he said. "If we all put our heads together, maybe we can figure out what's best to do." Anyone might say that he had no business interfering. He wasn't the children's teacher, like Anna, or even a real neighbor, like Aunt Ella.

But he had something else. He had a history of an unhappy family life. And an abusive father. That gave him an insight that ought to allow him to help.

The township fire hall appeared on the right ahead of them—a cement block building with parking lots on two sides, surrounded by a couple of flat acres that were used for festivals, carnivals, and mud sales.

He pulled up near the door to the building and stopped to help his aunt down. "I'll go park and come back and find you."

She was already heading for the door. "I'll get a schedule to see what's going to be auctioned when. Keep an eye out for Anna."

Of course he would, and not solely because Aunt Ella wanted to talk to her. He followed the gravel road toward the place where buggies would be parked.

Even though they were early, it looked like others had been even earlier. Canopies covered areas where the various livestock would be auctioned. Smaller stands were springing up all over the place, some for food, others for crafts. Soft goods like quilts and such would be auctioned in the fire hall itself.

And everywhere he looked, there were people, both Amish and Englisch. Supporting the volunteer fire company was important to the whole community. After all, anyone might need the fire company.

He found the row of buggies and parked, feeling thankful he hadn't yet seen anyone that he'd feel he had to talk to. But when he turned away from the buggy, he realized he'd been premature. Jogging toward him was Sam Miller, his red hair unmistakable.

Grinning, he pounded Matt on the back. "I heard you were back. Gut to see you after all this time. What have you been up to? Why'd you stay away so long?"

"Working," he said, answering the first question first. "Construction, mostly. As for why . . . you should know that as well as anybody."

Sam had been there the night James died. Drinking, just like everyone else, but not as much as some. Sam had a solid core of common sense under his exuberant exterior. He didn't easily get carried away.

And Sam had gone with him, trying to reach James before it was too late. They didn't make it.

"Yah, well . . ." Sam sobered. "That was a bad business, seeing him gone so fast. Not easy to live with. But you didn't have to run away."

He grimaced. "A lot of people were glad to see the back of me. Including my parents."

"Everyone knew what they were like." Sam

136

waved them away with a sweep of his hand and seemed to think he'd best change the subject, because almost immediately he nodded toward Aunt Ella, coming away from the registration table with a large number on a placard.

"You're staying with Miz Ella, I hear. Better you than me. I was always scared to death of her."

"That's because she caught you trying to raid her apple tree. As I recall, she chased you with a broom."

"And threatened to turn her dogs on me," Sam added. "I never ran so fast."

"Dogs." Matt jeered at him. "One old hound who spent all his time sleeping and a puppy who might have slobbered you to death, that's all."

"They sounded ferocious enough."

"That was your guilty conscience." Funny, to be back on such easy terms with Sam again. As if none of it had happened. As if they were both still teenagers, and James was waiting for them around the corner.

"You think she still holds a grudge? If so, I'll see you later."

"Don't be a dope." Matt elbowed him. "Komm along and act like one of the grown-ups."

"Hey, she's talking to Teacher Anna. I haven't seen her for a while. Have you seen the Stoltzfus family since you've been back?"

Matt nodded. Anna was talking to Aunt Ella,

and the two of them had their heads together. He trusted they were talking about the Burkhardt children, not him.

"Yah, I've seen them. Matter of fact, I've been helping Simon on the farm for a few days."

Sam nodded, understanding. "I guess Simon could use a little help. Trouble is, every time anyone asks, he says he's fine." Sam eyed him. "Course you were always close with James. Maybe he feels different about you."

He shrugged, not sure how to answer Sam's comment. Did Simon feel differently because of his relationship with James? Or was he sorry for the guilt Matt carried? How could he tell? But there was one thing he knew for sure, and he'd best warn Sam about saying anything to remind Anna.

"Listen, watch what you say around Anna. She wouldn't want to hear anything about that night."

Sam looked at him in some surprise. "But hasn't she asked you anything about it? After all, you were there. You'd think, after all this time, that she'd want to hear about how it happened. I would, I know."

"You're not Anna." He'd best be blunt with Sam. Sam wasn't anyone to take a hint. Or even notice a hint. "Just keep quiet about it."

Sam eyed him shrewdly. "Does she know you tried to save James?"

"I don't know. Just watch what you say."

"I always watch what I say." He sounded injured. "But I'd think she'd be glad to know we did what we could to save James."

Matt shook his head. "You don't know anything about how Anna feels. Just don't mention it, okay?"

Sam shrugged. "If you say so. I'll try."

He wished he had a little more confidence that Sam knew when to shut up. Things had been a little better with Anna since they'd been trying to help the Burkhardt children. He didn't want to ruin that, not now. Anna had always been special to him, and she still was.

Anna had seen Matt's great-aunt gesturing to her. She hesitated and then smiled and waved. It was too late to pretend she hadn't seen her. Turning her back on the breakfast stand, she'd veered to join her.

"It's gut to see you. Did you bring anything to sell?" She knew that sometimes Ella donated hats, scarves and mittens that she had knitted or crocheted.

But Ella shook her head. "Just shopping today. My knitted work goes better in the fall auction for the school," she said, gesturing with her auction number as if to point toward it.

"Yah, for sure. I wasn't thinking about that."

Ella didn't seem to be listening, and she looked

worried. "I must talk to you about those kinder, but not here. Too many people around."

A little jolt of fear went through Anna. Foolishness, probably, but she couldn't help asking. "Has anything more happened?"

"I've hardly seen them at all." Ella shook her head, probably at her own worrying. "And that's strange, this time of year. It's not normal for kinder their age to be cooped up in the house when it's getting warm out."

"No, it's not, but—" She lost the rest of what she was going to say when she saw Matt coming toward them with Sam Miller by his side. Sam, who'd been one of James's good friends, now beaming because he was with Matt again.

"Look who I found, Aunt Ella." Matt's smile extended to Anna. "You're out early."

Anna tried to relax her throat. Even after all this time, something as simple as seeing Matt and Sam together brought her brother to mind, as if she could almost see him standing with them.

"Yah, Mammi insisted I come, too. I think she didn't expect a lot of help from the others." She glanced at Sam and tried not to feel hurt that he'd seemed to forget James so easily. She forced a smile. "It's gut to see you, Sam."

Sam's broad smile and freckled face seemed to turn him back into a ten-year-old again, ready to follow the other two into mischief.

"I was just telling Matt that it was time he came back here. Almost feels like old times, like when James—" He broke off and glared at Matt, rubbing his arm where Matt had nudged him. "All right, all right. It's not like Anna doesn't know we used to hang out together."

Matt looked as if he'd like to gag his friend. Anna glanced from one to the other. Had they been talking about James? Or about her?

Maybe Matt had cautioned him in regard to saying anything about James. If so, he should have known that would do no good. Sam was the sort of person who blurted out things other people thought but didn't say.

"Yah, that's right." She tried to look as if it didn't matter. "I'm on my way to get coffee for Mamm. She sent Sally, but Sally must have forgotten." Far more likely that Sally had found something else she'd rather do. "Ella, would you like something? Coffee, a doughnut?"

"Coffee, denke," Ella said, and Anna turned away quickly.

But Matt was just about as quick, falling into step with her as she moved the few yards to the breakfast stand. "I'll help carry things. Sam, you can entertain my aunt."

Glancing back, Anna was diverted by the horrified look on Sam's face. "What's wrong with him? He looks as if you told him to handle a live snake."

141

"He claims to be afraid of her." Matt grinned. "Apparently she chased him with a broom when he helped himself to apples from her tree."

Anna couldn't help but laugh. "I should think Sam would be impervious to that sort of trouble. It happened to him often enough."

She had meant to be cool and polite when she saw him, avoiding any personal chats. Already she'd lost her way with the intrusion of Ella and Sam into the mix. She couldn't very well be cool to Matt and friendly to the others in the same breath.

They'd reached the coffee stand by then, so she bought coffees for everyone. Matt leaned over the counter. "We'll take a dozen of the doughnuts, too."

She blinked. "I'm happy to get doughnuts for Aunt Ella and Mamm, but who are all the rest for?"

"Sam and I are still growing boys. He could probably eat a dozen himself without gaining an inch. And I'm paying for them." He put a bill down on the counter before she could react. "What about Sally?"

"What about her?" she said, nettled by his assumptions that they were in this jointly.

He nodded toward the tent where sheep were being auctioned. "Isn't that her with Joseph? Shouldn't we bring her something?"

She followed the direction of his nod and saw

her sister, standing far too close to Joseph and looking up at him adoringly.

"She was supposed to be getting coffee for Mammi. She doesn't deserve anything. And as far as Joseph is concerned—"

"Watch it. Don't say anything you might regret." He said it teasingly, and the twinkle was back in his eyes.

The food was ready to take by then, saving her from saying something even more cutting. Just as well, she supposed. She shouldn't be revealing her exasperation with her sister outside the family. Although if Matt wasn't aware of Sally's behavior by now, he hadn't been paying attention. She didn't think anyone could accuse him of that.

"I guess it wouldn't help matters if I scolded her in front of a crowd, would it?" She picked up the box of doughnuts.

Matt juggled the cardboard container that held the coffees, spoons, packets of sugar, and milk. "Better leave it to your mamm and daad. They raised you and James. I imagine they can cope with Sally."

Her jaw clenched at his mention of James, but almost immediately relaxed. In a way, it felt comforting to hear James spoken of in that natural way.

They could see that Ella and Sam had joined Anna's mother, who was setting up a table to hold the potholders and small quilted items she'd made.

"Sam must be getting over his fears of your aunt. He's still there," she pointed out.

"Probably because he sees the doughnuts coming." Matt looked relieved, she realized. They'd skated past a mention of James without any show of anger from her.

Anna glanced at Sam again, seeing pictures from the past of Sam, Matt, and James together. So often together. A question popped into her mind—one she hadn't thought to ask before.

"Was Sam there that night?"

If the abrupt question startled him, Matt didn't show it. His face tightened for an instant, that was all.

"Don't you know all about it by now?" He seemed genuinely surprised.

She shook her head. "The police didn't release names. Some in the community knew, but Daadi thought it best not talked about. I guess people respected that."

And what about her? Had she been hiding her head in the sand, trying not to think about what happened? Did she have her vision focused on Matt, knowing he'd gone with James only because he always did?

She didn't want to consider what that said about her. But if she had been hiding, it was past time she confronted the truth.

Anna studied Matt's face as he walked beside her. It was a rigid mask, lips in a straight, tight line, giving nothing away.

"Was he?" she said again.

He didn't react for a moment, and then he let out a long breath. "I think that's a question you'd better ask him."

CHAPTER EIGHT

Anna couldn't possibly ask Sam a question like that here. In fact, it was a wonder no one had overheard what she'd said to Matt. She glanced at Matt as they approached the others, and managed a whispered word.

"Sorry."

Then she put a smile on her face and held up the bag of doughnuts. "Look what we have."

Sam grinned. "Anna, did I ever tell you you're my favorite person in the world?"

Mamm swatted at him with a crocheted pot-holder. "Schnickelfritz," she declared.

Ella actually smiled. "He always was."

Anna and Matt began unloading on the end of the table. "Before you get too fond of me, you'd best know that the doughnuts were Matt's idea."

That didn't deter Sam, of course. "You're both my favorite people." He grabbed a napkin and picked up a doughnut, dropping powdered sugar down his front. "Jelly filled. My favorite."

"Anything to eat is your favorite," Matt said, handing out coffees.

"Denke to both of you," Mammi said. "Ella, do you want sugar for your coffee?"

In a few minutes everyone had what they

146

wanted. Anna sipped the steaming coffee gratefully. This would clear her head, she hoped. Not that she didn't always get up early, but she generally didn't rush around as much as they'd done this morning.

The area around the fire hall was becoming increasingly crowded as cars began pulling into the area marked for parking. With each extra person and vehicle the mud grew worse, but nobody minded. The more people, the better for the cause. And as for the mud, it wouldn't be a mud sale without the results of spring rains.

Sam studied the remaining doughnuts and then shook his head. "Can't manage another, much as I'd like to. Just as well, I guess, because I told my daad I'd check the farm equipment that's up for sale."

"You can come with us, then," Ella said briskly, putting her empty cup in the trash barrel. "Help us look for a harrow while you're at it."

"If you need the garden done, Ella, Matt can use ours," Mammi offered.

"That's good of you, but I wouldn't mind having a decent used one around. If we don't find one, I might just do that. Denke."

Anna exchanged a glance with Matt. That was Ella, all right. Always wanted to be independent, as she always had, but she seemed happy to have Matt to rely on. Maybe she was hoping he'd stay and make his home with her.

Something seemed to quiver inside Anna at the thought.

Would Matt decide to stay? Originally he'd said he was only here for a month or so, she'd thought. But as he settled in this place, he seemed more at home all the time. If he did decide to stay, she wasn't sure what she felt about that.

"Anna!" Her mother called her out of her thoughts. Mammi was already clearing away the remains of their snack and arranging her tables for selling. "Check the cashbox, please. I think there's fifty dollars in change, but we must be sure so we know how much we raise."

Anna pulled the metal box out and opened it. "Yah, that's important, ain't so? You wouldn't want other folks to donate more than you do."

"Giving is important, no matter what the amount," Mammi said, and then she smiled. "But yah, I wouldn't want to think we did worse than anyone else. That's pride, I'm afraid. I should be ashamed."

"The fire company won't care what you feel about the money you raise," Anna said firmly. "It's raising enough for the new equipment they need that's important, ain't so?"

In truth, she didn't think Mammi was being proud of her handiwork. She just wanted to give her share. Probably all of those who did direct sales felt the same way.

Everyone knew that the bigger items, the

148

auctioned ones, made more money for the cause. But one way or another, everyone wanted to help, and if you didn't have anything to auction off, you could help another way.

"It was gut to see Sam and Matthew together again," her mother said, smiling again. "You could tell how happy Sam was by the way he was clowning. Just like he used to. He hadn't been doing that lately, and it was nice to see it again."

"It doesn't . . ." Anna hesitated, but maybe it was best to say the thought in her mind. "It doesn't remind you that James isn't here?"

Still smiling, Mammi shook her head. "It reminds me that James had lots of happy times with his friends. The fact that his time here was short makes that even more important, ain't so?"

She hadn't thought of it in that way, Anna realized. In fact, there was a lot she hadn't thought of. She began to think that she had been stuck in one place since her brother died, until Matt's return forced her to move again, one way or the other.

Several Englisch ladies stopped by the stand. Most of them were familiar residents of Promise Glen, but one was apparently a visitor, because she was talking about buying something to take home with her.

"What about these quilted potholders?" Anna showed her the variety that Mamm and the girls had made over the winter. Grace's sewing had improved a lot recently, but she couldn't say the same for Betsy's. Betsy always had something else on her mind. Or maybe she just liked more active things than sewing.

While the woman was sorting through them, Anna spotted one of Grace's early efforts with stitches pulling loose, and she put it aside. She could fix it when they had a break.

The woman was enthusiastic, picking out a half dozen to buy, and they made several more sales to her and her friends. One of them noticed the coffee cup Anna had set on a box behind her.

"Coffee, that's just what I need about now. Where did you find it?"

Anna stepped out from behind the table to direct her to the coffee stand. When she turned back, Mammi was frowning.

"That reminds me. Did you see Sally anywhere when you went for the coffee? The coffee she was supposed to get," she added, looking exasperated.

Anna hesitated, not wanting to be a talebearer, but unable to lie about it. "Yah, but not to speak it. She was over by the tent where they were auctioning the sheep."

"With Joseph, I suppose." Her mother shook her head. "I don't know what to do with that girl. You were never like that at her age."

Not sure whether the comparison was good or bad, Anna sought for a peaceful response. "When I was Sally's age, I was already assisting the teacher at Orchard Hill School. I was so excited about the idea of becoming a teacher that I didn't have a lot of time for boys."

That seemed to make her mother stop and think, and Anna was grateful. As annoying as Sally was, she really didn't want to see her in trouble with Mamm and Daad. Surely she just had to find her way.

"That's true," her mother said slowly. "Sally seems to like working with the dressmaker, but not in the same way you like teaching. If there's something else she'd rather do, I haven't seen it, though."

"She's young yet, even though she doesn't think so," Anna put in.

"I wish she realized it." Mammi shook her head, smiling a little. "You four girls are all so different. I'd never have believed it before I had children of my own. And as for Micah . . . he's different still." A shadow crossed her face. "Sometimes I think he's too serious about helping your daad. He forgets that he's too small to do a grown man's work."

Anna nodded. She'd noticed that, too. Apparently raising a family was even more complicated than teaching a school of eight different classes.

"He'll be all right." It was the only thing she could think of to say, and once the words were out, she decided she'd seldom said anything more useless.

"There's Sam again," Mammi said, glancing toward one of the auction tents. "Looks as if he's checking out the goats."

Anna almost asked Mamm then. *Was Sam at the party that night?*

She bit her lip, experiencing a flood of conflicting emotions. Maybe it was best not to know any more than she did. James was gone. Probing and questioning wouldn't bring him back.

Accept. Forgive. That was what the church said. But since Matt came back, she hadn't been able to do either of those things.

Matt hadn't expected his return to Promise Glen to become as complicated as it had. He wove his way through the crowd to the field where a variety of farm wagons and equipment were displayed, but his thoughts were on people, not things.

Seeing Sam again had moved him more than he could say. He'd missed him, just as he'd missed James, and once he was out in the Englisch world, they'd seemed about as far apart. He should have told Sam what he'd intended before he disappeared, but it had seemed impossible to talk about it to anyone. He'd just wanted to get away, as far and as fast as he could.

At first it had taken all his thoughts and energy simply to make enough to eat. Then, once he had a decent job, he'd immersed himself in it, trying not even to think of the past. He'd just wanted to do good work, be accepted, belong out there.

Now he knew the past had been here all along, still waiting for him.

He hadn't noticed Aunt Ella for a few minutes, so he looked around, spotting her just a few yards away, glancing through a stack of hoes and rakes.

Before he took more than a couple of steps in her direction, someone hurtled into him from behind. He swiveled to find young Micah, his grin a replica of his brother's at that age, hanging on to him.

"I'm here," he declared.

"Hey, Micah, I didn't know you were coming." He put his hand on the boy's shoulder. Since the day they'd worked on the brooder coop together, they'd gotten closer than had seemed possible that first day, when Micah had eyed him so cautiously.

Micah's spring straw hat had been pushed back by his enthusiastic greeting, so Matt settled it squarely on his head. "You weren't with your mother and Anna. How did you get here?"

"Grossdaadi and Grossmammi brought me. The girls, too. They're going to help Mammi." He looked relieved to be spared that, obviously thinking it was girls' stuff. "Grossdaadi is fun to go places with. He tells stories while he drives."

Matt had to smile at that. "Yah, I remember your grandfather's stories. I learned a lot from them." The old man had a gift for teaching without letting on that that's what he was doing.

"He told us about the time James pulled you over the fence and tore your pants. And about how you and James tried to climb to the top of the barn roof and got stuck."

"I remember." Actually, he remembered all of it. The scenes played through his mind vividly, as if he could step back into them again. Seemed like he and James both should have learned a little caution, but they never did.

Micah tugged at Matt's sleeve, encouraging him to bend closer. "Look what I have." He opened his hand to show a crumpled and sweaty dollar bill. "Grossdaadi gave it to me to buy something."

He was so serious that Matt had to reply in the same way, although he didn't think the boy would find many things he could get for a dollar.

"What are you going to spend it on?"

"I don't know. Do you think anybody would have some pink lemonade? I really like that kind. Mammi only makes yellow lemonade."

"I'd think we could find some somewhere." And if it cost more than a dollar, he'd make up the difference as discreetly as he could. Micah was obviously proud of having that crumpled bill to spend.

He caught sight of Aunt Ella gesturing to him. "First I have to find a harrow for my aunt. You want to help?"

"Sure." Micah swung around, eyes searching the field. "I'll find one for her. Be right back." He darted off.

Smiling in spite of himself, Matt made his way to where his aunt waited. After a shy beginning, Micah had certainly come out of his shell with him.

"What is young Micah up to?" Aunt Ella was watching Micah, who by now was jumping up and down and waving his arms, then pointing to something on the ground behind a clump of dead grass.

"Helping," he said. "Looks like he's found a harrow for you."

"We'd best get over there, then." She sounded as gruff as usual, but her face crinkled in a smile. "He reminds me of someone."

"Yah, I know. He's like James at that age." Funny that he could say it out loud and find it didn't hurt.

Aunt Ella's smile extended to him. And then they walked over to Micah.

"Look, Matt." Micah stood between two different harrows. "There's a small one and a big one."

Matt knelt to examine the finds more closely. "This is a double one." He indicated what the boy had called the big one. "This is like your father has."

"The single harrow is best for me." Aunt

155

Ella stepped a bit nearer. "I'll just use it for the garden. Maisy can pull this easily."

Tipping it up on edge, Matt brushed off the accumulated mud. "What do you think? It's in pretty good shape, yah?"

Micah mimicked Matt's gesture, brushing the mud off the other side of the prongs. "Yah, pretty good," he said.

Aunt Ella's lips twitched. "What do you think it will go for?"

"I'm out of the habit of auctions," Matt said. "Twenty? Maybe more if someone really needs it, but I don't really know."

"It's worth a try, anyway," she said. She consulted the list in her hand. "An hour until they auction this batch. We may as well get something to drink."

"Lemonade," Micah said quickly.

"Pink lemonade," Matt added, laughing. "Let's go look for some."

As they walked back to the circling crowds, Matt found himself wondering what Anna might think if she saw her little brother hanging out with him. If she didn't like it, he wouldn't be surprised.

Still, he wasn't going to rebuff the child. And whether Anna liked it or not, he wished he could find a chance to be a help to the boy.

But it wasn't Anna who caught his gaze just then. It was Carl Burkhardt, walking toward them with his two children. Not surprising that he'd come to the mud sale. But what was surprising was that Carl actually looked relaxed and smiling as he pointed something out to Rebecca.

As if he sensed someone was watching him, Carl turned until he was looking at Matt. Considering their last encounter, it wouldn't be surprising if Carl took his children and headed in the opposite direction. Instead, he came right toward them, holding his daughter's hand, his smile still lingering.

"Gut day for a mud sale, yah?" He spoke to Ella, nodding to Matt and Micah. "I brought the young ones along to see the sights."

"Your wife didn't care to come?" Aunt Ella probed a bit.

A shadow came over his face. "No, she didn't feel like going out. She was going to take a nap." He brightened again as he looked at the children. "We'll take her a treat when we go home, yah, kids?"

"Funnel cakes," Thomas said. "That's Mamm's favorite."

Aunt Ella began to give him directions to the funnel cake stand while Matt watched them, bemused. It was unusual, to say the least, for a relatively young Amish woman to go to bed during the day unless she was sick. Maybe all the odd things they'd noticed had that simple an explanation.

Had Anna's imagination been running amok, to say nothing of his?

It was possible that they'd misinterpreted their limited conversations with Carl and his wife, but he didn't think Anna could be wrong about the children and their problems. He'd like to see them together, just to find out what she made of this version of Carl Burkhardt.

Anna finally persuaded her mother to take a break, leaving Anna in charge of the handwork stand while she checked out the other stands and got something to eat. Grace stayed to help Anna while Betsy took advantage of the moment to decide she should go and get lunch.

Grace lined the array of potholders up neatly. "People mess them up when they look at them," she complained.

"True, but they look through them to find the color or the kind they want, and then they buy. So cleaning up afterward is part of the job."

Grace nodded, her expression serious. "I'll remember. When I get bigger, I'll make things to sell for the fire company, too."

"You already have." Anna pulled out the quilted potholder, its loose stitches repaired. "You made this, didn't you?"

Grace examined it carefully. "I guess. But those stitches look smaller than mine." She eyed Anna, who laughed.

"I had to fix it a little bit, but otherwise it's fine. You used pretty colors, and I'm sure someone will buy it. Let's put it on top, where people will notice it."

Smiling, Grace nodded and arranged it carefully on top of similar colored ones.

This was the nice part of being a big sister, Anna reflected. Doing things with the younger ones. Teaching them. Too bad that little sisters grew up to be troublesome teenagers. Although Grace, with her calm attitude and core of common sense, seemed unlikely to go floating on a cloud as Sally did. Or to flatly refuse to move on, like Betsy.

"There's Micah," Grace said a few minutes later. "Look, he has Rebecca Burkhardt with him."

Anna blinked, wondering if Grace was imagining it, but sure enough, Micah and Rebecca came up to the table, hand in hand.

"Rebecca's daadi is talking to Matt and Ella about harrows, and Rebecca wanted to see you. So he said she could come with me to find you. Is it okay?"

"Of course it is." Surprising, but okay. She gestured for them to come around the table. "I'm glad to see you. Do the two of you want to help us for a while?"

Micah looked at Rebecca and then nodded, seeming to appoint himself her spokesperson.

159

"Yah, Rebecca would like to do that. I'd rather go see what Grossdaadi is doing."

"Fine." Anna smiled at him, brushing the fringe of corn silk–fine hair out of his blue eyes. "Do you know where Grossdaadi is?"

Micah took a shortcut by scrambling under the table and emerging on the other side like a jack-in-the-box. "Grossdaadi is helping with the harrow, too."

Waving, he hurried away, almost, but not quite, breaking into a run. He knew that would earn him a scolding from someone. It sounded as if he enjoyed being involved in grown-up kinds of things. Or maybe he was enjoying being with Matt. It wasn't the first time she'd seen him seeking out Matt's presence.

It troubled her, and she didn't quite know why. Aside from her own prejudice against Matt, her parents and grandparents had accepted him. Daadi had even asked Matt to teach Micah how to do certain work, and to work alongside him. That was how Amish children learned, working alongside someone who already knew how.

She glanced at Rebecca, who looked up at her and smiled. She was arranging dishcloths by color.

"I like that, Rebecca. It looks like a rainbow." Rebecca nodded, a small, secret smile on her face.

Maybe this was a good time and place to get

the child talking a little. "Did you come to the mud sale with your daadi?"

Rebecca nodded, so Anna smiled, tipping her head to one side and cupping her ear.

That got a giggle out of her. "Yah," Rebecca said. "And Thomas."

"Gut." Anna gave an encouraging smile. "Did Mammi come, too?"

Her good fortune came to an abrupt end. Rebecca's small face shut down, and her lips formed a firm line. She shook her head.

"Ach, well, it doesn't matter. Maybe she'll come next time."

That didn't seem to warm the child up any. She returned her gaze to the dishcloths, her little hands deft and quick as she arranged them.

A shadow fell across the table. "What's going on over here?"

Matt's voice gave her a jolt. She looked up to see him standing on the other side of the table, smiling at them.

"I have a new helper," she said, indicating Rebecca.

"So I see." He bent over the dishcloths, and Rebecca spread them out for him to see as if she were an experienced saleswoman. "Maybe I should buy some of these for my aunt Ella. I think hers are looking a little shabby."

"You're using the dishcloths a lot, are you?" She implied doubt, laughing at him.

"I'll have you know I've been helping with the dishes every night. If someone's good enough to cook for me, the least I can do is wash dishes, right, Rebecca?"

She nodded solemnly.

"Suppose you pick out five pretty ones for me to give Aunt Ella." He slanted a laughing glance in her direction. "I assume I get a discount for buying five at a time, ain't so?"

"I'll think on it." She moved a step or two away, turning slightly away from the child. She lowered her voice. "I heard you were talking with her father. Really talking?"

"Yah." Matt glanced at Rebecca to make sure she wasn't paying attention. "He's like a different person today. Talking, relaxed . . . he even offered to buy the harrow Ella needs and do her harrowing for her so she doesn't have to buy something she'd only use once a year."

Anna's eyebrows shot up. "That's a change. Why this show of friendship after trying so hard to stay away from everyone?"

"I don't have a guess," Matt said, frowning a little. "The kids seem happier, too." He shrugged. "Maybe they're just happy to be here. Or maybe things are better at home."

"If so, I just hope it lasts." Her words were heartfelt, but she didn't quite believe in them.

People didn't change that abruptly, did they? The man who'd slammed the door in their faces the last time they'd seen him . . . the man who'd hustled his wife away from a conference with the teacher, he wouldn't become friendly overnight.

Matt seemed to hear the doubt in her voice. "You're not planning to do anything, are you?" There was a quiver of nervousness in his voice, and he looked at her as if she were a stick of dynamite about ready to blow up.

"Ach, relax. If I do, I'm not involving you in it anyway. But I just don't believe in sudden transformations."

"You think the tiger can't change his stripes."

There was an odd note in his voice, and his face had hardened when she looked at him. He thought she was referring to him, she realized.

Well, maybe that was true. She didn't believe he had changed, any more than she accepted the idea that the Burkhardt children's problems were solved, just like that. The days of sudden miracles were over as far as she was concerned, and she didn't think she could change, even if she wanted to.

Did she want to? She honestly didn't know.

CHAPTER NINE

Anna drove home from school alone on Tuesday, sending her brother and sisters to walk home with their classmates while she stayed to correct a few papers. Instead, she'd found her thoughts fully occupied by the question of what to do about the Burkhardt children.

Things had seemed brighter when the children were enjoying themselves at the mud sale. Unfortunately, after an off-Sunday spent at home, the Burkhardt children seemed back in whatever problems kept them sullen and silent at school. It hurt her heart, not knowing what to do for them.

As the mare turned in automatically at the farm lane, she was forced to realize that she'd have to talk to Matt and find out what had been happening at the Burkhardt farm since Saturday. Had he seen anything more of the family? He might have some new insight, and she wouldn't find out by avoiding him.

Pulling up at her usual spot to unload, she spotted Micah and Grace coming down from the stand of trees at the upper side of the pasture. They waved with something in their hands, and as they got closer, she realized that Grace held a cluster of spring wildflowers.

"Look what we found." Grace was almost

dancing as she arrived, her face lit with pleasure. "We're the first to bring Mammi spring flowers. We beat everyone else."

"You did." She slid down from the buggy seat to take a closer look. "Do you know what these are? Mammi's sure to ask."

Mammi had been determined to pass her love of wildflowers on to her children, and she'd begun taking them for early spring wildflower walks as soon as they could toddle. They should not only find and admire, but also be able to identify.

"Yah, for sure," Grace said, and then corrected herself with her usual caution. "Well, I think so anyway. This little blue one is hepatica, ain't so?"

"Right." Anna touched the tiny, deep blue petals lightly. "And the little white ones?"

"That's . . . um . . ."

"You don't remember," Micah chuckled. "You said you'd remember but you didn't."

"Yah, I did," she flared up. "It's bloodroot." She hesitated. "Isn't it?"

"Better go and ask Mammi," Anna said, laughing a little as her mind jumped ahead to the idea of doing a lesson on wildflowers with her younger scholars. "I think it's chickweed. Bloodroot flowers are bigger, I think."

"Okay, I will." Grace darted off toward the house, but Micah had already started to take the harness off.

"Grace always thinks she knows more than

me," he observed, not in any irritated way, but just as if he were stating a fact.

"Well, she is older, so she's had more time to learn."

Micah wrinkled his nose as he considered that fact. "You mean I'll always be the youngest. That stinks."

"Don't use language like that," she said with little hope that he'd pay attention.

"But I'm the only one who's a boy now," he announced, sounding as if that was a source of pride. Maybe his determination to use words she didn't like stemmed from the same source.

Her heart winced at the reason he was the only boy. "I guess you are. What does that have to do with whether you know the names of the flowers?"

"Nothing," he admitted. "But I have other things to learn. I need to be like James."

What was in his mind? she wondered. "I'm sure you will be," she said gently, hoping that was the right response. "It just takes time."

"I guess." He looked a bit discontented at that. Was he discontented with the time it took to grow up? The years between the older children and the youngest of a big family could seem forever, she supposed, especially if you were only eight and you wanted to do a man's work.

"Denke, Micah." She reached for the harness to hang it up, but he held on.

166

"I'll take it. I have to go in the barn anyway."

Nodding, she took the mare to the paddock.

Funny, the things children found to worry about. If Micah was concerned about being good enough to take over the farm, he certain sure didn't need to be. Grossdaadi claimed he was a born farmer, and Grossdaadi should know.

Anna guessed it was that same issue again . . . some people wanted to leap ahead to the next stage of life while others held back. She stood for a moment, leaning on the paddock gate and watching the mare cropping at the grass.

Pushing ahead, or holding back . . . which was she?

Movement beyond the mare caught her eye, and she saw Matt at the far corner of the paddock, apparently working on a fence post. Well, she had to talk to him, so it may as well be now. Slipping inside the gate, she headed across the paddock toward him.

He glanced at her and then turned back to what he was doing, his hands on a rail he was screwing into place.

"Do you have a minute to talk?"

"If you can hold this board steady while you talk, I can."

She put her hands on the board, holding it in place. "Why not just nail it in?"

"Because that mare of yours likes to lean on it, trying to reach the apple tree. Your daad says he's replaced it twice because she managed to pop the nails out. Maybe this will defeat her."

"Knowing Daisy's stubborn streak, I wouldn't count on it." She watched his hands, strong and skilled, as he screwed it into place. She knew she needed to talk to him about the Burkhardt children, but for the moment it was satisfying to stand in the afternoon sunlight and watch him work.

"There." He straightened, dropping the tools in a canvas bag at his feet. "What's—" He broke off abruptly, looking over her shoulder toward the barn, his face freezing.

She spun, heart clenching with fear, and saw what he had—Micah, pushing himself through the loft window at the back of the barn, looking up as if to find something to hold on to.

"Micah!" She tried to cry out to him, but her throat could produce only a quavering note of fear.

Then Matt had pushed past her, racing toward the barn, throwing words over his shoulder as she ran after him.

"Go. Get your daad or grandfather—the long wooden ladder. Hurry!"

"Micah . . ."

She was beside him now, running step for step, but he thrust out his arm and deflected her.

"Get them. The ladder. It's the best thing you can do for him."

It took all she had to turn and lose sight of that

small figure, standing now on the edge of the window. Matt was right. Help—more help and the ladder.

Thank the Lord she saw them coming out of the refurbished brooder coop. She waved her arms, and they started hurrying toward her.

"The big ladder," she gasped as soon as she could get out the words. "Matt says . . . bring the big ladder . . . Micah . . ."

They must have filled in the words. Daad's face went white, but he ran instantly toward the machine shed, Grossdaadi hobbling after him. Anna stood for an instant, torn in both directions, but she knew how heavy the wooden ladder was. Daad would need her. She'd have to trust Matt now.

Trust Matt. Her heart wrenched. Sending up a wordless prayer, she ran to catch the end of the ladder as Daad pulled it from its hooks. *Please, Lord. Please.*

Heart pounding so loud he couldn't hear anything else, Matt raced to the barn. What had possessed Micah to think of doing such a thing?

He flung himself at the ladder to the loft, willing himself not to think about the height at the peak of the barn, not to think about reaching, straining every muscle, trying to catch something . . . anything . . . to stop a downward plunge. Not to think about failing.

Reaching the loft, he paused for a split second to orient himself and then spun toward the back. Through the window he could glimpse trees and sky, but no small figure blocked it. Micah—for an instant a horrifying picture filled his mind, but he struck it away.

Micah hadn't fallen. If he had, Matt would have heard the cry. So Micah had somehow climbed beyond the window.

A few hurried strides took him to the open space. He thrust his head through, swiveling to look up, and his breath caught.

Micah clung to the barn, one foot balanced atop the shutter that could close the window when needed. His other foot seemed to grope for purchase on the flat boards. He had managed to just touch the hoist that was used to lift hay into the loft.

Careful, Matt warned himself. *Don't startle him into a sudden movement.*

"Hey, Micah," he said, trying to speak naturally through his knotted throat. "What are you doing?"

Micah glanced over his shoulder, his face crinkling into a smile so that he looked like a mischievous monkey. "Just climbing." He seemed to try to sound cool, as if this were something he did every day.

"Yah, you sure are. How about coming back in here with me?"

He reached out, twisting his body around so

that he could get his upper torso through the opening. "Just grab my hand, and I'll pull you back in."

Micah shook his head. "Not coming in. I'm going on top of the barn roof."

Matt's heart lurched, and he fought for calm. Where was Anna? Where was the ladder?

"You don't want to do that. Think about how much trouble you'll get into." Matt strained, the edge of the window cutting into his back. "Just take my hand."

"James climbed up here." His voice sounded so calm, even natural, though he was a heartbeat away from disaster. "I can, too."

So that was it. Poor little guy was so determined to live up to his big brother.

"Listen, Micah. James didn't make it to the top, not when he was your age. In fact, he didn't get clear to the top until he was a lot older, and then he used a ladder."

"Then I'll do better than he did, ain't so?"

"No, you'll just get yourself in a peck of trouble, that's what'll happen."

Matt struggled to assess the situation calmly. There was no good news that he could see. Micah wasn't tall enough to reach the hoist, and he didn't have the arm strength to pull himself up. There was no possible way for him to reach the top.

He had to get to him, at least close enough

to stabilize the boy until the ladder got here. He could hear voices shouting, and he risked a glance away from Micah, thinking they might be in sight.

The world spun dizzyingly. His stomach lurched, and he gripped the rough edge of the window until it cut into his hand. That was enough to chase away the vertigo.

The others weren't in view yet, and any minute now Micah could lose his grip. Matt couldn't take the chance of waiting for them.

He squirmed around until he could force himself farther out, talking to himself all the time.

Sit on the window ledge. Reach for a handhold on the shutter. Don't think about how far down it is. Stay calm.

"How about it, Micah?" How he kept his voice normal, he didn't know. "Just take my hand, okay? I'll hold you. See, I'm right here."

"I don't need—" Micah's words cut off. For the first time it seemed he looked down. His eyes widened, the bright blue darkening. His face paled.

"Look at me." Matt snapped the words, pulling Micah's attention to him. "I'm coming."

He forced the rest of his body through the window, using the shutter for leverage. Once out, he balanced on the edge, praying the shutter screws would hold, wondering if God would listen to someone like him. Flattening himself against the wall, he looked up.

"Matt . . ." Micah's voice had become a thin wail. "I'm scared."

Me, too. Matt reached out, straining, and grabbed the brace for the hoist with one hand. His arm muscles screamed as they took his full weight, but he got his other hand on Micah's leg.

"I . . . I can't hold on . . ." The boy's voice trembled.

"It's okay. Just slide right down against me. I've got you now."

He must have sounded sure enough, because the boy followed his orders immediately. He let go and slid down the boards. Matt pressed his body against the boy's until Micah could get both arms tight around his neck. They clung together, and Matt was afraid to breathe for fear of disturbing their precarious balance.

Simon's voice from below sounded almost calm. "Ladder coming." A thud shook dust from the planks of the barn as the ladder struck just a couple of feet from them.

Feet sounded on the ladder. Matt didn't dare to attempt reaching it or even looking that way. He could only stay where he was, holding Micah safe, trusting his muscles wouldn't give out, no matter how much they screamed.

And then Simon's deep voice sounded next to him. "All right now. Pass Micah over to me."

Matt managed to nod. Micah still clung to him like a monkey, but they managed to coax and pull him over onto the ladder with his daad's arms strong around him.

"Now you," Simon said.

Matt shook his head. "Take Micah down first." He couldn't move, not for a moment, anyway. He could only be grateful when Simon didn't argue.

Simon slipped down quickly. Matt heard voices—Anna, her grandfather—as they grabbed the boy. Then Simon was next to him again, his hands firm and strong as he helped Matt onto the ladder.

Matt clung there for a moment, his face pressed against the rough wood. Slowly, a step at a time, slow as an old man, he made his way down.

Finally his feet found firm ground. He took one step, then slid down to his knees. He could hear voices exclaiming, and then Simon.

"Leave him alone for a moment. Komm, get Micah to the house."

He was alone, finally. He could let himself retch, spasms wrenching his body, until he could finally lie still, his face buried in the damp grass.

How much later he couldn't guess, he realized someone was kneeling next to him. Then a warm, wet cloth was passed over his face.

"All right now." Anna's voice was soft. "Sit back against the wall for a minute. Everyone is all right."

• • •

For a moment, Anna thought Matt wasn't going to respond at all. Then he grasped the cloth from her hand, pressing it hard against his lips. Finally he gave what might have been a nod and pushed himself back onto his knees.

She grasped his arm, easing him into a sitting position against the wall. His face was almost gray, and the skin seemed to have shrunk against the bone.

Pity surged through her, wiping away any other feelings in the urgent need to help. She rinsed the cloth in the pail of water she'd brought, then pressed it against his face, longing to wipe away that look of despair.

"It's all right," she repeated. "Honest. Micah is fine." Her throat clenched as she thought of what might have been, and she had to swallow before she could go on. "You saved him."

The words reverberated as if they shivered in the air. Matthew had saved Micah from a fall that would surely have resulted in broken bones if not worse. And she was seeing the cost to himself.

His head moved painfully from side to side in negation. "Doesn't make up," he muttered.

"Komm." She tugged at him. "Let's get in the house. You need some coffee. You'll soon feel better."

At that his eyes focused on her almost angrily. "Leave me be."

"Matt, you're scaring me. You aren't making sense." Again she pulled at his arm in a futile attempt to raise him.

He yanked his arm free. But it seemed the anger was pulling him out of whatever daze he'd been in, and she was thankful. Matthew angry was easier to deal with than Matthew lost in his own pain.

"You wanted me to suffer for what happened to James, ain't so? Well, this is it, so take a gut look."

"I didn't—" She started to protest, but he swept on, grabbing her hand to keep her from pulling away.

"Yah, you did. And I thought I could deal with it if I got away from here, but I was wrong. I carried it with me, no matter where I went. James died, and the rest of us were still alive. It didn't seem fair. And then the accident on the job . . ."

His frown deepened, but she saw that his color was better. Whatever was driving him to talk, maybe it was helping.

"You said there was an accident on your job, so you had some time off. I thought you got hurt." He hadn't really said that, she realized, looking back at that conversation.

"Nobody got hurt but somebody could have died." His fingers tightened, biting into her hand. "Boss's son, new on the job. Cocky kid who thought he could handle himself."

Anna struggled to follow. "This kid . . . what happened to him?"

"Playing around on a girder. I yelled at him." His eyes glazed, as if focused on the scene in his mind. "He mouthed off, turned, and fell, just like that. He was dangling, hanging on. I got to him, grabbed him—other guys rushed to help. He was okay. But I wasn't. Couldn't stand being up there. He was back at work the next day like nothing happened. Not me."

Anna struggled to understand. It was James's accident that was at the heart of it, that was certain sure. She tried to untangle the feelings that ricocheted back and forth—his, hers, and back to his again.

"You said your boss gave you time off. He didn't blame you." That was evident.

"Right." His mouth twisted. "I've still got my job, but I can't do it if I panic every time I'm fifteen feet from the ground."

"But you saved that boy. And today you saved Micah. Even if you were sick afterward, you did what you had to do."

Anna wasn't sure what side she was arguing, but it was all she could find to grab hold of. He'd done what he had to.

He didn't respond. She realized he was still gripping her fingers so tight that she was losing feeling in them. She put her other hand on top of his, pressing it lightly.

"Komm, that's right, ain't so?"

"Yah." It was grudging, but she could feel him relax a little. His grip loosened, his fingers flexing as if they had been locked tight and had to be released slowly.

"Losing someone we love is just about the hardest thing there is."

She spoke slowly, feeling her way along, afraid of saying the wrong thing. He'd said she'd wanted him to suffer, but if she had, she didn't any longer.

"I guess we're bound to make some mistakes in dealing with it, yah?" She continued watching his face, hoping to see some agreement or understanding there.

She saw the muscles in his face begin to relax. The color began to return, as if welling up from beneath his skin. At last his eyes grew warm, and she seemed to feel that warmth touch her face.

Matt looked down at their clasped hands with the slightest of smiles. "I guess God's not finished working on me yet."

"Me, either." She'd have to think that through, but she felt as if she was finally on the right path.

She drew her hand away from his, and just as gently, he released his grip. She took a breath, searching for something that would move them forward. Her heart was full with a complicated mix of feelings—love, pain, pity, sorrow . . .

"Komm." She tugged at his arm again. "You'd

best go inside with me to have that coffee, because if you don't, Mammi will be coming after you herself."

He smiled, his gaze warm on her face. "I guess we'd better." He started to push himself up, and she grasped his arm to help, feeling the hard muscles tremble. Finally he was standing steady next to her. They turned toward the house.

Anna walked next to him, still holding his arm and feeling the change in what lay between them. It was different now. She wasn't sure how, but she knew that much anyway.

CHAPTER TEN

When they reached the back porch steps, Anna realized she was still holding Matt's arm—with no good reason, because he was walking fine now. She dropped her hand, pressing it into her skirt and hoping the heat she felt in her cheeks didn't show.

She hurried ahead of him into the kitchen. Just Mammi and the grandparents were there, making her suppose that Micah had been taken off for a private talk with Daadi.

"There you are at last." Mammi rushed at Matt, grabbing him in something between a hug and a shake. "You sit right down here and have some gut hot coffee. Something to eat, maybe a big slab of shoofly pie?"

Anna could see Matt lose his color a little at the mention of shoofly pie, but he let her push him into a seat at the table.

"Coffee, denke. Nothing else."

Mammi looked about to urge something more on him, but Anna managed to catch her eye. She gave the tiniest shake of her head, and Mammi backed off and began to pour out coffee, the pot rattling as if she couldn't quite control her hands.

Anna took a cup for herself and put one in front of Matthew, giving him a reassuring smile before turning to fetch milk and sugar. With her back turned to the table, she took a couple of deep breaths. At least Mammi hadn't seen what she had, looking up and seeing Matt clinging to the barn wall like a fly, holding Micah safe against him.

"What possessed that boy?" As usual when she was upset, Grossmammi was scolding. "Micah's old enough to know better."

"It was my fault." Grossdaadi sagged in his chair. "I never should have told him that story about James trying to climb the barn roof. What was I thinking?" He rubbed his face with his palms, as if trying to scrub away the image of Micah.

"Don't be so foolish, old man." She turned the scolding on Grossdaadi. "He needs to hear the family stories. Nobody would think he'd go and try it all alone."

"We love your stories, Grossdaadi." Anna reached across the table to rub her hand down his sleeve. "You can't ever stop telling them. How will we keep all our memories if you don't?"

Grossdaadi patted her hand. "You're a gut girl, Anna. But it was foolish of me. It was my fault."

"Now that's plain ferhoodled," Matt said firmly. "He's a boy, and he's going to take risks." He paused, seeming to remember some examples, though she didn't know if the examples would be from his own life or her brother's.

"He was thinking he should do what his bruder did," Anna said. "James climbed up there, so he had to try it, too. Daadi will make sure he knows how silly that was."

"And that he remembers it," Mammi said. She patted Grossdaadi's shoulder. "Whenever something bad happens, we all think we're to blame, but he certain sure didn't go up there just because of what you said."

"He was feeling his oats," Matt said, his voice easing. "Silly little monkey, scrambling around like that. If he'd been a little bit taller, he'd have made it, too."

Mammi shivered slightly. "Don't say that to him, or he'll be trying it again."

"I won't, that's for sure." Matt looked up at her, his face creasing in a shadow of his old smile.

Matt hadn't smiled all that much when they were kids, as Anna remembered, but when he did, it warmed his whole face. Anybody watching just had to smile as well. It had been all the more touching because it had been so rare. His parents hadn't given him much to smile about.

Tears stung her eyes suddenly so that she had to blink them away as Daad and a very subdued Micah came into the room.

"Still some coffee in that pot?" Daad asked, his voice almost normal.

"Just a little." Anna reached the stove before her mother could get up. "I'll make another pot."

182

"No, just give me what you have. Then we'll need to get that ladder put away."

Micah tugged at Daad's sleeve. "Can I help?"

Daad's weathered face crinkled into a smile. "What do you think, Matt? Can we use another helper?"

"Sure thing," Matt said easily.

"Gut." Daad gave Micah a meaningful look, and Micah slipped around the table to Matt's chair.

"Denke." Micah seemed to struggle with something else he wanted to say, and then the words burst out in a rush. "I was scared. I'm glad you came." He leaned his head against Matt's arm, and it seemed to Anna that Matt was too moved to respond.

Then he squeezed Micah's shoulder. "Know what? I was scared, too. But we're okay now, yah?"

Micah nodded violently, and Anna's throat grew tight. If Matt hadn't seen him in time . . .

Daad rose, putting his cup in the sink. "Ready? Let's take care of that ladder."

All of the men went out together, with Micah hopping and jumping alongside. The door closed behind them, and Mammi wiped her eyes with a quick movement.

"We . . . we must be thankful Matthew was there."

"Yah." Grossmammi nodded. "It's right that

183

he's come back. I just hope he stays here. Promise Glen is his home."

Anna realized that she hadn't even thought about him going away again in days, maybe longer. Her vision of Matt disappearing as suddenly as he'd come seemed to thin away to mist.

"The house where he was raised belongs to other people now," Mammi said. "But it was never a happy place for him. Still, the people, the community, his aunt are here for him." She looked at Anna as if challenging her. "And we are here for him."

Anna understood that challenge. Mamm was reminding Anna of her own responsibility in the matter.

"Matt's mother was a strange woman," Grossmammi said in a considering voice. "She could never accept anything less than perfection, not in herself, or her husband, her house, or her son. And we all know that nothing's perfect on this earth." She shook her head as if pitying the woman. "It causes a lot of pain, thinking that you can have everything just perfect in this life."

Anna couldn't help but feel as if her mother and grandmother were holding up a mirror to her. Challenging her to look in it and see herself.

What did she see? A teacher, yah, and someone who cared for the children who were her responsibility. An obedient daughter who loved her family even if she wasn't always patient with each of them.

But there was another side that she hoped not to see—a side that was too much like Matthew's mother . . . too critical, too demanding of perfection.

Too quick to blame. To blame Sam and the other boys who'd gone with James that night, and mostly to blame Matt, as if he and he alone could have prevented what happened to James.

What about the rest of them? What about her parents? Herself? What could they have done to prevent James's accident?

Blaming. She saw that in herself, suddenly, and she didn't like it. She didn't want to be that person—blaming, unforgiving.

If she was to be different, she'd have to start now. And she'd have to start with Matt, if she could.

Matt had to smile at Micah's enthusiasm over helping with the ladder. He and Matt reached the spot first, and Micah danced around, eager to help and getting in the way.

"I can help take it down." He grabbed the side of the ladder and started pulling on it. So Matt grabbed him, moving him firmly out of the way.

"Daad said I could help." Micah's face screwed into a pout. "He did."

"Yah, he did, but we have to wait for him to

get here. He's the boss. You know what that means?" He'd know, all right, but that wasn't an expression he'd have used much, if at all.

The pout was replaced by a look of concentration. "It's the person who's in charge, ain't so? Like you said your boss gave you time off after the accident."

The words, in Micah's childish treble, jabbed Matt, reminding him of too much he didn't want to think about.

"That's right." He pushed the unwelcome thoughts away. "So he was the one who decided on the work plan every day, and he'd tell each of us what to do."

Micah nodded in understanding, but he shot a look at the ladder anyway. His gaze swept up it to the top, making Matt wonder what he was looking at, and whether the height would feature in Micah's dreams tonight. Or nightmares, if that's what it was.

Simon came around the corner of the barn just then. "Now we'll get to work. Matt, you take that side. Micah, I need you to stand back here where you get a gut view of the top of the ladder." He positioned Micah well out of range with his grandfather.

"But that's not helping," the boy protested.

"Yah, it is." Simon's voice was firm. "We have to lower it toward the right, because if it goes the other way, it might hit the paddock fence.

186

So your job is to watch the top. A heavy wooden ladder isn't the easiest thing to manage. If you see it start to sway in any other direction, you sing out nice and loud. Okay?"

Micah nodded, seeming to feel the weight of the responsibility on his small shoulders. "I will."

Simon gave him an approving look and came back to grasp the ladder with Matt. "Over to the right, yah? I had this thing come over backward on me once, and when it starts to move, it would take a giant to stop it."

"I remember that. You had James and me standing back to warn you, but there was nothing we could do but watch you jump out of the way."

"Yah, I'd forgot that." His face crinkled. "We won't do that this time. On the count of three."

In a matter of minutes the ladder lay on its side, and Micah hurried over on his daad's signal to grasp the ladder. At a word from Simon, they lifted together, and then they carried it toward the hooks from which it hung.

Matt kept an eye on Micah as they went. They'd had enough disasters for one day.

His face tightened. How was it that every time he thought he was settling in and being useful here, something came up to challenge that idea? Maybe life was telling him this wasn't the right road for him after all.

By the time they'd finished, Simon's father was

heading toward them in the two-seater buggy. He pulled up next to Matthew.

"Hop in. I'm driving you home."

Before Matt could protest, Simon had leaned over to put his hand on Matt's shoulder. "Komm. Get in. It's the best thing to do. You must feel like you've been kicked by a mule after all you did today."

"I can walk, but seeing as you're all so set on it, I'll have to say yes." Come to think of it, he did feel that way. Seemed like hanging on to the side of a barn took something out of a person.

"Can I go, too?" Micah was already reaching for the seat to climb up, and this time it was his father who grabbed him and pulled him back.

"You cannot," he said firmly. "You're going to feed the chickens before supper, so you'd best get started."

Micah looked as if he considered arguing, reviewed his day, and decided to obey. "Yah, right." He turned away. "See you tomorrow, Matt." He trotted off.

Raising his hand in farewell, Matt climbed somewhat stiffly into the buggy next to the grandfather. "Denke. Micah doesn't seem to be a bit slowed down, but I am."

The old man clicked to the mare, and they moved off. "When you were that age, you'd bounce, like he's doing. Not now."

"That's certain sure." His jaw tightened as he

considered the words. "Maybe being afraid takes it out of you." He could hear the bitterness in his own voice, but he couldn't take it back.

"Funny thing about courage." The grandfather looked ahead, between the horse's ears, but it felt as if he was studying Matt. As if he looked into Matt's heart. "Courage is in the doing, not the feeling. Whatever you felt, you went after him, ain't so?"

Matt nodded, not wanting to claim any courage for himself. But that was more or less what Anna had said, too. If he could believe it . . .

"You youngers grew up together, you, and James, and Anna. You were ready to try anything, the three of you."

"I guess so." Matt studied the old man's lined face . . . lines that spoke of living and working and doing. Laughter lines, too. It was a good face, belonging to a good man. Maybe at his age, a man's face reflected the life he'd lived.

"I think I'm a bit more cautious now than I was then," Matt reflected. "As for Anna, well, I don't know. She seems like she's serious and adult now, but once in a bit I see the girl she used to be, ready to try anything."

"And James?"

The question startled him, stinging. "James didn't live to show us who he'd be when he was grown up."

The old man shook his head. "Don't you

believe it. Folks don't change, not really. What you are when you're young stays with you." He was silent for a moment, and Matt didn't have anything to say.

"James was a good person and a good friend. I don't see that changing. So were you." Isaac turned to study his face. "You tried to stop him that night. And when he got in trouble, you went after him."

Matt felt as if Isaac had thrown a bucket of cold water in his face. "How did you know? Sam just promised he wouldn't say anything to Anna because it would upset her. But right after it happened—"

He shook his head. "I didn't need young Sam to tell me anything. Simon felt it best that it not be talked about, and they all respected that. He didn't want anybody blaming anyone else. But I knew you, and I knew our James. That's the only way it could have happened."

Matt stared down at his hands, clenched so tightly together that he couldn't feel his fingers. "Yah, I went after him. But I wasn't in time. I couldn't stop him." He held his breath for an instant. "I should have, but I couldn't."

"No. You couldn't work a miracle. We all know that. Seems like you're the one who doesn't."

Matt shook his head slowly. He felt as though someone had opened him up and looked at the inside of him.

Isaac didn't speak for a bit. The lines in his weathered face seemed deeper than they had been when Matt went away, and his beard was almost entirely white now. Only his eyes hadn't changed—still a clear blue, always questioning, but always wise and kind. Matt had always thought him the wisest man he'd ever known.

"It's gut you came back," Isaac said finally. "It's gut for us, having you here, helping us. And not just with the farm work."

He paused, looking at Matt as if to be sure his words sank in. "I think being here is helping you, as well."

Anna sat down on the bench at the picnic table in the schoolyard, as glad as the scholars were that recess time was here. She must have been affected by the previous day's adventures more than she'd realized, because her gaze had been returning to Micah again and again throughout the morning's lessons.

Naturally, he'd been seated at his desk, working as diligently as he usually did . . . which meant he was enthusiastic where arithmetic was concerned, but not so eager to work on his writing. Or spelling, for that matter.

She'd seen it with boys enough not to be alarmed, and other teachers said the same. Was it that Amish boys saw more need for numbers in their lives? Or maybe the fact that numbers were the same in Pennsylvania Dutch and in Englisch? If so, girls seemed to master that crossover to Englisch easier than boys, for some reason.

Anna watched him now, throwing and catching a baseball with some of the other younger ones. They were probably hoping to emulate the older boys, who had a pickup game of baseball going in the field.

To her surprise, Thomas Burkhardt was playing. It seemed that since the mud sale on Saturday, he'd been a bit easier to approach for the older boys. She hoped it would last.

As for Micah—well, Micah was fine, she reminded herself. Sooner or later the image of him dangling from the barn would fade from her mind, and she'd stop feeling that she had to have her eyes on him all the time. He wouldn't appreciate having her fuss over him, that was certain sure.

As always when they were outside, Anna counted heads almost automatically. Most of the younger girls were trying to play jacks and spending much of their time chasing the ball. She looked, and then looked again. Rebecca Burkhardt wasn't with them. She wasn't in sight.

Thrusting down a stab of panic, Anna rose and walked casually along the side of the school building, her eyes darting from side to side. She had to be here somewhere. Rebecca was much too shy to wander very far. They'd all come outside together, and Rebecca had been with the rest of her class. So where was she?

Anna reached the corner of the building and glanced around the back. The shed that held equipment needed for maintaining the building and grounds was kept locked, so she couldn't be there. The open-sided shed for her mare didn't allow for many hiding places.

A small sound alerted her. Rebecca sat on the floor in the corner beyond the stall, her head on her knees and her shoulders shaking in silent weeping.

Heart clenching, Anna approached her quietly. If Rebecca heard, she didn't react, seeming lost in her own world. Murmuring a wordless prayer for wisdom, Anna knelt beside her.

"Rebecca." She said the name softly, touching the child's shaking back.

At the touch, Rebecca jolted upright, revealing her tearstained face, her eyes wide.

"It's all right. It's just me."

Rebecca's neck moved with the effort of swallowing her tears, and she nodded. She rubbed her eyes with her hands, as if to scrub away the evidence of crying.

"Was ist letz?" Anna murmured. "What's wrong?"

Rebecca shook her head.

"Komm, tell me. How can I help if I don't know what's wrong?" She touched the child again, very lightly, and this time Rebecca didn't wince away. But she didn't speak, either.

"Please tell me." Anna sat on the ground next to her, longing to put her arm around the child but afraid that would scare her off. This was like approaching a newborn foal, when every movement had to be slow and gentle.

Rebecca looked at her and seemed reassured by what she saw. "Micah," she said softly.

Anna's thoughts skittered wildly. "What about Micah? Did he . . ." But she couldn't think of anything her little brother was likely to do that would account for tears.

"He told me." Rebecca looked down at her fingers, twisting themselves in her lap. "He said . . . about the barn . . . how he almost fell." Her small face was tight with fear, and the gaze she turned on Anna was pleading for something . . . Anna didn't know what.

"But he didn't." She tried to sound reassuring, but Rebecca's words were like an echo of her own fears. "He was all right," she said more firmly. "Really. He didn't get hurt a bit."

"Up so high." Rebecca looked up at the very top of the school building. "He could have."

"No." Anna moved her arm gently around the child. "No, he couldn't, because Matthew was right there. You know Matthew. He lives right next to you, ain't so?"

Something of what she said seemed to catch

194

the child's attention, pulling her out of whatever image she had when she looked up.

"Matthew is strong," Anna went on. "You know that. He wouldn't let Micah fall. He kept him safe while we brought the ladder. He wouldn't let Micah fall." She repeated the words, knowing them to be true.

But she couldn't start thinking about Matt right now. She had to keep focused on the child.

"Micah was foolish to climb up so high. He knows that now. He promised never to be so foolish again. So you don't have to worry about him."

She couldn't tell whether that was what was going on or not. Rebecca didn't seem completely reassured by that response. But what else could she be worried about?

"Don't look down," she whispered, and turned her face into Anna's sleeve.

Anna scrambled for sure footing in this strange conversation. Had something happened to Rebecca? Perhaps she'd been in a similar situation.

" 'Don't look down' is good advice if you're climbing." She tried to sound cool and practical. "I climbed too high in the oak tree once, and when I looked down, I got dizzy. Daadi told me just to look at the next step. So I did, and I was fine." That was probably good advice for a lot of things.

Rebecca seemed to be trying to push her face clear into Anna's arm. Praying it was the right thing to do, Anna snuggled the child against her.

"It's all right to be afraid of things that can hurt you."

Rebecca sucked in a breath and looked up at her fleetingly. She nodded. "Mammi . . . she . . ." The words came out in a rush and then stopped, as if they'd hit a wall.

"What did Mammi do?" Anna asked softly. If there was a clue here to what was troubling this child, she had to follow through.

But Rebecca pressed her lips together. She shook her head.

Anna patted her gently. "If you tell me, maybe I can help."

For a moment, Anna thought Rebecca would speak. The words seemed to hover on her lips, but then she shook her head again.

"You would tell somebody if I did. Nobody must know." Rebecca said the words as if they were some sort of rule.

Anna wanted to promise that she wouldn't tell. But how could she? Whatever was going on with the Burkhardt family, it was probably something that needed adult help. The bishop, a doctor . . .

No, she couldn't promise not to tell anyone.

"All right," she said finally. "But when you want to tell me more, I'm here. I'll listen." She managed to smile when the child looked at her.

"Everybody needs someone to tell things to. Even grown-ups." *Even me,* she added silently.

Rebecca clearly wasn't going to say anything more now, so Anna got up and held out her hand to the child. "Anytime," she said. "Anytime you want to talk, you can come to me."

Rebecca studied her face as if wondering how much it was safe to trust her. Then she reached out and took Anna's hand.

Better, Anna thought, leading her back around the school. It was a step forward, and that was good.

CHAPTER ELEVEN

"You sure you don't want me to take the wagon to the lumberyard for you?" Matt watched as Simon pulled himself up to the wagon seat. They'd just finished the noontime meal, and he'd figured Simon might want a break before starting on the afternoon's work.

Simon shook his head. "We'd best take advantage of this warm, sunny weather while we've got it. I'll pick up what we need in town, and if it stays like this, we can get an early planting started tomorrow." He smiled, his eyes twinkling. "Besides, I don't want to miss any of the gossip going on."

"The lumberyard's the right place for that," Matt agreed, wondering how much of the gossip would be about his return. "Or maybe the hardware store."

"Yah, that's so. Might have to stop there, too." Simon snapped the lines and clicked to the big gelding. "Plenty of other things for you to take care of this afternoon. Don't worry about it, Matt. You're earning your keep."

Nodding, Matt stepped back, watching as the wagon creaked slowly down the lane. Maybe Simon did want to make the run to town, or maybe he was sparing Matt the annoyance of enduring the stares of people speculating about his return.

He shook that off. He must be getting a swelled head, thinking that folks were always talking about him. The novelty of his return had surely worn off by now. Folks had other things to talk about, and he had other things to do. He'd best find Isaac and get to work.

As it happened, the old man was coming out the back door of the grossdaadi haus, carrying a flat of plants that he set in the wheelbarrow. Matt hurried over to him.

"Can I take those someplace for you?" It was a flat of cabbage seedlings, he saw once he was closer. "I thought Simon said we weren't going to set those out for a few more days."

Isaac sent him a sharp glance. "The ground is thawed, and there's no frost coming. I've been farming for a lot of years, and I know a bit more about planting than anyone else around here."

Isaac sounded annoyed, and that was unusual enough to be concerning. "Something wrong?"

Scowling, Isaac shook his head. "Not so's you'd notice. Just that son of mine telling me to take it easy this afternoon. Easy! A farmer doesn't get ahead by sitting in the shade drinking lemonade. And I was figuring out when to plant things when he was in diapers."

Matt struggled to repress a smile. "I guess you were. What do you want me to do?"

Isaac seemed mollified. "Go and bring out the rest of the flats of cauliflower and cabbage we've got in the daadi haus. Then we'll get them put in. No use wasting a good afternoon."

Escaping inside, he found Isaac's wife looking for him. "What is that man up to now?" She bustled to the window. "I thought he was going to take a little rest after we ate. It's gut for him, but you think I can get him to listen?"

Matt wasn't eager to get into the middle of their disagreement. "He says he wants to get the cauliflower and cabbage planted."

"Well, there they are." She waved a hand at the folding table set up by the window. It was lined with seedlings. "Why he couldn't wait until tomorrow like Simon said, I don't know."

"He's used to doing it, ain't so?" He tried to reassure her.

"Silly old man," she muttered. "Simon wanted to spare him from trying to do it by himself, so of course he has to prove he can." Her eyes focused on him. "You make sure he doesn't do too much now, you hear?"

"I'll try." But he couldn't see himself talking someone like Isaac out of anything.

He picked up a couple of flats and headed for the door. "Don't worry."

"Don't fuss, you mean," she said tartly, holding the door open for him. "It's best to let him do whatever he's got his head set on, I guess." She sniffed. "Thinks he's still twenty-four or so, and that's been a lot of years."

"I'll do my best to keep him from doing too much. Honest." He went out.

He didn't suppose for a minute that she wouldn't worry. She'd been fussing over Isaac for . . . what . . . close to fifty years, most likely, and she wasn't going to stop now. Still, what could happen to him setting out cabbages and cauliflower, and with Matt right alongside?

When he'd loaded the last of the flats, Matt took the handles of the wheelbarrow, beating Isaac to them. "Where to?"

"Up along the side of the harrowed section." He gestured. "We'll set out these at the top."

"Right." The ground sloped gently upward here, then more sharply where the woods ran up to the top of the ridge. "It's looking more like spring every day, ain't so?"

Isaac paused while Matthew spoke, as if taking a moment to get his breath. "Beautiful, ain't so? Some folks like fall better, but give me spring. It's as if the good Lord is creating the land all over again."

Matt hadn't thought of it that way, but he nodded. Maybe Isaac had a point. The valley was responding to the warmth and sunshine, coming to life again after the cold of winter.

"Seems to me that you're coming back to life since you've been here." Isaac spoke as if he'd read Matt's thoughts.

"Maybe so. When you drove me home, you said my coming back had been gut for me."

"You fit in here." Isaac paused, huffing a little to catch his breath, and Matt slowed his stride. "You should stay."

It was the first time someone had said that out loud. Matt couldn't deny he'd thought it a time or two, but he'd carefully avoided letting those thoughts linger.

"I have a place out in the Englisch world," he said. "A good job, and a decent place to live."

"That's not everything."

They'd reached the designated point, so Matt set down the handles and bent to lift out the first flat and a trowel. "Want me to start at the far end and work toward you?"

Isaac didn't seem troubled by Matt's silence in response to his comment. "Yah, might as well. I'll start here." He reached for another flat, but Matt was already grabbing it.

Isaac took it back firmly. "I'm not so old I can't pick up a flat of cabbage. Did Simon tell you to make sure the old man took it easy?"

Matt was relieved that he could answer truthfully. "No, he didn't. My aunt Ella's the one who taught me to help older folks."

Isaac's face reddened. "Sorry. I shouldn't have said that. But I guess your aunt wouldn't like it if folks acted as if she couldn't put in a day's work anymore."

"I guess she wouldn't. But she's pretty sensible about pacing herself."

Something was clearly caught in Isaac's craw, and it had to do with the whole idea of getting old. It was a bit surprising, in a way. Isaac understood the nature of things, like anyone who lived close to the land. He was the one who'd talked to Matt and James about the nature of living and aging and dying when James's old dog had died.

Probably it was different when it was yourself you saw slowing down. And certainly when a man like Isaac saw his grandson go before he did. Aside from his grief, he was struggling to fill in for the loss of James in running the farm. That would explain his determination not to slow down. He wanted to keep going until Micah was big enough to take over.

Before Matt could find something reassuring to say, Isaac put his hand on Matt's shoulder. "Ach, forget what I've said. Things are changing, and like a crochety old man, I don't like change." His hand gripped tightly all of a sudden.

"Think about staying, Matthew. You're needed here. By all of us."

The words were heartfelt, and for a moment they warmed Matt, giving him an image of a world in which he was back here, fitting in, filling up the hole in his heart from losing James.

But it wouldn't work. It couldn't. His life wasn't

here any longer. It was out there, in a world that didn't even notice he was missing.

Anna was still feeling a spark of hope in her heart when she drove home that afternoon. It wasn't only that she'd sensed a connection with Rebecca during those few moments of recess. For the rest of the afternoon, Rebecca had seemed brighter, more involved. She'd even smiled when one of the other girls had asked her to be her reading partner. That was a positive step.

She just wished she'd been clever enough or knowledgeable enough to know what Rebecca had meant by those fragments of conversation. What was it that she was afraid to share . . . so afraid she would rather live in fear than have it be known?

She could guess, of course, but guessing wasn't good enough. The mare came to a halt at the barn, and Anna yanked her thoughts back to her present environment. Unless they were dawdling in the woods, the children should be home by now, but she didn't see them.

A sweeping glance found two figures coming down toward the house from the plowed field. Grossdaadi moved slowly, with Matt right next to him. As they turned slightly, she realized that Matt held her grandfather's arm, supporting him.

Anna's heart stopped for an instant and then began beating wildly. She had leaped to the ground before she could wrap her mind around what was happening, and she started running.

Hurt? Sick? Something was wrong. Something had happened. A silent prayer filling her head, she raced along the side of the field, stumbling a little on the rough ground, and nearly falling when her foot hit a clump of dead grass.

Panting, Anna came to a stop at Matt's outstretched arm.

"Easy. It wouldn't help any to knock your grossdaadi over, ain't so?"

"Ach, Anna, I'm fine." Her grandfather's fingers closed around hers. "Don't look so frightened. Matt is just being too fussy." He flashed a smile at Matt. "He's as bad as your grandmother, yah, Matt?"

Matt smiled back, but his eyes were dark and serious. "If you don't want anyone to fuss, you shouldn't keel over when you're trying to plant a cauliflower."

"What were you doing out there planting . . ." Anna let that question trail off as she caught Matt's expression and saw the slight shake of his head.

She took a breath, pressing down the need to demand answers. She understood, none better, that it wasn't a good idea to make an accident worse by overreacting. Still, as she walked close to her grandfather's side, she knew she wouldn't be content until she had answers.

But at the moment her grandmother came

hurrying out of the grossdaadi haus, grabbing everyone's attention.

"What did I tell you?" she demanded, grasping Grossdaadi's hand as Matt helped him up the steps into the house. "What did I say? I told you not to go out and do all that bending over, planting all those seedlings that could just as well have waited until more people could help. And now see what happens."

The door banged shut, and Anna yanked it open again. Matt eyed her cautiously. "Maybe we should leave them alone. Sounds like she has plenty to say to him."

Anna had to admit that he had a point. "I'll just make sure she doesn't need any help," she said stiffly. She wanted to say that they were *her* grandparents, but caught the words back just in time. Instead she hurried in, to find her grandmother still scolding.

"Old fool," she was muttering, slapping the kettle on the stove and then turning to pat Grossdaadi's cheek gently. "I told you, didn't I?"

"Yah, Abigail, you told me. You always tell me." He grabbed her hand and held it against his cheek. "But I'm just fine. I got a little dizzy, that's all. And Matt was right there to help, so stop your fussing."

Grossdaadi gave Anna a sharp look, and she realized that was meant for her. No blaming Matthew, that was what he'd been saying.

He started to move, and her grandmother shoved him back down on the chair.

"You stay right where you are. You're going to have some hot tea with lots of sugar in it and something to eat, that's what. And then you're going to put your feet up and rest until supper. No arguing."

Grossmammi didn't sound as if arguing would do him a bit of good, and as far as Anna could see, Grossdaadi wasn't going to try. He settled back in the chair, a little smile on his face.

His gaze caught Anna's. "You go along now, child. Your grossmammi knows all there is to know about taking care of me."

She couldn't argue with that, so she headed outside. "Just pound on the wall if you want anything."

He chuckled. "No need."

Closing the door behind herself, Anna shook her head. Nobody was more stubborn than Grossdaadi, even though it seldom showed. He'd decided to treat whatever had happened lightly, and that was that, although she might find out a little more from Matt.

She spotted him at once, turning the mare into the paddock, and hurried toward him.

Matt closed the gate and waited, watching her. "Are you going to yell at me for not taking better care of your grandfather?" He raised his eyebrow questioningly.

"I don't suppose you can convince Grossdaadi

to take it easy any better than anyone else can," she admitted. "What happened?" She leaned against the gate next to him.

Matt shrugged, frowning a little. "He seemed like he was determined to get those plants set out today. I knew your daad intended to work on that tomorrow, but . . ."

"But Grossdaadi insisted he knew better, ain't so?"

"That's about it." Matt studied her face, obviously concerned. "Has this been going on long?"

It was her turn to shrug. "I'm not sure. It seemed like it happened gradually over the last year or so." She hesitated.

"You mean since James died," he said. "You can say it."

His voice had that tinge of bitterness she'd noticed before, but it didn't give her any satisfaction.

"Don't." She put her hand over his where it lay on the top bar of the gate. "I know I've been blaming you, but it's not as easy as that. I see that now. When something happens, everyone blames themselves, like Grossdaadi thinking it was his storytelling that made Micah do something foolish."

"That's true enough." He sucked in a breath. "Let's start again. Your grandfather feels like he needs to do everything he used to, especially since James isn't here to take over."

"Yah, I guess so." She watched him, noticing again how he'd changed. But she had, too. It seemed that James's death had changed all of them. She shook her head, trying to shake off the thought.

"I tried to talk him out of doing all that planting, but it didn't stop him. I took over as much as I could." Matt looked baffled and frustrated. "What else could I do?"

"Nothing," she said promptly. "Unless you were willing to hog-tie him, you couldn't do anything else." She squeezed his hand, meaning it to be comforting.

His lips twitched. "If you want to try that, I'll help."

Anna's tension relaxed in a bubble of laughter. "Grossmammi would help, too."

"She would, wouldn't she?" His voice broke in a chuckle. "She was so exasperated with him you wouldn't believe."

"Yah, I would. She's in there right now, bossing him around and making him drink hot tea, and he's sitting back in his chair and enjoying it."

"I guess they've been doing it that way for fifty years or so, so it must work." He clasped her free hand in his, as if inviting her to share his amusement, and his warmth seemed to flow through her in a flood.

Startled, her gaze flew to his. Laughter was there between them, but something more . . .

something that sparked from him to her and back again.

Matt's eyes darkened. His hand slid up her arm, trailing warmth in its wake.

She should pull away, should break this contact, but she didn't want to. She wanted . . . what?

A door banged somewhere, and the sound of the young ones squabbling broke into the moment. Matt blinked, as if the noise awakened him, as it had her. His hand dropped slowly, and he took a step back.

The moment was over, she told herself. But it had happened, and she couldn't ignore it, no matter how she might try.

Anna found the easiest way to block Matthew from her mind was not to see him. It really hadn't been too hard to avoid him for the next couple of days, because he seemed just as eager to avoid her. When she came home from school, she could always head straight to her room to prepare lessons for the following day. By the time she emerged, Matt had gone back to his aunt's. True, his name kept coming up in conversation, especially when Micah was around, but she managed.

Now it was Saturday, and she knew he'd be at the farm most of the day, because Daad had decided that everyone should help with the planting. The next day was the Sabbath, so they wouldn't be doing any work then, and rains were predicted for several days in a row.

The younger children had been jabbering about it at breakfast, obviously excited to be helping. Sally didn't look very enthusiastic . . . and then Anna remembered that Sally was going to work at the dressmaker's today.

Sally hadn't looked especially happy about being relieved of the planting operation, but come to think of it, she had been rather quiet for the past couple of days.

Anna rinsed an oatmeal bowl in hot water and passed it on to her mother to dry. "Sally was awfully quiet at breakfast. I'd expected a talk on how skilled Joseph was at planting."

Mamm shook her head. "Something's wrong, that's certain sure. Something at work yesterday might have been a problem. She's been cross since she got home." She shrugged. "Maybe Ada found fault with her work. If she's mooning around about Joseph Miller at work the way she is at home, it's no wonder."

Anna gave some thought to Ada Schultz, local maker of dresses and shirts for those Amish who didn't have a good seamstress in the family or didn't have enough time to sew their own. That was the case for more women than one would think these days, with so many people having businesses.

"Ada's not exactly a patient person to work

211

for, I think," Anna said carefully. It didn't do to criticize a sister in the church, but she'd do almost anything rather than that job. Still, Sally seemed to like it well enough.

"Yah," Mammi said, and darted a look at Grossmammi to see if she had noticed. But Grossmammi was bent over the mending she was doing, and she didn't seem to be paying attention. "Maybe you could get her to open up to you, Anna."

Anna opened her mouth to find an excuse not to do that and closed it again. She could hardly point out that Sally was more apt to do the opposite of anything Anna might say. She finally nodded. "I can try."

The last dish was washed, so she rinsed out the cloth and hung it to dry, then dried her hands. "I'll go out and see if I can help," she said, thinking that with so many people working, she ought to be able to avoid saying anything personal to Matt.

Her mother nodded. "If they need another pair of hands, send someone in to tell me. Otherwise, I'll get started on the noontime meal. I want to make a gut, hearty beef stew with everyone working so hard."

Anna grabbed her sweater from the hook and headed out into the bright sunshine. They'd had more sunny days than usual this spring, but it sounded as if the April showers would be coming their way soon.

As she passed the phone shanty, the phone began to ring. Quickly, before the answering machine could pick up, she scurried to answer it.

"This is Anna Stoltzfus." She reached for the pencil that hung from a nail on the wall.

"This is Ada Schultz. Where is Sally? She should have been here a half hour ago." Ada didn't sound happy.

"I'm sure she's on her way." Anna tried to sound as if she were sure. "Maybe she's had some problem getting there."

"If she's not going to be responsible, I'll have to get someone else." Ada didn't sound soothed. "I have a lot of work on hand."

"I'm sure she realizes that," Anna said. "I'd best go after her in the buggy. Don't worry. She'll be along soon."

She hung up before Ada could vent her annoyance any further. Yah, Anna had been right. She wouldn't enjoy working for Ada, not for a minute.

But where was Sally? She'd left right after breakfast, hadn't she?

Anna hesitated for a moment, undecided. Had she left? Now that she thought about it, Anna realized she hadn't actually seen her go out the door. Well, a quick look in Sally's room would answer that question.

Not wanting to run into Mammi, she went around to the side door. The sound of Mammi and Grossmammi talking about apple cobbler came faintly from the kitchen, but she could slip silently up the back stairs to Sally's room.

She paused for a moment outside the closed door, feeling a little silly. Most likely Sally had stopped to talk to someone. Maybe Joseph had happened to be along her route to the shop. Still, it only made sense to check whether she was here.

"Sally?" She eased the door open, prepared to find the room empty. But it wasn't. Sally, fully dressed, lay across the bed, her face buried in her pillow.

"Sally!" Anna rushed to her sister, catching her by the shoulders. "Are you sick? What on earth is going on?"

Sally turned over at her touch, exposing a tear-stained face and red-rimmed eyes.

Anna touched her cheek gently, overwhelmed with memories of the little sister who'd run to her with every bump and scrape, looking to her for sympathy and something to make it feel better. Sympathy she could provide, but whatever was making Sally cry would not be easily fixed with a kiss and a bandage.

"Tell me," she said softly. "Tell me why you're not at work. Ada called a few minutes ago."

"Ada can call until she's blue in the face." Anger flared up briefly and was gone just as fast. "Ach, it's not Ada's fault."

"Whose fault is it?" Anna rubbed her back gently, just as she had when Sally was young. "Is it Joseph?"

"No!" she said. "It's that Mary Ann Dahl. I hate her!"

"Hush, don't let Mammi hear you. And you don't hate anybody, not really."

Mary Ann Dahl, Anna thought. A little older than Sally, with bright red hair and big blue eyes. To say nothing of having a sassy manner that her parents should have clamped down on a few years ago.

"What did she do?" she asked, thinking she probably knew. Only one thing could make Sally this upset. Joseph.

"She was at Ada's, getting measured for a dress. I was in the corner, working at the machine. So Ada asked her about the color for the dress. And you know what she said?"

Sally didn't wait for Anna to guess, which was just as well.

"She said Joseph Miller told her that she looked wonderful in blue, so she was getting a blue dress just to please him. And she knew I was there, Anna. She looked right at me when she said it."

Anna sat down next to her on the bed and put her arm around her sister.

"I always did think they spoiled that girl rotten. Now we see how she's turned out," Anna said.

Sally looked at her, blinking. "I didn't think that was what you were going to say."

"Well, it's true, isn't it? She's not a very nice person, and it shows."

Sally sniffled. "Joseph doesn't seem to see it."

"He will." She hid a smile. "If he's the person you think he is, he will." She hugged Sally for a moment, pleased when she didn't draw back. "Now, are you going to work or are you going to quit? You'll have to decide."

For an instant Sally didn't move. Then she straightened, her head coming up. "I guess I'd best go. Ada's okay once you know how to handle her. I'll try not to cut Mary Ann's new dress into little tiny pieces."

They rose together, and Anna felt ridiculously proud of her little sister, despite all her foolishness.

"Gut girl. I'll call Ada and let her know you were delayed." She hesitated. "Nobody else realizes that you didn't leave right after breakfast."

Sally hesitated and then wrapped her arms around Anna in a warm hug. "Denke," she whispered, and then spun like a leaf in the wind and was out the door.

CHAPTER TWELVE

With Sally off to work and the message called in to Ada, Anna started once more toward the field Daad had decided to plant first. Shielding her eyes from the morning sun, she picked out the figures clustered around Daad, waiting to start. The children were there already, with Grossdaadi, while Daad stood on the cart pulling the plow.

For a moment Anna didn't see Matt. Good, that meant she didn't have to focus on showing how cool and collected she was. Then he moved from behind the cart and glanced back toward the house. His tall figure paused. Was he staring at her? Did anyone notice?

Warmth flooded her cheeks. She felt as if she'd been dipped in boiling water. Clenching her hands, she resisted the urge to clap her palms to her cheeks. That would be a dead giveaway.

No one could see whether she was blushing or not from this distance, not unless she gave it away herself. If she stopped thinking of what happened between her and Matt, then no one would know. She had to be in control.

The only problem with that assertion was that she didn't *feel* in control, at least not when she thought of those moments when the world paused while they looked at each other.

She sucked in a deep breath. A few stolen kisses and furtive hugs during her rumspringa years had generated nothing remotely resembling what she'd felt in those moments with Matt. Their lips hadn't even touched, and yet she'd sensed that each had moved into the other's very being.

Nonsense, she told herself firmly. And even if it wasn't, at least she and Matt were mature enough to keep it to themselves. At least she was, and she trusted Matt would do the same.

Anna had been walking steadily toward them while she argued with herself. She reached the group as the big Percherons pulled up at the edge of the field, and she went to pat the leader. "Getting back to work again seems to suit Max."

She glanced at Micah, who wasn't much higher than that horse's belly. He was standing a safe distance back, and the animal probably looked like a mountain to him.

"Want to say hello to Max?"

He hesitated a moment and then ventured forward, reaching out tentatively.

"Best put a little energy behind patting him."

Anna nearly jumped at Matt's voice, sounding right behind her. She hadn't heard him come so close, but now she was way too aware of his nearness.

Then she saw Micah's eyes on her. What was he noticing? He was the observant one, while

218

Betsy and Grace just chattered away to each other.

"Matt's right," she assured him. "If you touch Max too lightly, he'll think it's a fly and try to whisk it off. You don't want to get his tail in your face. It's likely to knock you flat."

Micah nodded, stepped up bravely, and patted Max with a firm hand. Then he looked at Anna, and they exchanged smiles.

"He'll like getting the plowing done, ain't so? It'll be something exciting for him to do. Daadi, can I ride on the cart?"

Daadi turned from the conversation he was having with Grossdaadi. "A little later, Micah. I want to be sure everything's working smoothing first. Will you help Grossdaadi plant some peas first?"

Looking a little disappointed, Micah nodded. Grossdaadi handed him a bag of seeds, and Micah brightened a little. Soon everyone was busy, with Daad and Matthew plowing for the planting of early corn, while Grossdaadi directed the others in the fine art of planting peas.

The earth turned by the plow looked as rich as chocolate with the sun shining on it, and she loved to see the massive horses working steadily together, leaving the furrows behind them as even as could be.

When the plow came back from the second row, Daadi stepped down. "Anna, you're the one

I need. You go up and watch for any problems with the plow blades while Matt drives. Looks to me as if one blade might need to be straightened, but I want to get this corn in first."

Not giving her any time to argue, he handed her up into the cart. "I'm going to check the planter before we hook it up." He headed toward the barn with long strides.

Very aware of Matt seated inches away with his back to her, Anna balanced herself where she could see the plow blades, not wanting to take a tumble.

Matt glanced over his shoulder. "Don't worry."

"Worry about what?" she said quickly, telling herself to be calm. Or at least to sound calm.

"I promise not to hit anything and knock you off." Amusement laced his voice.

"Are you taking up mind reading now?" This time she kept her voice light.

"Only with you." He looked back again, and her heart skipped a beat.

"You'd best look right between Max and Manda if you want a straight furrow."

"I'll try, but I find having you right behind me distracting."

"Don't." She hoped she didn't sound desperate. "I don't want to talk about it." She didn't have any doubt that he knew exactly what she meant.

Matt was still for a few heartbeats, staring ahead, his eyes fixed. "Yah, all right. We'll talk about something else. Your daad always gets his first corn planting in earlier than anyone else."

Anna tried to untangle her thoughts. *Think about corn,* she ordered herself.

"Daad says it's better to take a chance and have his corn first. You know how crazy everyone is about the first fresh sweet corn. If we get a hard frost . . . well, we replant, so we're not really later than anyone else."

Matt nodded, and she could sense the movement even though she was staring religiously at the plow blades.

"I always have liked your daad's attitude," Matt commented. "He never gets all tense and upset about things that can't be changed."

She knew exactly what he was talking about. Maybe she was as guilty of mind reading as he had been. When you'd known someone since childhood, it seemed that a couple of years apart didn't make all that much difference.

Matt's father had always been the exact opposite of Daad. Tense was a good word for it. He'd been so determined that everything be perfect that he couldn't stand anything slightly out of line. And Matt's mother had been just as bad.

When they'd left the area, folks had taken a deep breath and relaxed, and that was a terrible thing to say about anyone who had been a brother or sister in the church.

Matt and Anna had reached the end of the row,

and she could feel the strong muscles of Matt's arm brush against hers as he pulled up.

"Your daad's coming," he said, gesturing toward the barn. "We'd best wait for him before we start another row, ain't so?"

"I guess." She turned around, resting her hand on the back of the seat. "Matt . . . you understand, don't you?"

Again, she didn't need to explain. He gazed at her, his face seeming deliberately blank. "I understand that something happened between us. And instead of talking about it, you want to pretend it didn't happen."

Anna felt the color flooding her cheeks. "It's not that. How could we even do it? I just feel that I don't want half the town gossiping about us before we know what's what."

When he didn't answer, she put her hand on his wrist, feeling warmth and strength through his sleeve. "Please, Matt." She looked at him pleadingly.

But his gaze wasn't on her face any longer. He was looking over her shoulder, and her heart sank. She followed the direction of his gaze to find that her three youngest siblings were staring at them, open-mouthed.

This was definitely not the way to keep a secret.

With the next day being Communion Sunday, Matt had arranged to go with Aunt Ella for the morning, but he'd be leaving then. The communion service was only for those who were members, something he didn't suppose now that he would ever be.

As he walked out of the barn where morning worship had been held, his gaze searched the crowd for Anna despite his best intentions. Anna would be staying, of course. She had been baptized into the church in the fall after her brother died. She was now a full member of the community. She'd taken a step ahead of where he was.

People often made that decision when they were thinking about marrying. Clearly that hadn't been true for Anna, and that made him think again about why she had made the decision when she did. Was it because James had missed that important rite?

A hand grasped his arm, and Matt swung around to find Bishop Paul at his side, studying him gravely. His stomach twisted. What now?

A warm smile spread across the bishop's face. "It's wonderful gut to see you here at worship again, Matthew. I can see how happy it's made your aunt Ella to have you with her for a time."

Bishop Paul must be in his seventies by now, but he didn't look it. His back was straight, and as far as Matt could see, his chestnut beard contained very little gray yet. He held Matt by the arm, but his grasp was gentle. Matt could easily pull away, but why would he want to get away from the kind gaze or the welcoming smile?

"I'm glad to be able to give Aunt Ella some help," he muttered, wondering if the bishop thought he should have done that months ago.

"And you're helping the Stoltzfus family as well, I hear," the bishop said. "That's gut. They need it now that James has passed."

Matt nodded, wondering whether he'd brought that up to measure his response to a mention of James. Bishop Paul would have known the truth of James's death, no matter what gossip went around. He always did seem able to discern the truth. Would he also know that Matt hadn't come to stay?

"I hope I can stay long enough to help them get the spring planting done, at least. That's always a time when a farmer needs some extra hands."

There, that should set some boundaries about his being here. He took a step back before the bishop could prolong the conversation.

"I must get moving. I promised to take the Burkhardt children home in my buggy."

"I'll let you go then." Bishop Paul patted Matt's arm. "Maybe by the time Fall Communion comes around, you'll be joining in the full services."

Before Matt could collect himself to respond, the bishop had moved on to speak to someone else, leaving him dumbfounded. What did Bishop Paul mean? Why would he think Matt would even be here in the fall, let alone be a member?

Matt had just as much as told him that he planned to be leaving soon.

Then he saw Anna's younger sisters watching him, and thought he understood. They'd been talking—talking about seeing him and Anna. How much had they said? By now, half the valley might be talking about them, thinking they were pairing up.

But there wasn't much to say about him and Anna, he assured himself. A brief glance, a moment of handholding . . . you couldn't make a lot out of that.

Just enough to embarrass Anna, he supposed. He didn't know his own feelings yet, let alone Anna's.

Shaking off that line of thought, he strode through the crowd looking for Thomas and Rebecca. He and Aunt Ella had agreed to keep an eye on the Burkhardt children, and they'd barely seen them. Maybe he could remedy that today with some conversation on the drive home.

He found Thomas waiting next to Aunt Ella's buggy, clutching his little sister by the hand. A few yards away, Sally was loading up her younger siblings. Micah, seeing him, darted away from his sister and ran to Matt. Matt had to grab him to prevent him from barreling into the buggy wheel.

"Slow down, Micah. What are you up to?"

"Going home," he said. "Can't I ride home with you?"

"You could if we were going the same place, but we're not," Matt told him. "Guess you'd best go with your sisters."

"Silly," Betsy said, with an air of superiority. "You ought to know that. He's taking Thomas and Rebecca, because they live next to his aunt. In the house where he used to live."

"Oh. Yah, I remember now." Micah's bottom lip came out. "I think Matt would let me drive." He darted a look at Matt, as if asking him not to give him away to his sisters.

"Next time." Matt clapped him on the shoulders. He didn't know what it was like for a boy to have four older sisters, but he could guess. "See you tomorrow."

Micah scrambled into a seat next to Grace, and Matt turned back to his own responsibility. He found Thomas eyeing him with speculation.

"Would you really let him drive?"

"Maybe." He figured he knew what Thomas would say next.

"Can I drive? I'm plenty older than him."

"Yah, you are." He turned his back to the Stoltzfus buggy as Sally began to pull out. "I'll drive first, so they don't notice. Then I'll stop and switch with you."

Thomas considered that, then lifted his sister into the buggy. "I wouldn't mind showing off in front of that Betsy."

Matt chuckled, taking up the lines. "Yah, but

if you did, then Micah would feel bad. Us guys have to stick together."

Thomas considered that for a minute, as if he hadn't run across that idea before. Then he nodded.

They followed the other buggy down the lane, continuing behind them until they reached the turnoff. Then, as they started down the narrow country road, Rebecca tugged at his sleeve.

"Will you really let my bruder drive?" she whispered.

"Sure thing," he whispered back, liking it when she smiled.

"You're not supposed to whisper," she said, giggling.

"Why not? You did." Matt pulled over to the side, and he and Thomas changed places.

As he'd expected, the boy was a competent driver. Not that it mattered a lot, as Aunt Ella's gelding would take them home no matter who held the reins. Since they'd turned off the main road, they weren't in the stream of Amish buggies headed home, although they could see them across the width of several fields.

They rounded a bend with a stand of trees on either side, and the road and the buggies vanished from their view. They jogged along peacefully alone.

Matt looked down at little Rebecca, who sat between him and her brother. She was rolling a handkerchief in her hands—a man-sized one, which made him think her father had handed it to her to amuse herself during the service.

He bent and whispered to her. "Do you know how to make babies in a cradle with that?"

This time she relaxed enough to giggle at his whispering.

"Is that funny?" he whispered again.

"You're a grown-up," she said, so loudly this time that her brother turned to look in surprise. "You're not supposed to whisper."

"Maybe we can both talk out loud. It hurts my throat to whisper very long."

She considered, studying his face, and finally nodded. "Okay." She held out the handkerchief. "Show me."

Smiling, he folded the handkerchief into a triangle and then started rolling from each side. "We roll it into the middle, like this," he said. "And now, very carefully, we take hold of this point, separate the bottom one, and pull it down." He suited action to words. Grasping it by the points, he let it swing between them like a cradle.

Rebecca let out a long whoosh of air. "It's babies—two babies in a cradle." She looked up at him. "For me?"

"Yah, for you." He put the ends in her hands and showed her how to rock it. "You can sing them a lullaby. Like Mammi . . ."

"Like Daadi does," Thomas said quickly. He caught Matt's eye with a slight shake of his head.

"Right." He certain sure didn't want to upset Rebecca or scare her back into her shell, but he did wonder about it. Did the problems in the family come from the mother, not the father?

Thomas looked as if he was trying to think of something to distract him, and meanwhile, Rebecca rocked the handkerchief cradle, seeming to have forgotten or not noticed his error.

"Glad you could bring us home," Thomas muttered at last. "How come you didn't have to stay for communion?"

Matt's hands clenched against his knees. "I jumped the fence a while back. You knew that, didn't you?"

"We heard something, I guess. Some folks are blabbermauls, that's certain sure."

"Yah." Matt blew out a long breath. "So I wasn't here about the time when my friends were getting married, joining the church, having their first communion."

He bit off the last word, thinking about what Anna would be doing right now, as the words of communion were said. Would she agree that she was in love and charity with her neighbors? With him, in particular?

"Sorry," the boy muttered.

A small hand made its way into his. Matt looked down to find Rebecca's eyes fixed on him.

Pity? Sympathy? He wasn't sure what she was feeling. But he did know that he'd set off to try to be a help to these children. And instead, they had turned the tables on him. He was the one being comforted.

When Anna reached home after the service, she found the sense of peace she'd taken from communion slipping away. She'd tried to forgive. She'd thought she'd succeeded. So why was there still a knot in her heart?

Sally was stirring a pot of beef vegetable soup on the stove when she reached the kitchen. "You're home earlier than I thought you'd be."

Anna nodded, trying to hang on to the look of peace that she felt she should have after the communion service. "That smells gut, and you look happy. I saw you talking to Joseph after worship this morning. Is everything better between you now?"

Flushing, Sally smiled. "Yah, I guess."

"So Mary Ann isn't going to find her new dress in tiny pieces?" she questioned.

"Not this time. Denke. I was glad you talked me out of it. I wouldn't want to lose my job." A thread of laughter flowed through her voice. "And you know what Joseph said?"

"No, but I think you're going to tell me." She perched on a stool to watch as Sally began rolling out biscuit dough. It was nice to see her sister looking so cheerful, even if it meant that her romance was back on again.

"I asked him right out about what Mary Ann said. And he told me it was all so mixed up. That he happened to be in the store when she was, and she held up a bolt of blue material. She's the one who said it looked good with her eyes, not him. He felt like he had to nod, that's all. So there."

Because Sally seemed satisfied with that explanation, Anna decided to accept it as well. It was well worth it to be back on good terms with her younger sister.

"I'm glad, Sally. It did seem kind of funny that Joseph would have said something like that." Actually, from what she could see of him, Joseph was still as shy and awkward as he'd always been. Clearly Sally saw him differently.

Sally nodded, focusing on the biscuits she was cutting. "I just . . . I got to thinking about Easter coming, and I don't want to be fussing with anyone, especially my own family. I don't know what's wrong with me sometimes."

Anna slid off the stool and went to put her arm around Sally's waist. "It's all right. We love you anyway."

She was bemused about Sally's mood. Maybe the morning's sermons had gone home. Or maybe she was just growing up.

Sally turned to hug her, getting a little flour on

her dress. "And I'm sorry. For saying you didn't understand because you hadn't been in love." Her cheeks grew pinker. "I mean, how would I know if you had or not?"

"That's right." Grossmammi must have come in from the grossdaadi haus in time to hear the last bit of the conversation. "Sometimes a person doesn't even know when she's in love herself."

Anna hurried to arrange the cushions in Grossmammi's rocking chair. "Is that a story?"

"Yah, tell us when you fell in love with Grossdaadi," Sally added, putting biscuits on a baking sheet. A thought seemed to strike her. "Were you ever in love with anyone else?"

"Ach, no." Grossmammi settled in the chair. "Nobody at all. But I certain sure didn't think I'd fall in love with somebody like your grandfather who'd been teasing me all my life. I'd have said I didn't even like him." She shook her head.

Anna smiled, knowing where the story was going because she'd heard it more than once.

"But one day I dropped a whole basket of blackberries I was picking when he startled me. He bent down to get them just when I did, and we bumped heads. I was going to yell at him, but I looked at him, and it was like I'd never seen him before. He was everything I wanted."

She smiled, her eyes growing misty as if she looked far back into the past to see that day again.

Anna's eyes grew misty as well, and her throat

seemed too tight to speak. Grossmammi might have been speaking of her and Matt. Was that love?

Even if it was, she didn't know if Matt felt the same about her. And she didn't know if she still held any blame in her heart for him. How could she love him if she did?

Geh lesse. The bishop had said those words in his sermon, and he might have been speaking directly to her. *Geh lesse* meant let it go, stop trying to figure it out, accept what is.

If only her heart knew she felt it without a doubt. *Geh lesse.* Acceptance.

CHAPTER THIRTEEN

Anna was relieved to get back to school on Monday. The weekend had raised too many questions in her mind. There had been good things, of course, like the Communion service and those moments when she'd felt closer to those she loved.

But somehow she'd still felt unsettled. She felt as if the people she knew were all changing in one way or another, and she didn't know how to cope with it. At least here, in her schoolroom, she was in control.

Anna always found extra things to do on Monday morning, arranging her classroom to suit the lessons she'd planned and any breaks in routine during the upcoming week. This week would be a short one, because Good Friday meant no school or work for the Amish community. It would be a quiet day, for the most part, a time of remembering.

With Easter so late this year, fitting everything in before the end of school seemed more rushed than usual, and she wished she felt more confident that the plans she'd made were going to work out. Somehow no matter what she intended, there were the unexpected interruptions, for better or worse.

Taking a step back from the chalkboard, Anna glanced from the list of spelling words on the left to the map of the United States she'd pulled down on the right. In geography, they were focusing on the locations of the various Amish settlements.

Anna had to smile. She'd found that to be a sure way to get the scholars interested in the map. They might not care where Texas or Oregon were, but if they had relatives or friends moving to an out-of-state Amish community, it became fascinating.

Most of her scholars found it fairly easy when it came to Pennsylvania and the surrounding states, where many of them had traveled for family occasions. There were sometimes vacation trips, as well, like the bus trip several families from Promise Glen had made to Niagara Falls last year.

She glanced at the map again. The Burkhardt family had moved from Indiana, hadn't they said? Perhaps Thomas could show the class where they'd lived. Strange that she hadn't heard more about their previous home . . . Knowing might help to build up her picture of the children's lives before they came here.

It was nearly time to ring the bell, so she moved to the doorway, where she could look around the schoolyard. As usual, the older girls and the older boys had clumped into separate groups, but she didn't see Thomas.

She reached for the bell, smiling as the younger ones began lining up at the steps before she reached it. Anna did a mental count of the primary scholars. Rebecca was missing too.

Her fingers clasped the rope, and the bell sounded its call to lessons. She greeted each child coming in the door, but the back of her mind was busy with wondering about the Burkhardt children.

The last of the eighth graders came through, and she shut the door. They might be late, but that was unusual.

Starting toward the front of the classroom, she paused at the desk of Jasper Miller. The Millers lived not far from the Burkhardts and usually seemed to arrive together. Jasper was a sensible boy who wouldn't make anything of Teacher Anna asking about them.

"Thomas and Rebecca?" Jasper shook his head. "We waited a couple of minutes at the lane where we usually meet, but they didn't come. Maybe their daad is driving them today."

"Maybe so. Denke, Jasper." She went on to her desk, but a slight frown had settled between her brows.

By the end of the day, the frown had escalated to a full-scale headache. There'd been no word of the Burkhardt children. After sending her siblings off with the others to walk home, Anna walked quickly around to the shed for her buggy. Her gaze fell on the spot where she'd found Rebecca last week, hiding from her own fears.

No, she couldn't just head for home. She'd have to stop by the Burkhardt place to see what was going on. It was unusual for any child to be sick without the parents sending word about the absence. And for both of them . . . well, it just didn't happen unless the teacher knew about it.

The mare waited patiently while Anna harnessed up. Far more patiently than Anna, it seemed, whose fingers fumbled with the buckles. Her uneasy feelings about the children just wouldn't go away. The only answer was to see for herself.

As they came out onto the main road, Anna had to check the mare for an instant before turning her to the left. Daisy knew which way home was, and she didn't like any departure from the usual.

Anna felt the same way, but a much stronger feeling directed her toward the Burkhardt place. She'd been worried about those children from the moment they'd entered her school. Maybe she was developing a teacher's instinct for knowing when something was wrong, just as her mother did about any of her own children. She wouldn't rely on a feeling without facts, but she couldn't ignore it, either.

In a few minutes she passed Ella's place, waving when she spotted Ella coming out the side door with a basket of laundry. Anna turned in at the next lane. As she drew up to the hitching post, she realized that the family's carriage wasn't in its usual place. Were they away after all? Some emergency?

Hurrying to the door, she rapped firmly. Nothing. Anna stood for a moment longer, then rapped again. "Mrs. Burkhardt? Are you there?" She stood listening for a response that didn't come. It almost seemed the house listened, too.

Foolishness, she scolded herself. Foolish to be worried, she supposed. But she'd stop at Ella's before she headed home, just to see if she knew where they'd gone.

Matt's aunt was folding shirts before putting them into the basket, but she stopped to stare as Anna drew up in her lane and slid down from the buggy seat.

"Is something wrong?" she called out before Anna could reach her.

"I hope not." Anna walked quickly to her. "The kinder weren't in school today, so I thought I'd stop to see why." She shrugged. "I guess they must be away. No one answers."

Ella frowned, unclipping a sheet from the line. Anna automatically caught the bottom edge, and together they shook it out and started folding. "I don't see how they can all be away," Ella said. "The only person I saw go out was Carl. That was about an hour ago, and he headed toward town by himself."

"It doesn't sound like an emergency, then." Wondering, Anna started on the pillowcase that was next on the line. "I supposed maybe they'd been called away by some family issue. I can't understand why they wouldn't have sent word if they wanted to take both youngsters out of school."

"They're not away, that's certain sure." Ella looked over Anna's shoulder toward the Burkhardt house. "Didn't you say no one answered? Looks as if Thomas just came out. He's coming toward us."

Sure enough, Thomas was running across the intervening field. As he drew closer, Anna saw his distraught face. A bad feeling gripped her stomach as she hurried to meet him.

"Mammi," he gasped as he came close enough to be heard. "She . . . we thought she was taking a nap, but we can't wake her up. Please komm."

"Yah, of course." She was aware of Ella hurrying along to them. "Did you try shouting? Did you shake her?"

"Everything." His face was white, and he looked on the verge of tears. "I don't know what's wrong."

Anna nodded, pity for the children flooding over her. "Where is your father?"

"He went to town." Thomas seemed to choke back tears. "Mammi wanted a prescription filled. It was from where we used to live, so Daadi said it might take some time. He told me to keep an eye on her, but I didn't think there was any harm in her taking a nap."

"For sure. Don't fret about it." Ella sounded as sensible as always, if breathless. They'd reached the house by then, and Thomas pulled open the door.

"This way." He was already pounding up the steps.

They followed, panting on the stairs, and rushed into the bedroom at the front of the house. Anna found herself praying wordlessly even before she saw what awaited them.

Elizabeth Burkhardt lay back against a pillow, a quilt scrunched up around her as if she'd been cold. Her face was very white, and for an instant Anna thought the worst before she noticed the shallow rise and fall of Elizabeth's chest.

"Look." Ella pointed at the small table next to the bed. A pill bottle lay on its side, open and empty.

Matt arrived home from work to see Anna's buggy parked at the hitching rail. Waiting for him? He'd like to think so, but more likely she was talking to Aunt Ella about something.

He started on toward the barn and then stopped. The side door of the house was standing ajar, as if Aunt Ella had just run out for a moment. Her laundry basket sat in the grass with a few things in it, and a shirt dangled crookedly from a single clothespin. Frowning, he jumped down, and pushed the door open to shout.

"Aunt Ella? Anna? Are you here?"

Nothing. As he came away from the door, his gaze caught movement over at the Burkhardt place. Thomas was running from the phone shanty back to the house. Running. Without stopping to think about it, Matt ran, too, compelled by an urgency he couldn't reason away.

He reached the house a step or two behind Thomas. The boy grabbed his arm and pulled him inside.

"Mammi." Thomas pointed up the stairs. "They're trying to help her. She won't wake up."

Matt's mind worked swiftly. "You called 911?"

"Yah. They said for me to stand out by the road and wave them down when they come. But . . ." He looked at the stairs, and it was clear he was torn.

Matt clamped his hand on the boy's shoulder and shook his slightly. "Listen. If my aunt and Teacher Anna are with your mother, they'll do all that can be done. I'll see if I can help. You go flag down the paramedics. It won't help if they go to the wrong place, ain't so?"

Looking grateful to have the decision made for him, Thomas dashed off down the lane. Matt moved to the stairs, feeling out of his depth. She wouldn't wake up? What did that mean? He just

241

hoped Anna and Aunt Ella knew what to do, because he sure didn't.

"Thomas? Is that you?" Anna's voice came from the top of the steps. He moved where she could see him.

"No, it's me. He's gone out to the lane to watch for the ambulance. Where's Carl? Anything I can do?"

Anna looked worried, but she was keeping it under control. "He went for medicine, Thomas said. See if you can find Rebecca. She's not up here, but she must be in the house somewhere."

Relieved, he nodded. "Will do."

Anna was out of sight in an instant. Clearly she didn't have time to answer questions. If he wanted to help, he'd find Rebecca.

A small hand seemed to clutch his heart as it had clutched his hand the previous day. Poor little kid. Bad enough for Thomas at his age, but Rebecca was far too young to understand any of this.

"Rebecca?" he called out tentatively. "It's me, Matthew. Tell me where you are, and I'll come get you."

He walked slowly through the familiar down-stairs, looking and listening. There were plenty of places for a small kid to hide in the old house. He'd used all of them when his father was in a rage.

"Rebecca," he called again. "Help me find you, okay?"

Maybe in the cellar . . . then he stopped. A sound came from the pantry, a squeak as if something had been pushed along the floor. He'd hidden in there more than once, but never very successfully. He opened the door.

Rebecca was squeezed between a box and the bottom shelf. Only her shoes were showing.

"It's just me," he said, keeping his voice very soft, remembering how she'd giggled about his whispering. "It's going to be all right." He hoped he sounded sure.

The shoes moved, and then Rebecca's face peeked around the box, her eyes reddened with crying. He reached out his hand, and after a moment's hesitation, she took it.

"Let's get out of the pantry, yah?"

When she nodded, he picked her up and carried her out into the kitchen. "Listen, now. Teacher Anna and my aunt are looking out for your mammi. They'll take care of her. You know that, yah?"

Rebecca nodded, clutching him tightly.

"Besides, the ambulance is on its way. Thomas is watching for it. They'll know just what to do."

Her eyes widened at that, and she looked out toward the lane.

"They'll know just what will make your mammi feel better," he repeated. He tried to think what else might be troubling her. "Your daadi will be home soon. And we'll all take gut care of you."

She seemed to relax a little, and she put her face near his to whisper in his ear. "Teacher Anna?"

He might have known that Anna was the one she'd ask for. Anybody would. He patted her.

"Teacher Anna is here for sure. Meanwhile, let's go out and see if we can see the ambulance coming."

Still carrying her, he went back out the side door, glancing down the lane to where Thomas was waiting.

"Look, there's Thomas. He's waving." The boy had stepped out on the road, waving both arms. Matt heard the siren even before he spotted the blinking lights through the stand of trees. "The ambulance is coming. We'd better tell Teacher Anna."

Rebecca wiggled to get down, and they hurried inside together. "The ambulance is coming," he called. "And I have Rebecca."

"Good." Relief sounded in Anna's voice. "Send the paramedics right up."

Even now, the wail of the siren trailed away as it came to a stop outside the door. He pushed it open, pointing to the steps. "She's upstairs."

The paramedic looked vaguely familiar to him. Someone he'd known in his teens, maybe?

Carrying equipment, the senior man gestured for a younger woman to follow him. Then he turned to Matt. "You know anything about this?"

Matt shook his head. "Only what the boy said,

that they couldn't wake up his mother. His father should be back soon."

At least, he hoped Carl would get here quickly. Someone needed to explain all this.

The paramedics tramped upstairs, and Rebecca made a move to follow them. Matt caught her before she could get far, and lifted her into his arms again. Her face screwed up with the effort not to cry.

"It's going to be okay," he said, wishing Anna could be the one comforting the child. She'd do a much better job than he could. "They're going to take care of your mammi."

Thomas came in, his face taut and worried. He kept his eyes on the top of the stairs and moved closer to Matt, who put his free hand on the boy's shoulder. He understood. Thomas needed contact with his own kind just now, even if it wasn't his blood kin.

It seemed hours, but it was only minutes before Anna appeared at the top of the stairs.

"They're bringing her down to the ambulance." She started down, white but composed. "We'd best get out of the way."

He nodded, handing Rebecca to her when the child reached out. "You take care of the kinder. They might need help with the stretcher on the stairs."

Once this had been his house. These had been his stairs. He didn't have many happy memories of this place, but he did know the trick of getting around the tight corner at the bottom of the steps.

Anna led the children to the door, but before they went out, she looked back at him. "Denke." She murmured the word, but he thought he understood. At this moment, she was glad he was here.

Anna stood outside, holding Rebecca. The child had her face buried in Anna's shoulder. Obviously she wanted to block out what was going on, poor thing. She murmured soothing words, she hardly knew what, hoping they had some benefit.

Thomas was old enough to know what was happening, but at least he was able to help. Anna knew from experience how much of a help that was in trouble.

Just now he stood by the door, ready to open it the instant the stretcher arrived with his mother. His face was tightly controlled, and Anna had the sense that he might shatter at a touch.

In another moment she heard the sound of low voices as they maneuvered their way down the narrow stairs with their awkward burden. She could pick out Matt's voice, and she heard the strain in it. Did it make it better or worse that he had grown up in this house? Better, certainly, for the paramedics, because he'd long been familiar with the awkward turn at the bottom with the low headroom and the twist toward the door.

She moved slightly when Thomas opened the door so that she could see them come down the last few steps. Matt's face was set, his muscles straining as he lifted the end of the stretcher over the bottom of the banister to make the turn. She held her breath, praying silently, and then they were clear and moving out the door.

Anna had been concentrating so hard that she hadn't heard the approach of a buggy, but at that moment she realized that Carl had arrived, and her mind scrambled to think how to explain all of this in a few words. Impossible, but maybe all that explanation wasn't needed. He'd know what had led to this, if anyone did.

Obviously seeing the ambulance, he ran the buggy onto the grass and leaped down, letting the horse drop his head and crop at the grass.

"What is it? Elizabeth?"

Anna didn't think she'd ever seen such a tragic look on a man's face. "Thomas found her unconscious. It looks as if she'd taken pills . . ."

She let that trail off at the startled look on his face.

"She said she didn't have any. That's why she sent me to the drugstore in town. She said—" He stopped, clearly realizing what must have happened.

"You're the husband?" The senior of the paramedics reached them by then, bearing the head of the stretcher.

Carl nodded, but all his attention was on his wife. He bent over her, murmuring brokenly as he touched her face.

Matt and Ella joined them. "He is Carl Burkhardt, and his wife's name is Elizabeth. Will he be able to ride with you? If not, I'll call for a driver."

"That's okay. Once we get her into the rig, he can ride with us. You'll notify anyone else who needs to know?"

Matt nodded, then helped as they lifted the stretcher into place. He grasped Carl's arm as he stumbled, not wanting to let go of his wife's hand.

"They'll take you in with them. In the meantime, we'll take care of the kinder and everything here."

"God be with you," Anna murmured, and hugged Rebecca tightly as the doors closed and the ambulance moved off. Ella put her arm around Thomas's shoulders, and he didn't pull back.

Anna discovered she was trembling in the aftermath of events. She'd been pushing forward on adrenaline, she guessed, and it seemed to have run out. The others probably felt the same. Best to find something for all of them to do.

"Now," she said, assuming her teacher's voice,

248

"we should call the bishop. He'll want to go to the hospital or send someone if he can't."

Ella nodded, clearly glad to have a plan. "Let's go over to my place, and we'll get some food on. Or at least something to drink, yah? Matt?"

"Thomas and I will check on the animals and take care of things here. Then we'll join you." He looked at Anna. "You'll take care of calling the bishop?"

"Yah." She understood. No doubt he still felt awkward around the bishop. She looked at Thomas. "Try not to worry. I'm sure either your father or Bishop Paul will let us know what's happening soon."

Thomas managed a nod and then went quickly to the buggy his father had abandoned. Probably like all of them, he yearned for something to do.

"Keep him busy," she murmured to Matt.

He nodded, reaching out to pat Rebecca's back. His hand brushed Anna's and lingered for an extra moment. "You'll help Aunt Ella and Teacher Anna, yah, Rebecca?"

Rebecca felt the child's head move as she nodded, and her arm tightened a little around Anna's neck.

"We'll be all right," she murmured, and her gaze locked with Matt's, feeling relief that she wasn't alone. Whatever her tangle of feelings about Matthew, at this moment she was glad she had him to share this burden.

CHAPTER FOURTEEN

An hour later Anna left the phone shanty at Ella's and walked back to the kitchen door. Bishop Paul had sounded concerned, that was certain sure, but he seemed fairly confident, too. Now all she had to do was persuade the children of that confidence. Taking a deep breath, she put a smile on her face and walked into the kitchen.

The four people in the room froze in what they were doing, all staring at her with a mix of hope and apprehension. She could only hope her smile was convincing.

"We're just getting supper on," Ella said, putting a heavy dish of chicken potpie on the table. "Komm, eat, while you tell us what the bishop had to say."

Rebecca jumped down from the stool where she'd been helping Ella with the dishing up. She tugged at Anna's skirt, looking up at her with wide eyes. "Mammi?"

"Mammi is doing much better. Bishop Paul says so." She hugged the child and then sat her on a chair at the table.

"What was wrong?" Thomas sounded as if he needed much more detail to comfort him.

"It looks like your mammi forgot how many pills she had taken. Maybe she thought she hadn't had any, so she took another dose. That's happened to a lot of people. So the extra medicine made her sleep so soundly that we couldn't wake her." She focused on Thomas, longing to reassure him that he wasn't to blame.

"You said she was better. How did they make her better?" It seemed he wouldn't be satisfied with just a little of the story. His face wore its sullen, stubborn look.

"Bishop Paul said they gave her something to wash the medicine out of her system." She certainly hoped he didn't want details. "Then she was awake and talking to your daadi, and she felt more like herself."

"What did she say?" Rebecca piped up. Apparently she'd followed more of that than Anna had hoped.

Anna patted the child's cheek. "She said you should be good and eat all your supper. She's going to have some soup and pudding in a little bit."

Rebecca considered that. Finally she nodded. "And then she'll come home, ain't so? She needs to put me to bed."

Anna's gaze met Matt's, and he looked as baffled as she felt.

"Not yet, sweetheart. She's going to stay there overnight, and your daadi will stay with her."

Rebecca shook her head at the words. "No. She can't." Her eyes filled with tears.

251

Anna knelt next to her. "Now listen. She has to do what the doctor tells her, because he's the boss. He wants her to stay overnight so that he can be sure she's doing okay. You wouldn't want her to come home too early, now would you?"

A couple of tears spilled over onto Rebecca's cheek, but she managed to nod. "Okay," she whispered. "But where am I going to sleep?"

"You'll come home with me," Anna said. "You know my brother and sisters, ain't so? And they all want you to come. Then we can all go to school together tomorrow."

"What about Thomas?"

Thomas looked as if he was about to say that nothing would persuade him to sleep at the teacher's house, so she hurried into speech again.

"Your daadi says that Thomas should stay here so he can take care of the animals."

"That's right," Ella said at once. "He'll stay here at our house, and Matthew will help him take care of everything at home."

Thomas's mouth set in stubborn lines. "I'll be fine in my own house. And I don't need any help."

Anna wasn't sure how to handle that, but Ella seemed to have no doubts. She put her hand on Thomas's shoulder and held him lightly.

"We're neighbors," she said. "Neighbors do things like that for each other. Like your daad helping get my garden ready for planting. We share the good days and help each other on the bad days. You understand?" She cupped his chin in her hand and made sure he looked at her.

Thomas blushed, but he nodded. "Yah. Denke," he muttered.

Anna exchanged glances with Matt. He didn't seem surprised at his aunt's handling of a difficult teenage boy. Maybe she'd practiced on him, but if so, Anna hadn't realized it at the time.

It would have been difficult, she thought. Ella was related to Matt's mother, not his father, and from what she knew of that family, his father had ruled with an iron hand. He wasn't the type who'd have accepted advice from his wife's aunt, no matter how good.

"I'm sure your daad will be home tomorrow," Anna said, hoping that would encourage the children. She suspected that it would be a while before Elizabeth came home, from what the bishop had let drop.

It would be getting dark soon, and she wanted to get the buggy home before then, so she'd best start moving. She held out her hand to Rebecca.

"Let's go over and pack a few things for tonight. You'll need a nightgown, and whatever you're wearing to school tomorrow, and . . ."

"And my dolly," Rebecca added, sliding off her chair. "She always sleeps with me."

"Good idea."

"I'll bring your buggy over to the Burkhardt

house while you're packing." Matt got up quickly. "You'll want to leave as soon as you can, or you'll be driving by moonlight."

"Right." Taking Rebecca's hand, Anna hurried out, starting across to the other house.

Matt was being helpful, of course, but she suspected he was also looking for a moment alone with her to learn what she'd left out of Bishop Paul's account.

She couldn't blame him for that. It seemed their interest in the children had led them into more responsibility than they'd bargained for. She wasn't backing down. Since she was a teacher, such involvement was part of her life.

But what about Matt's plans to go back to his job soon? Had he made any decisions about it? She realized suddenly how long it had been since he'd mentioned anything about his new life out there in the world. She had stopped thinking about it, too, as she got used to having him around. Still, that didn't mean he'd forgotten it, or changed his mind.

They'd barely started on packing Rebecca's things in a small bag when she heard the clop of Daisy's hooves. Then Matt was calling up to her.

"Anna, can you come down for a minute? There are a couple of things I forgot to ask about."

"Yah, right away." She smiled at Rebecca. "You put everything in this bag that you want to take to my house, okay? I'll run back up and help after I talk to Matt."

Rebecca nodded, seeming more interested in which nightgown to take than in what Matt might have to say, so Anna felt fine about leaving her to it.

Anna found Matt outside by the buggy, and she plunged into speech before he could ask the question that was clearly on his lips, eager to get the information out while the children couldn't hear.

"According to what the bishop said, the doctors fear it was a suicide attempt and not just an accident. The depression she had after her last baby died was severe. She had so much trouble that she was in the hospital for weeks."

Matt winced at hearing it, much as she had. "I wish Carl had trusted someone here with the information. People would have helped. But I guess I understand."

"Too many people still have an odd attitude about any sort of mental or emotional illness. I'm afraid some communities might lag behind the outside world." Anna rubbed her forehead. It looked as if her headache was back. "With just moving here, it would be hard for them to know who to trust."

"I see how that could happen. If they'd only been more open with my aunt . . ." Matt let that trail off. "You know how Aunt Ella is. She might have a sharp tongue, but there's no one better to have on your side when there's trouble."

Anna nodded. "Now that Bishop Paul is on the job, I'm sure everything will be done that can be done."

She left unsaid the fact that there would be difficult days ahead, even with Elizabeth getting the care she needed. Poor little family.

"What about Thomas?" Matt frowned down at her. "He's probably going to ask me questions. Once his daad is here, he'll take over, but in the meantime, I'm on the spot."

In her opinion, there wasn't anyone better suited. Matt knew what it was to have trouble with your parents.

"You'll do fine. At least he knows you well enough to have some confidence in what you tell him. Just try to be hopeful without telling any stories."

"Yah." A smile lit his eyes for an instant. "Like you quoting what their mother said, you mean?"

Anna felt her cheeks grow hot. "Maybe she didn't actually say that, but if she'd been herself, she would have." She'd had to say something encouraging to the children.

Matt squeezed her hand. "I suspect the good Lord would forgive that one. And the bishop, too."

His grip was comforting, and it reassured her to feel they were in this together.

"I'd best help Rebecca finish up." But she

clung to his hand for another moment before turning and hurrying back to Rebecca.

Matt was up the next morning just as the sky was lightening, but early as he was, he found Thomas ahead of him. Aunt Ella was in the kitchen putting coffee on with a bowl of eggs on the counter next to her, looking prepared to feed any number of people breakfast.

"Coffee before you go out?" She lifted the pot in Matt's direction.

He glanced at Thomas, who shook his head. "We'll milk the cows first and then come in."

"Come back hungry, then," she said.

They stepped out into a chilly early morning. "Maybe do yours first, then I can see to Aunt Ella's stock," he suggested.

Thomas just nodded. He wished he knew what the boy was thinking, but he hated to ask. Thomas was young to have this trouble as well as this responsibility thrust on him.

He tried to think what he'd been like at the boy's age. Troubled, no longer trusting, but still longing for someone he could trust. That ought to give him insight, but he still couldn't think of anything to say.

They reached the cowshed and set to work almost automatically. As far as Matt was concerned, having work to be done was a good antidote for worrying. Should he say something like that to Thomas, or keep his mouth shut?

"My daad . . . we'll hear from him this morning, yah?" It seemed Thomas's words came out almost against his will.

"Yah, I'm certain sure. Either he'll call or come." He paused, wishing Anna were here to say the right thing. "Until then, we'll just carry on with the work."

Thomas started to speak but then looked back at a sound from the door.

Aaron Miller, whose farm adjoined the Burkhardts' on the west side, stood hesitating for a moment, then came in, followed by his eldest boy, Jasper. He stood speechless for a moment, then cleared his throat and spoke to Thomas.

"Sorry for your trouble, Thomas. We'll do this or whatever you need." He nodded to Matt, seeming unsurprised to find him there.

Thomas flushed a bit at the attention, but he stood tall as he glanced toward Matt, seemingly for guidance.

"How about if Aaron and I finish milking. You can take Jasper and feed the rest of the stock, okay?" It might be good for the boy to be with someone his own age.

Given the way Thomas relaxed, that seemed to be the right response. He and Jasper went out, not talking.

Aaron took his place. "Any news from the hospital yet?"

"Not since the bishop called last night. Elizabeth was doing better then." Hard to tell what sort of talk was going around, but he certain sure didn't want to add to it.

At least Aaron wasn't the chatty type. He set to work quickly, and they had the few cows finished in short order. Once they'd cleaned up, they stepped outside. The sun had cleared the top of the ridge, warming them even though the air was chilly. The two boys came toward them from the chicken coop. They weren't talking much, either, but they looked comfortable together.

"Aunt Ella's got breakfast on. She'd be glad to have you and Jasper," Matt began.

Aaron shook his head. "The wife's expecting us. She says to tell your aunt she'll bring food over later. Jasper, you stop here on your way home from school and help."

"Yah, Daad." He looked at Thomas. "Will you be in school?"

Matt understood Thomas's look of uncertainty. "Not sure," the boy mumbled.

"Okay. See you later." At a nod from his father, Jasper headed off. Aaron paused for another word.

"Gut to see you, Matt. Seems like you got home just when you were needed, ain't so?" He walked away before Matt could find an answer.

As soon as they were out of earshot, Thomas spoke. "I can't leave until I hear something about Mammi."

He looked ready for an argument, but Matt certainly wasn't going to give him one.

"Sounds right to me. Let's get some breakfast."

They'd no sooner started on their food than a car pulled up. At the sight of his father getting out, Thomas bolted from his chair and raced out to him.

"Best let them have a few minutes together." Aunt Ella moved back to the stove. "Then tell Carl to come in and eat. You can't meet trouble on an empty stomach."

Matt glanced out the window and saw the two of them, heads close together, Carl's arm around his son's shoulder. He looked away. That was too intimate for anyone else to watch.

After a few more minutes, he risked a look and saw that they were coming toward the door, so he went to open it. "Breakfast's on," he said.

"Denke." Carl moved up the steps slowly, as if he'd aged since yesterday. It would have been a long night, he guessed.

Once they were all in the kitchen, Aunt Ella started putting food on the table as if they all must be starving.

"Eat, eat. Everything's better when you've had something to eat." She looked sharply at Carl. "And then some sleep for you."

Carl rubbed his hand over his haggard face. "Yah, I'll take a rest before I go back to the hospital." He hesitated, maybe wondering how much to say to them. "Elizabeth's better this morning. No more problems from the pills."

Aunt Ella whispered something that was probably a prayer of thanks.

"Way I understand it, the doctors think they can put her on some medicine that will help her. Stabilize, that's what they said." He paused, looking at his son. "They're needing to keep her in the hospital while they try out the new medicine. The doctor says that's important."

It seemed to take an effort for Thomas to form the words. "How long?" he managed to say.

"About a week. Maybe not so long." Carl gulped a huge swallow of coffee and then shook his head. "She's upset, wanting to be with you and your sister."

"For sure she would be." Aunt Ella put a hand on Carl's shoulder. "But you make sure she does what's best for her, yah?"

He managed a small smile. "Yah, I will." Carl looked from her to Matt. "I don't know how to thank you. And Teacher Anna. And the Millers . . . Thomas says they were here helping already. The bishop . . ." He wiped his hand across his eyes as if to dash away tears. "He made arrangements for somebody to drive me back and forth. Everyone is so kind—" His voice broke then, and they were tactfully silent until he regained control.

"Don't you think another thing about it, now," Aunt Ella scolded. "What kind of people would we be if we didn't help each other?"

Carl nodded. "I think I'd best sleep a couple of hours before the driver comes to take me back to see Elizabeth. But first I should go along to the school with Thomas. I have to see Rebecca."

"Don't worry about anything here," Matt said quickly. "Your family is the important thing. We'll take care of the rest."

"I'm most grateful—" Carl began, but Aunt Ella cut him off.

"No more of that. Matt has it right. Your family comes first." She gave him one of her rare smiles and turned to Matt. "You see, Matthew. There's a reason why you came home just when you did. It was time, and you were needed."

His aunt's words echoed in Matt's mind as he set about what had to be done. Aunt Ella talked as if it were settled. As if this were home, and he were here to stay.

He'd convinced himself that was impossible. But maybe, if it were possible, if he could step back into his place here, was that what he wanted?

He wasn't sure. First, he had to assure himself that he was healed. If he didn't, then he'd never know if he'd really made a choice to stay or if he was hiding from the truth.

A chill went down his spine, and his stomach

twisted. There was only one way to know, and that was to go back to where it happened. Back to Hawk Cliff.

Anna was growing concerned about Rebecca as she drove her home late that afternoon. It had been arranged, after much leaving of messages, that she would bring Rebecca and her belongings to Ella's house and have supper with them. Then Rebecca could go home with her father and brother afterward.

It sounded like a good plan, and certainly Carl was eager to have his kinder back under their own roof. It should be the best thing for them, but why was Rebecca so quiet?

Anna settled her a little closer on the buggy seat. "Are you getting sleepy? My sisters didn't keep you awake last night, did they?"

Mammi had set things up so that Rebecca slept in with Grace and Betsy. She'd seemed fine about that, and when Anna went back to check on her about a half hour after she'd tucked her in, she'd found all of them asleep.

Rebecca shook her head. "It was nice," she said. After a long pause she seemed to think that wasn't enough. "I never had any sisters to share a room with. Do they like it?"

"I think so." Anna had better be cautious, because there was no telling whether Betsy and Grace had embarked on one of their squabbles.

"Sometimes they argue a bit, but that's natural in a big family."

She considered that. "I think it would be nice to have sisters. We were going to have a baby, but it died. Did you know that?"

Anna's throat grew tight. She'd assumed, wrongly it seemed, that Rebecca didn't know about that. She couldn't have been very old.

"Yah, your daad mentioned it." She rubbed Rebecca's back. "Maybe someday there will be another baby."

"Maybe." The child slipped back into silence.

"You can share my sisters if you want to," Anna said, trying to sound cheerful, but Rebecca didn't respond.

Apparently Elizabeth's problems had started with the loss of a baby. Depression after a birth or a miscarriage wasn't that unusual, but it seemed Elizabeth's had gone on a long time. Carl had talked a little more to her when he'd come to the school to see Rebecca.

Two years ago, it had been—an eternity for little Rebecca. Carl had told a story of improvements and setbacks that must have been discouraging. Small wonder the whole family had been affected. He'd said they'd hoped the move to a new place would help, but instead . . .

Mammi's cousin, Hettie, had suffered from depression, so Anna knew a little about it.

Enough to know that encouraging someone to cheer up didn't help.

Cousin Hettie was doing well now. Maybe it would be a good idea to talk to her. She was very open about her problem, saying that it might help someone else to know. Hettie might suggest things that would be helpful in dealing with Rebecca and Thomas.

Teaching, Anna realized every day, was more than a matter of helping her scholars know how to read and spell.

"We're almost there," she said. "If you've forgotten anything, I'll bring it to school tomorrow."

Rebecca nodded, but she seemed sunk back into whatever it was that occupied her, snuggling her faceless stuffed doll against her. A thought struck Anna.

"You know that your mammi won't be there tonight, yah? She has to stay in the hospital a few more days."

"I know. Daadi said. I hope she's home for Easter. We always have eggs on Easter, and Osterbrot."

"We do, too." At least that was something she could deal with. "I help my mother make it, and we'll bring an extra loaf over to you. Just in case. All right?"

Rebecca actually smiled at that, and because they turned in the lane at Ella's just then, Anna didn't have to struggle to come up with anything else reassuring to say.

Carl seemed much more cheerful today, and by the end of supper, Rebecca had finished her meal and was sitting on his lap, looking contented. Anna's gaze met Matt's, and she suspected that he was thinking the same thing she was. This little family had a long way to go, but at least they were started in the right direction.

After supper the men and the children scattered to do chores, and she set about clearing the table.

"Ach, Anna, you don't need to do that." Ella tried to shoo her away, but she was determined not to be shooed.

"I don't need to, but I'm going to. I have plenty of time to get home before dark. And you look as if you could use a good night's sleep."

Ella actually chuckled. "I must say I haven't stayed this busy since I don't know when. But really, since Matthew came home, I feel like I'm getting younger. It's nice to know I'm still of use in this world."

She'd never thought of how Ella must have felt once Matthew's family disintegrated. Ella didn't have any other close relatives, and Anna felt shamed at not realizing how lonely it must have been for her.

"I'm certain sure that Matt needs you, and it looks like your new neighbors do, as well."

The back door rattled as Matt came in,

looking at them curiously. "Did I hear my name mentioned?"

"Eavesdroppers never hear anything good about themselves," Anna said, teasing him.

"Yah, you'd best be careful what you ask about," Ella added. "Are they getting settled?" She nodded her head toward the neighboring house.

He nodded, coming to the sink and taking the dishcloth out of her hand. "I think so. I'll finish this. You go put your feet up before you drop."

"I'm perfectly able to wash the dishes . . ." Ella began, but Matt wasn't impressed.

"Maybe so, but we'll finish these in no time without you."

"Well, since you're that eager to be alone with Anna, I guess I'll have to."

Anna knew she was flushing, and hoped neither of them noticed. It was just teasing, that was all.

Once Ella had gone, Matt gave her a sidelong look. "Should I apologize for my aunt?"

"I know she was just teasing." She didn't look at him, but she seemed to sense a change in him—a determination she hadn't seen before. She didn't know what he was determined about, but it was there.

"You could look at me, you know." Matt was teasing again, but she couldn't confess that she hardly dared to look at him when he was in this teasing mood with his eyes laughing. What might he say next?

She composed her face and looked at him. "I should probably get going soon. I don't want to be on the road after dark."

With a glance at the clock, Matt shook his head. "You have plenty of time. Don't rush away."

"No, I . . ." She put down her dishtowel and started to turn away, but Matt caught her hand. His was warm and soapy. "You'll get dish soap all over me."

"I wouldn't want to do that, but Rebecca left a message for you. Don't you want to hear it?"

She stopped pulling and looked into his face. "Of course. Why didn't you say that to begin with?"

"I hoped you'd stick around without it." He shook his head, his firm mouth easing into a smile. "Rebecca said to tell you good night, and she'll see you at school in the morning."

His fingers were wrapped around her wrist now, and she wondered if he could feel her pulse racing. She seemed to hear it thundering in her ears.

"She wanted to kiss you good night," he said softly, and his face was very close to hers. She couldn't keep herself from tilting her face to his, any more than she could pull back when his lips claimed hers.

Nothing seemed to exist in the world except the touch of his hand on her skin and the warmth of his lips on hers. She'd never felt this way before, never even imagined it. She wanted the moment to last forever.

But it couldn't. Seizing what remained of her common sense, she pulled away. "I can't," she murmured, blinking back a rush of tears. "I can't," she repeated, and fled.

CHAPTER FIFTEEN

By the time Anna reached home, she felt she'd give anything for someone to tell her what to do about Matthew. But she couldn't talk about it to anyone when she could still feel his kiss on her lips. She hurried from the barn to the house, pausing on the back porch long enough to rub the back of her hand over her mouth. It didn't help.

The kitchen should be quiet by this time, but she found her mother busy at the stove while Sally, flushed and excited, tried to convince her of something. Betsy came in from the living room, realized what was going on, rolled her eyes, and vanished back where she'd come.

Anna's lips twitched in spite of herself. Maybe Betsy had the right idea where Sally's love life was concerned. In any event, it seemed clear she wasn't going to have an opportunity to ask Mammi's advice, even if she had felt she could talk about Matt and what had happened between them.

Mammi turned toward her, and Anna realized she'd been filling a hot water bottle. "Anna, gut, you're home. I hope the Burkhardt kinder are settled." She didn't wait for an answer, but thrust the hot water bottle at Anna. "Take that in to your grandmother, please."

"Is someone sick?" She slung her jacket on its hook and seized the bottle, alarm bursting through her own concerns.

"Your grandfather is coughing, and Grossmammi wants to put a poultice and some heat on his chest." She glanced at Sally, who was still talking. "Sally, do be quiet for a moment."

"I'll take care of it," Anna said quickly. The last thing she wanted was to get in the middle of one of Sally's periodic crises. Tending to Grossdaadi was certain sure the better choice.

"No one wants to listen to me," Sally was declaiming when Anna closed the door to the grossdaadi haus behind her.

Anna blew out a breath and went in search of her grandparents.

She found them both in the big bedroom that looked out over the meadow toward the east. Grossdaadi was in bed, protesting, it sounded like, while Grossmammi ignored him and rubbed a strong-smelling salve on his chest.

"I've brought the hot water bottle," she said. "Maybe I should go back out and come in again."

That caught her grandmother's attention and diverted it from scolding Grossdaadi. "Ach, Anna, you know I only scold him for his own gut."

Grossdaadi coughed, and she could hear the rasp in his chest. Since he'd had pneumonia three years ago, no wonder her grandmother was upset. She was, too.

"Your grandmother thinks she can scold me into feeling better." His eyes twinkled as he looked at Anna, and she felt better herself.

"Maybe you should listen to her. She does seem to know best."

"There, you see. Anna agrees with me." Grossmammi handed her a long piece of flannel. "Wrap the bottle in that, and then put it on his chest while I wash this off my hands." She held up sticky hands and hurried off toward the bathroom.

Grossdaadi smiled at her, coughing again. "I don't suppose you could wipe this stuff off me while your grandmother is out of the room."

"Not a chance," she said lightly, putting the hot water bottle on his chest. She buttoned his nightshirt and pulled up the quilt. "You know Grossmammi rules the roost when it comes to sickness."

"Yah, yah." He leaned back against the piled pillows. "Seems like she taught you a thing or two. Did I ever tell you she was the prettiest girl in the valley when I snatched her away from all the other boys?"

"Why wouldn't she be?" She smoothed the quilt out. "She says you were the handsomest boy."

He chuckled, coughing a little. "Don't let her give me any more cough medicine."

"I'll try. Now you behave."

His eyes were drifting shut. "Guess I could take a little nap."

She patted him, listened to his noisy breathing, and went quietly in search of her grandmother.

"He's going to sleep, I think," she said, meeting Grossmammi coming out of the bathroom.

"Gut. I'll heat up some chicken soup for him later." She linked her arm with Anna's, suddenly looking tired. "Komm, have a cup of tea with me."

"Only if you let me make it."

Her grandmother nodded and sank down on her chair at the kitchen table. Her grandparents had turned the grossdaadi haus into their own haven, using only the ground floor as a small apartment with living room, kitchen, bedroom, and bath. Several things that she remembered from the main house during her childhood were here now, like the framed family tree. She thought her grandmother liked the fact that the young ones had to come to her for family information.

Anna busied herself with the teakettle. Nothing like coming home to distract her from her own troubles, she realized. That was what it was to be part of a big family like the one represented on that family tree.

"What was Sally fussing about, do you know?" she asked, carrying two filled cups to the table and sitting down close to her grandmother. If Sally was still complaining, at least Anna didn't hear it here. The only sound in her grandmother's small kitchen was the tick of the clock on the wall.

"Something about going somewhere with that Joseph, what else?" Grossmammi said. "She thinks she's in love, but she doesn't even know what it is yet."

She studied Anna's face, her eyes wise with years of experience. "But you do, ain't so?"

Somehow Anna wasn't surprised. She'd felt when she came in that it was written all over her face, but Mammi hadn't seemed to notice.

"I . . . I'm not sure." She hesitated. Grossmammi would understand, but she didn't want to bother her when she was already worried about Grossdaadi.

Her grandmother clasped her hand. "Stop being afraid you'll upset me. There isn't anything I haven't heard in the last seventy years. It's Matthew, of course."

Anna nodded, looking down at their hands. Grossmammi's was all bones and blue veins to look at, but it was still strong and very comforting.

"I don't know what to do. I don't know what I feel."

"I can see how you feel easily enough," Grossmammi said. "What does he?"

"He didn't say." Come to think of it, he hadn't said anything about his feelings. He'd just had that odd, determined air that puzzled her. "He kissed me."

"You've been kissed before, ain't so?" Grossmammi said.

"Not like this," she said, and had a sudden urge to laugh at the idea of having this conversation with her grandmother.

But Grossmammi just smiled. "You were a long time falling in love. So was Matthew, I'd guess. I don't think he'd kiss you unless he meant something serious. So you'd best decide what you want to do. If you love him, what's standing in your way of telling him?"

She took a deep breath, trying to think what to say first. "When he came, he said he wasn't going to stay. What if he still wants to go back to the Englisch world? And what about James?"

"What about James? He would be pleased to think his sister was marrying his best friend, ain't so?"

"It's not that." Misery settled on her. "What if I committed to him and then all that resentment I felt about James's death came rising up again?"

"Ach, Anna, I thought you'd gotten over that. What happened to James was no more Matthew's fault than it was yours or mine or your father's or anyone else's."

"I know. I know in my head that's true." She blinked away tears. "But what if those feelings came back?"

"I'd say that's his business. If he wants to risk it, it's up to him." Grossmammi's voice softened, and she smiled. "I don't think it's much of a risk. And if he loves you, he knows he has to stay."

"Yah, but—"

"But nothing. You need some plain talking between the two of you. Decide what you feel. Ask him what he feels. That's the only way to know." She leaned forward and kissed Anna's cheek. "Don't be afraid of the future, Anna. It's waiting for you."

By the time Matt got to work on Wednesday, Anna had already left for school. That was just as well, because he still hadn't figured out what had possessed him to kiss her the previous day. It wasn't as if she'd given him any encouragement.

But she hadn't pulled away, either. She must have felt the same thing he did, hadn't she?

He shook himself mentally. He may as well stop thinking about it. He'd already decided that he had no choice but to face Hawk Cliff again before he could make any plans for the future.

He was just coming out of the barn when Sam drove up with a wagonload of lumber. Matt raised his hand in greeting. "Where are you headed with all those two-by-fours?"

"Right here," Sam said, grinning as he jumped down. "We finally had time to cut the lumber Simon wanted. Sorry it took so long."

"Don't tell me, tell him." This must have been set up before Matt had come, because he didn't know anything about it.

"I already did. And Simon said you'd help me

unload and stack it in the back of the barn."

"You sure you didn't make up that part of it?" He went with Sam to the back of the wagon and watched him slide off several of the long pieces. He followed suit.

"Nope." Sam balanced them on his shoulders. "Come on, man, can't you carry more than that?"

Matt grinned, glad to be back to exchanging the familiar insults that were part of their relationship. "When I see you take more, I will. So your daad is still running the sawmill?"

"Off and on." Sam gestured for him to go first. "Mostly off over the winter, but we're getting a good flow of water downstream now."

The mill Sam was talking about was a small, ramshackle affair, typical of a lot of the early mills. Settlers had put them up wherever they had a good spot—gristmills, lumber mills, whatever they needed to serve the folks in the immediate area. He remembered climbing all over the mill with Sam and James when they were kids.

"You remember when James got stuck on top of the waterwheel?" Sam was obviously thinking the same way, reflecting on times past.

"I remember that he figured out how to climb down when you said you were going to get your daad."

"Yah. Funny." Sam paused and then started to make a pile of the lumber against the back wall. "We did some crazy things and never told anybody about it, even when it was dangerous. If I have kids, I hope they've got more sense."

"I wouldn't count on it." Matt added his load, and they headed back out. "Their heredity will be against them."

Sam swung a mock punch at him. "No more than yours."

"True. So have you got anybody in mind for the mother of these kids of yours?"

Sam flushed, his fair skin turning nearly as red as his hair. "As a matter of fact, Joanna Kline and I are keeping company. Maybe by fall I'll get up enough courage to actually ask her."

Matt pounded Sam's back, trying not to think of his own precarious romance. "Gut news! It wonders me that a smart girl like Joanna should consider you, but they say love is blind."

"It may surprise you to know that Joanna considers me good-looking." Sam pulled out a couple more pieces.

"Poor girl." He took a load, too, and they headed back through the barn. "Tell me, have you ever been back to Hawk Cliff since . . . well, since the accident?"

Sam's flush returned. "I almost went a couple of times, but then I changed my mind. Seems like I didn't quite have the nerve or something."

"I know what you mean." Matt struggled with his thoughts until they reached the back. "I don't want to, but I think I should. Seems like . . . well, like I won't really feel healed until I do. I guess you think that's stupid."

"No, I don't. I think you're right." His sunny face grew serious. "I guess you need to be sure you're over it so you can go back to your job."

"Did I tell you about that?" He didn't remember bringing it up the only time they'd been together.

Sam shrugged. "Rumors, I guess. Somebody mentioned you had a job working construction. I just thought . . . well, you need to be able to deal with heights for that, don't you?"

The rumors had been more accurate than he would have expected. Anna wouldn't have said anything, but one of the younger ones might without thinking much of it.

"I wasn't prying." Sam sounded anxious.

"I know. I get it."

He almost said there was more to it than getting a job back, but he held his tongue. No matter how good a friend he was, Matt didn't tell anybody everything. He guessed that was a heritage from his parents. He hadn't talked, aside from that one moment when he'd broken down and told Anna more than he'd intended.

"Well, anyway, I'm going over there as soon as I get a chance. Seems like I ought to say goodbye to James, in a way."

He could sense Sam studying his face for a long moment before he spoke. "Gut idea. Tell you what, I'll go with you. If I'm really going to get married, it'd be best not to carry any extra baggage in the way of feeling guilty."

It was the first time guilt had been mentioned between them, and almost immediately Sam shied off in another direction.

"Can you believe how stupid we were in those days? Even thinking about climbing that cliff in the dark was crazy. It's dangerous enough in broad daylight."

"Yah. Young and stupid is a dangerous combination."

Was he any smarter to be thinking about going back there now? Oh, they could go without trying to climb, but he didn't figure they would. They'd be stupid all over again, but he didn't see any other way for him to move ahead.

Moving ahead meant Anna; he knew that now, no matter how he tried to avoid it. He thought about that kiss and knew he hadn't tried very hard.

It had always been Anna for him. He knew that now. Even when they were children, he'd felt they belonged together. Why else would he have spilled all of the secrets to her about his family? He loved her.

As she came home from school on Thursday, Anna reflected that Grossmammi's advice had probably been very good, except that she hadn't been able to follow it. She'd just spent a day and a half trying to be sure of what she felt and still didn't know. And as for talking to Matt . . . well, he'd managed to stay out of her way completely.

They hadn't said a word to each other since that kiss. Was that why he was avoiding her? There didn't seem to be another answer, but she couldn't quite accept that one. Matt, at least the Matt she'd gotten to know since he came back, didn't hide from things. Did he?

Or maybe the obvious answer was the right one—he'd regretted the whole thing and wanted to erase it from their memories. If so, this wasn't the way to go about it.

Her jaw tightened as she turned in the lane and headed for the barn. If so, it wasn't going to work. She'd made up her mind to talk to him the minute she got home.

The problem was, she couldn't find him. He wasn't anywhere near the barn, where she unharnessed the mare and turned her into the paddock. She could see the fields from where she stood, and she didn't spot him anywhere.

Frustrated, Anna headed for the house. As she neared the back porch, she noticed Grossdaadi, slipping out of the door from the grossdaadi haus, so furtive he was almost tiptoeing.

She came up behind him and tapped his shoulder. "Are you running away from home?"

He jumped guiltily and then chuckled. "Just trying to escape your grandmother. She keeps on feeding me chicken broth. I don't want broth. Now a good big slab of pie . . ." His eyes twinkled at her. "You're not going to tell on me, are you?"

"No, but don't blame me when she catches you."

He still looked a bit the worse for his cold, but she could sympathize. She didn't want chicken broth right now, either. They linked arms and walked toward the kitchen.

"Grossdaadi, do you know where Matt is? I need to talk to him."

He gave her a guarded look that made her suspicious at once. "I hear he asked your daad if he could leave early today."

"Why?" Her voice was too sharp. "I mean, was he going somewhere special?" He could easily be doing something for his aunt. Or even for the Burkhardt family.

"I did hear him say that he and Sam were going to Hawk Cliff." Grossdaadi hurried to the back door as if determined to avoid further questions.

Anna reached it first and grasped the handle. "What do you mean? Why would they be going to . . . going there?" She could hardly say the name.

Her grandfather hesitated, seeming to weigh what he was going to say. "I didn't talk to them about it. But sometimes people feel they need to remember, even something bad."

Anna felt that she was going to either explode

or cry. But neither one was aimed at Grossdaadi, just at Matt. Or maybe at her own confusion of feelings.

She couldn't stand here thinking about it, and Grossdaadi shouldn't be standing outside anyway, chicken broth or no chicken broth. She opened the door and piloted him into the kitchen, where they were instantly enveloped in noise.

The young ones were making colored eggs. It seemed they couldn't do that without commotion.

Grossdaadi sank into his usual chair, looking at the newspaper spread on the table and the cups of coloring. "We're just in time, Anna."

Before she could protest that she didn't want to color eggs, Micah was grabbing her arm. "Anna, these brown eggs will color, won't they? Betsy says they won't. She says they'll look funny. Will they?"

Anna gave him a hug to make up for behaving like his teacher all day. "How does Betsy know? This is the first year we've had any Rhode Island Red chickens."

Betsy made a face. "I think so. I didn't say I know."

"Well, then, let's try some and find out, yah?"

She grabbed a large apron from the peg on the wall and wrapped it around herself before anyone could spill egg coloring on her.

"I'm going to make all yellow ones," Grace announced. "Yellow is my new favorite color."

283

Anna couldn't even guess why, but she nodded and pushed the yellow coloring toward her sister.

If she were an only child, she would be in her own room right now, venting her emotions. Clearly she didn't have that choice.

Micah was holding his breath while he lowered a brown egg into red coloring with Grossdaadi's help. "You guys hurry up," he said when it was safely done. "We'll see whose egg colors first."

"No fair," Betsy said, sounding as if she were eight again.

"If you say something's no fair again, you can put an extra nickel in the jar for church," Mammi added from the stove. She met Anna's eyes, smiling.

Together they'd come up with the idea of fining the young ones for using the expression. It worked better than reminding them that life wasn't fair.

The children had probably picked the phrase up from some of their schoolmates, although no one in the school had ventured to say that to her.

The door from the grossdaadi haus opened and Grossmammi stalked in, looking as ruffled as one of those Rhode Island Reds.

"So here you are." She went straight to Grossdaadi and shook her finger in his face. "I told you to stay in the rocking chair while I made you some broth. Did you go outside?"

Grossdaadi leaned back in his chair with an

innocent face. "I'm just watching all the fun. No harm in that, is there?"

Grossmammi looked around the room, and everyone managed to hide their smiles and look in another direction. Betsy, getting carried away, slopped some of her egg dye on the table near Grossdaadi's arm.

Grossmammi grabbed the towel Betsy handed her. "Ach, well, we only color eggs once a year after all."

They all started talking at once, and the usual noisy turmoil erupted. Micah triumphantly fished his dark red egg from the cup.

"There, see!" The egg wobbled dangerously, and Anna steadied his hand.

Family was family, and she couldn't expect things to be any different. She gave up the idea of running to her room for a good cry without any regrets and turned to coloring the eggs.

Maybe it was best not to be alone right now, thinking about Hawk Cliff and why Matthew was there. That would lead her into all the questions she didn't have answers to. At least here she had the family to distract her from the way her heart was aching.

CHAPTER SIXTEEN

Anna woke as the sun started to lift above the ridge. She sat up, shaking, and pulled her quilt around her, trying to free herself from the remnants of her dream . . . no, nightmare.

She shuddered, realizing her nightgown was twisted around her legs and her bedclothes were half off the bed. She'd been struggling in her dream, struggling to get somewhere, struggling to save someone. Falling—

No. She wouldn't let herself hang on to that dream. It was the same one she'd had so many nights after James's death—she'd seen him falling, and no matter how she tried, she couldn't reach him.

Last night's dream had taken a turn that she might have expected after learning what Matt had intended yesterday. She'd seen what she thought was James, but when she saw the face, it was Matthew's. Matthew who was falling, Matthew who reached out for her to save him, and Matthew she lost.

Thrusting the quilt away, Anna forced herself out of bed and stumbled to the window. The sunlight had just begun to pour down the ridge, touching everything in its path. It was sunrise on Good Friday, and she straightened, shedding the last bits of the dream as she had the quilt.

Good Friday meant they would spend the morning in fasting and prayer. Last night, as usual on that night, Mamm had served a huge supper followed by an evening snack. She always said that it would help them not to be so hungry during the fast, but Anna had found that it didn't work that way for her. Her stomach seemed to expect food at the usual time, no matter how much she'd had.

Well, that was the point of fasting, wasn't it? It sharpened their hearts and minds to receive the Bible passages Daadi would read to them this morning.

Below her, she heard the back door open and close. The animals had to be taken care of, fast day or not, but after that was done, the family would gather in the living room. Dressing quickly and quietly, she began waking her siblings. The younger ones were easier, but for some reason, Sally and Betsy never wanted to wake up. She had to watch them until they'd gotten moving, or they'd have slid back into bed for a few extra minutes that might turn into an hour.

When she started downstairs, Micah came tiptoeing from his room to join her. He caught her hand, and she bent for his whisper.

"Can I sit with you for prayers?" He was looking very solemn and responsible this morning, so she didn't let herself smile at the question.

"Yah, that would be gut." Last year Micah had still been allowed to sit quietly at the kitchen table and color during the morning, but now that he was eight, he was old enough to participate along with the rest of the family.

She matched her steps to his as they went the rest of the way down and entered the living room, where Mammi already sat next to Grossdaadi and Grossmammi in the circle of chairs. With a silent nod in greeting, she led Micah to the widest of the upholstered chairs. It would be big enough for two.

The girls came down, with Betsy yawning and Sally rubbing her eyes. They settled on straight chairs, where they wouldn't stand a chance of going back to sleep again.

When Daadi came in, the prayers and readings began. Daadi always read the story of the happenings of Holy Week, with the emphasis on Friday. And then came the prayers, followed by another reading from the Old Testament. Then more prayers. It hadn't always been easy for her to focus the whole time, and she wasn't surprised when Micah's head sagged against her arm.

She let him rest, sympathetic, but he woke when she moved slightly. He blinked rapidly, glancing around as if to see whether anyone noticed. Halfway through the readings, Micah's stomach growled loudly enough to be heard. His cheeks flushed, and she snuggled him closer to her. She'd remind him afterward that this vigil was meant to make them humble and accepting, like Jesus. Micah's noisy tummy just showed that he was both.

When the last Amen had been said, Mammi scurried to the kitchen, followed by Grossmammi and Anna. The fast was always broken with a big meal, and Anna stayed busy flipping pancakes and scrambling eggs while Mammi made a mountain of sausage.

Not surprisingly, everything was gone when they'd finished.

Anna carried plates to the sink. "I sometimes think Betsy and Grace would keep eating as long as there was food in the house," she said.

"Just wait a few years until Micah reaches that stage," Mammi said, stopping Anna when she started to turn on the water. "We'll let the girls do the dishes. I want you to do an errand for me."

"Yah, of course." Anna dried her hands. "What can I do?"

Mammi led her to the pantry, where she indicated two baskets, already packed. "I told Ella that I would send food over today. She's feeding the Burkhardt family most of the time now, and she's not used to that. You don't mind taking these over, do you?"

She could hardly say so if she did mind. *Acceptance,* she reminded herself. At least this way, she'd see for herself that Matt had survived his trip to Hawk Cliff yesterday. Maybe then the shadow of her nightmare would leave her.

In a few minutes she was ready to go. Mammi met her at the buggy, and they loaded the baskets.

"Go along now before Sally sees you're going out," Mammi said. "She'll use any excuse to get out alone and see Joseph. I'm not having her do it today, of all days."

Anna clicked to the mare and moved off. She'd thought Sally had been a little better lately, but maybe she was just getting more adept at ignoring her. Mammi would know better.

What would she be like after another year of rumspringa? They could hope maturity would hit at some point.

Reaching the main road, Anna headed Daisy toward the King place and found she was thinking about Matt again. If only she and Matt could talk about James's death without an outburst of emotion on one side or the other, maybe they could see their way to the future.

But they hadn't managed to do so yet. What would Matt be feeling after going back to Hawk Cliff yesterday? And why had he done it at all? It seemed that each time she saw him, there were more unanswered questions.

Matt must have heard the buggy, because he came out of the house before she reached the porch.

"Anna." He stood watching her, his face expressionless. It was as if they'd gone back to the beginning again, before he'd begun to show her the person he was now.

She stopped, hesitated for a moment, and then swung down, gesturing toward the baskets. "My mother sent these over for Aunt Ella."

Matt blinked, registering confusion. "I see." He reached toward them. "I thought you came for another reason."

"You thought I came because you went to Hawk Cliff yesterday."

She hadn't intended to say it, but the words spilled out of her mouth before she could stop them. Whatever came of it, she had to know.

Matt froze for an instant. Even though he'd expected it, he still didn't have an easy answer. He knew it had been needful, but how to explain it to her?

Anna moved slightly, as if to turn away from him. Acting on instinct, he clasped her wrist, feeling her pulse beat against his palm. Now it was Anna who froze, staring down at his hand.

It looked like that had been the wrong move. He let her go, irrationally annoyed. Maybe she was waiting for him to apologize for touching her, for kissing her, for breathing the same air she did. He opened his lips, but before he could speak, the door banged behind him. He glanced back to see Rebecca running toward them. She jumped down the steps and flung herself at Anna, who bent to hug her, looking relieved.

"Rebecca, how are you? Have you been helping Aunt Ella?"

Rebecca produced a smile, which seemed more frequent than it was even a few days ago. Maybe she understood that her mother was getting help, despite all their efforts to shield her.

"Yah. We had prayers and then we had a great big breakfast and I helped make sausages. Did you?"

Anna caressed her face lightly. "I think we had the same breakfast you had, but my mother made the sausages while I cooked eggs."

Matt cleared his throat. Obviously neither of them could say anything meaningful right now. "Can I carry the baskets in for you?"

"Ach, yah, I was forgetting. Let's take them in. You can have that one," she said, pointing. "It's heavier. Rebecca and I can manage the other one."

They took the baskets, Anna sharing the handle of hers with Rebecca. Aunt Ella was already holding the door open.

"Ach, I told your mammi she didn't need to bother," she said, sounding flustered as usual when someone tried to help her.

"Don't say that," he said lightly. "Or Anna might take them back, and I see shoofly pie in this one."

"Mammi said to tell you it's just a few things

she thought you might need with all these people in the house." Anna started unloading the baskets onto the counter.

Rebecca tugged at Anna's skirt. "Did you hear? Daadi says Mammi might come home by the end of next week."

He suspected that Anna was wondering, as he was, whether it would be wise for her to be with the children again. But in the face of Rebecca's joy, all they could do was be happy with her.

"That's wonderful gut news." Anna hugged her.

"Ach, what am I thinking?" Aunt Ella bustled to the stove. "You'll stay and have some coffee, ain't so?"

Anna seemed torn for an instant. "That's kind, but I'd best get back home. Mammi has so much to do today and tomorrow, and she's counting on me to help."

"I'll walk out with you." Matt spoke quickly, sending a warning look at his aunt and gesturing toward Rebecca.

"Me, too." Rebecca started for the door, but Aunt Ella caught her. Good, she'd understood what he meant.

"Say goodbye for now. I want you to help with putting all these things away."

Rebecca nodded, seeming happy enough to have a role, and Matt steered Anna to the door. He was going to have a private word with her no matter what.

They reached the buggy without anyone inter-rupting them. "Look, let's start again." He tried to keep any hint of frustration out of his voice. "You want to know why I went to Hawk Cliff."

She wasn't looking at him, but she was listening. "Yah, I do."

He caught her by surprise and lifted her up to the buggy seat, then swung up beside her. "Drive around the bend in the lane, so we'll be out of sight. Rebecca is already peering out the window."

That surprised her into a smile. She picked up the lines and did as he suggested. Once the hedge of lilac bushes was between them and the house, she stopped.

Matt hesitated, not sure how to begin. Well, he guessed at the beginning. "Do you know what happened that night?" He asked the question abruptly, and she seemed taken aback.

"I don't . . . what difference does that make?"

"A lot." He spoke with more firmness than he felt. "If you don't know, then you won't understand what drove me to go there."

That went for Sam, too. Sam might have delayed returning to Hawk Cliff a little longer if not for Matt's going, but sooner or later it would have happened. He knew Sam.

Anna wasn't looking at him. She stared down at her hands in her lap. "I just know what everyone knew. That there was a party. That James fell."

She looked at him then. "There's one thing I have to know. Did someone dare him to climb?"

Relief went through him. At least he could reassure her on that point. "No," he said. "You can believe that, Anna. No one had even mentioned it until James brought it up."

She studied his face and then nodded. "Okay, then." She took a breath. "Tell me about it."

"Right." He hesitated, organizing his thoughts. "Some of the Englisch kids we knew invited us. They called it a picnic, but everybody knew what that meant."

"A drinking party, yah?"

He nodded. "I still don't know how they bought the beer, when they were all under twenty-one, but they did. Everyone had to pitch in ten bucks. James and Sam and I . . . we were the only Amish kids there. We all had to sneak out, I guess, but that just made it more exciting."

Anna's face twitched, her lips trembling. "I know. James and Daad had a terrible argument about it, and then he slammed off to his room."

"So he talked about it. I wondered. I knew better than to ask my parents."

If he had . . . well, his daad would have locked him in one of the outbuildings. Then he wouldn't have been there. He wouldn't have seen James fall.

He pushed himself to go on. "It wasn't really that wild a time—mostly drinking and telling tall stories. Then James mentioned about that group that climbed Hawk Cliff the year before." He shook his head. "I'd wandered away from the folks around the fire by then, so I just heard snatches of it. Next thing I knew, James was trying to talk me into climbing."

He gripped the front of the seat so hard that it hurt. "I told him no. Told him only an idiot would try that in the dark without any equipment. I thought he'd given it up."

He sucked in a breath, not wanting to go on, but knowing he had to. She was watching him, her eyes wide and dark, her face strained.

"A little later Sam came running to find me, stammering out that James was doing it, and we had to stop him." He skipped over the panic of running toward the cliff, tripping and stumbling, seeing that James was already up at least twenty or thirty feet.

"We started up, but it was hard to see the way with the shadows from the fire flickering on the rocks. I was yelling at James to stop, come back, we'd go down together, but he didn't pay any attention. Sam was falling behind. He kept stumbling and I thought he was going to fall, so I told him to drop back where there was a ledge and work over below James. Maybe he could break his fall."

"You tried to reach him." She said it as if she felt he needed reassurance.

"Yah, for sure. I thought he was stuck, so I told him to stay where he was. I was coming after him. I went as fast as I could." He stopped, feeling as if he couldn't breathe. "I didn't get there in time. I reached out, tried to grab him, but I couldn't."

He bent over, pressing his hands against the front panel, his head down. He'd failed. That's what it amounted to. He'd failed.

Anna touched his arm. She must have felt how taut it was, because she moved her hand in a comforting gesture. "Denke," she whispered. "Thank you for telling me."

He pulled himself upright, not looking at her. "You see why I had to go back? I have decisions to make, and I couldn't do that without going there again." He hesitated. That wasn't much of an explanation. "Maybe Sam said it best. He said we had to say goodbye to James."

He finally looked at Anna. Her face was wet with tears. Maybe he was imagining it, but in a way she seemed at peace.

Unable to look at her any longer, he moved suddenly, sliding off the seat before she could speak. Then he paused, hand on the buggy wheel.

"Whether I go or stay . . . well, I guess that depends on you, Anna. You know what I feel. I love you. I want a life with you."

She looked for an instant as if she'd speak, but he held up his hand, and she was silent.

"Don't say anything now. Just think about it."

There wasn't anything else to be said. They knew each other too well for there to be any mistake. He spun and walked back toward the house.

Anna slept in on Saturday after lying wakeful until after three in the morning. Her thoughts had been too jumbled for sleep until exhaustion finally took over. At that, she'd have expected to dream again, seeing Matt and Sam trying to save James and failing.

Oddly enough, she hadn't dreamed at all.

She considered that while she dressed hastily, unsure what that meant, if anything. Hurrying downstairs, she nearly ran into Sally plunging through the hall, clearly back in one of her moods.

Feeling unable to cope with Sally, she scurried to the kitchen to find Mammi and the younger girls already busy with the baking.

"Ach, Mammi, you should have waked me."

Grace grinned, looking up from the nuts she was chopping at the table. "I would have, but Mammi said to let you sleep."

"I'll help with the baking . . ." she began, but her mother shook her head.

"Not until you eat something. There's a plate staying warm on the back of the stove for you."

Her mother's tone didn't admit any argument,

so Anna grabbed the plate, nearly burned her fingers, and then poured a cup of coffee. "Don't finish the bread without me. I'll eat fast."

The table and counter were crowded with the evidence of baking. Mammi was in the midst of her annual Easter bread baking. The round loaves of Osterbrot were traditional for Easter morning, and her mother always made extra. She and Daadi would take them to friends and neighbors tonight after supper so they'd be ready for Easter morning. There'd be one for Ella and the Burkhardt family among them.

Betsy dusted flour from her hands, getting it on her dress instead. "It's a wonder Sally didn't wake you, as much noise as she was making."

Anna couldn't help rolling her eyes at that. "I saw she was in a mood. What did she want this time?"

"To go out with Joseph tonight. His brother invited them over." Betsy seemed contemptuous of Sally's idea of a good time. "Daadi said she couldn't go tonight and if she mentioned it again, she couldn't go to the next singing."

"That's enough talking," Mamm said briskly. "Sally's punishment is no concern of yours. Besides, the loaves are almost ready to bake. You two go downstairs and bring up the tins of slivered almonds and two jars of apricot jam. Hurry up, now."

Betsy and Grace raced each other to the stairs

and thundered down to the cellar, where shelves were filled with canned goods.

Mammi touched Anna lightly on the shoulder. "You talked to Matthew about going to Hawk Cliff, ain't so?"

Anna nodded, her throat tightening at the thought. "He told me . . . about what happened that night, I mean."

"Yah, I thought he would." Mammi didn't seem troubled by that, but when Anna looked at her face, she could see the deep sadness in her eyes. "Did it help you any?"

"I don't know." That was the most honest answer she could give. "Matt said that he and Sam had to go back there before they could move on. That they had to say goodbye to James." She struggled with the doubt that still clung to her. "It seems almost heartless, as if they want to forget him. As if they want to get on with their lives without him."

"Ach, no." Mammi touched her chin, tipping Anna's head up to meet her eyes. "We can't bring back those who are gone, child. We can only keep them alive in our hearts by remembering them. That's all any of us can ask for—to be remembered."

There wasn't time for anything else, because the thudding on the cellar steps said the girls were coming back. Almost simultaneously the timer rang, and Mammi began uncovering the loaves, full and round and perfectly raised.

"Can I cut the crosses this year?" Grace pleaded. "Please?"

Mammi looked at her skeptically. "You can do one. Then we'll see."

Each of the loaves had to be brushed carefully with an egg wash, and then the cross cut in the top with a razor blade or very thin knife. Anna could understand Mamm's reluctance to trust Grace with the blade. She watched her mother incise the sign of the cross on the first loaf, and she began to see something else.

For her mother, the marking of the Easter bread was a special act, even a part of the Easter worship. Anna could read it on her face. No wonder she didn't want to let go of it.

But Mammi finished, hesitated a moment, and then handed the blade to Anna. They went around the table, with everyone taking a turn, until the loaves were ready to go in the oven. When they came out again, the tops crisp and brown, it would be time to finish them with the apricot jam glaze and sprinkle them with almonds.

"All right, now." Mammi whisked a dusting of flour off the table into her hand. "There's plenty more to do today to be ready for tomorrow."

Her mother's prediction was true, of course. Anna decided that the busier they were, the better, as far as she was concerned. If she kept busy, she couldn't brood on Matthew and herself.

301

The day flew by, thankfully. Sally eventually reappeared and was drawn into the cleaning and food preparation, grumbling a bit, but in a minor way, as if she felt obliged to. A few showers fell, making her grandmother insist that Grossdaadi stay inside. Betsy, looking happy to escape the cleaning, joined Micah to go out and help Daad and Matt with the outside work.

By the time supper was over, the clouds had thickened. Daadi, taking a look out the window, shook his head. "We'd best hurry along with taking the bread, ain't so? We don't want it to get wet."

Mammi swatted her dish towel at him. "As if I wouldn't cover them securely. I'll be ready by the time you bring the buggy up. You'll see."

With Grossmammi and Anna helping, all the loaves were wrapped, secured in boxes, and covered with a sheet of plastic.

"Komm, Daadi's here." Her mother gestured to Anna to help carry. As soon as they were out of earshot of the kitchen, she went on. "Try to get your grandparents to go to bed early tonight, yah?"

"I will, but Grossdaadi is better, he says."

"He's still coughing at night, and neither of them have gotten much sleep, so keep the young ones from being noisy. We won't be late."

"If we don't get going, we surely will be late," Daadi grumbled, clicking to the horse.

Anna stepped back, waving, her lips twitching. Some things never changed. Mammi always had some last-minute directions to give, and Daadi always warned they'd be late. One way or another, everything got done.

She started back inside and spotted Matt walking toward the barn. Then he saw her and veered toward her. Her heart seemed to jolt and then began beating faster.

As soon as he was close enough, she spoke. "What are you doing still here?"

"I'm not still here, I'm back again," Matt said calmly. "Your daad was worried that one of the heifers was about to calve, so I thought I'd check. Any problems?"

She shook her head. "I . . . I have to go in." She hurried inside and only once the door was closed behind her did she realize what she'd done.

She'd run away. There was so much they had to say to each other, and she'd run away.

Anna stood for a moment, her hands twisting together. Did she even know what she wanted to say to Matt? Before she could make up her mind to go after him, Grace came looking for her.

"Have you seen Sally? She said she'd play a board game with us, and I can't find her." She made a face. "I should have known she wouldn't."

Anna was just as glad to focus on something else. "Well, let's find her, wherever she is, and rout her out. You can have one game, and then it's time to get ready for bed. Tomorrow's a busy day."

"We've looked everywhere," Grace complained, just as Betsy came in from the grossdaadi haus.

"Grossmammi and Grossdaadi are going to bed. She's not over there."

"Did you check everywhere? The basement?"

"Everywhere," Betsy said. "I know what she's done. She's run off to meet Joseph. Daadi will really let her have it this time."

"Hush." Anna spoke sharply, with a glance toward the door to the grossdaadi haus. "Don't disturb the grandparents." Her thoughts raced. No point in wondering how Sally could do something so stupid. She had to decide what to do.

"Listen," she said, interrupting an argument between her sisters about where Sally was. "You two go and play the game with Micah. Betsy, you're in charge. Make sure the younger ones get to bed on time if I'm not back."

"I can't—" Betsy began, but Anna cut her off.

"Of course you can." She pulled her jacket off the hook.

"Where are you going?" Betsy wailed.

"I'm going to bring her back." Anna flew out the door.

CHAPTER SEVENTEEN

Pulling her jacket around her, Anna rushed out of the house and headed for the barn. She'd have to harness up and go after Sally quickly.

Anna ran into the barn and came to a sudden stop. She'd forgotten that Matt was still here. He was looking at her, startled, with a question in his eyes.

She rushed into speech. "How is the cow doing? A calf coming soon?"

"False alarm," he said easily, walking toward her. "Maybe Bessie just wanted some attention." He watched, puzzled, as she led her buggy horse out. "What are you doing?"

"I have to go out." She didn't have to tell him anything else. She just led Daisy to where her buggy waited, thankful that Mamm and Daad had taken the large family one.

Not saying anything, Matt fetched the harness and began helping her. After a few moments of heavy silence, he shook his head. "You may as well tell me, Anna. What's going on? Where are you rushing off to?"

Anna pressed her lips together, but it was no use. If she didn't tell him, he'd pretty quickly guess the truth, even if one of the younger ones didn't spill it the minute he looked at them.

"It's Sally. She's run off someplace. I've got

to find her before Mamm and Daad come back." She fumbled with the buckle, her fingers not cooperating.

Matt put his hand over hers and fastened it for her. "Why? I mean, why go after her? Why not just let your parents deal with it?"

"You don't understand. Mamm and Daad left me in charge." Maybe an only child couldn't understand it. "They trusted me. I'm supposed to be watching out for the younger ones."

"Make sense, Anna." His tone was gentle. "They're not going to blame you for what Sally did. She's old enough to be responsible for herself."

Her jaw clenched. "You wouldn't think that if you saw as much of her as I have lately."

He backed Daisy between the buggy poles, and they finished quickly. "Are you planning on hiding it from your parents forever?"

"No, don't be ferhoodled. I just want to get her home before they come. If Daad has to go out chasing after her, it's going to spoil Easter for Mammi. She's so dedicated to having it just as we always do." She climbed up into the buggy. "Sally will have to tell them, but at least if she's here and safe, it won't be as bad."

She tried to pick up the lines, but she could hardly see them in the dim light, especially when her eyes were blurred with tears. The words came out before she could stop them.

"You said once that everybody had something to regret when it came to James's accident. It's true. I did. I heard him sneaking out and didn't stop him. I'm not going to do the same thing with Sally."

Matt took the lines from her, and she thought he was going to try to stop her. Instead, he climbed up next to her and clicked to Daisy.

She sent an anguished look toward the grossdaadi haus windows as they went, but most of the lights were out. No one was looking out at them.

"One thing," Matt said as they neared the road. "You have any idea where we're going?"

She stared at him blankly, and then the words came back into her head. "Something was said about inviting her to Joseph's brother's house. Eli, it must be. He's the only one married. And he's just as feckless as Joseph is." She shrugged. "For all I know, they may not even have invited Sally. This idea might just as easily have come from her."

"Not from Joseph?" he asked.

"Surely you remember Joseph. He couldn't say boo to a goose. If those two ever do get married, she'll rule the roost, that's for sure."

She thought he chuckled at that, but she couldn't be sure.

"Eli and his wife bought that small house on the corner of Appletree Road. It's not very far. If only we can get back before Mamm and Daad."

He nodded, turning to the left out of the lane. They were silent for a while as he concentrated on seeing in the dim light. The thick clouds hid the moon, and she tried to keep herself from straining forward anxiously.

"Do you want to tell me about it?"

The question, coming from nowhere, shocked her for a moment. Then she knew what he meant. He meant her failure to stop James.

She paused, biting her lip, but the desire to share was stronger than the longing to continue keeping it to herself.

"James and Daad had a quarrel about his going to that party. You know how it is, people say more than they mean when they get angry. James kept saying he was old enough to make his own decisions, and Daad was just as adamant that he didn't want James going to that party." Anna rubbed her forehead, remembering too clearly. "Daad and Mamm knew he'd been to Englisch parties before, and they hadn't said anything. But Daad thought this was dangerous, being so far out in the woods away from any help."

"He was wise," Matt said, a hint of bitterness in his voice.

"Yah. Well, James slammed his way to his room eventually." She stopped, struck by something. "Sally is just like him in that way. I never thought of that before. Anyway, I could hear him stamping around in his room, and after a while I decided to try to calm him down. But he just kept repeating what he'd been saying to Daad, and when I didn't agree, he pushed me out of the room."

"And now you're wondering if you should have said something different. Well, you couldn't have."

"No, I guess not, but that isn't all of it. I stayed awake for a long time. After a time the house grew quiet. Everyone was asleep. I was drifting off to sleep myself when I heard the board creak outside his bedroom door." She stopped to take a deep breath.

"I heard James creeping out. I knew what he was doing. I should have reacted. Instead I argued with myself about whether I should go after him or tell Daad or mind my own business. And while I was arguing, James left."

Matt reached across and wrapped his hand around hers. His was warm and comforting. "So you put yourself in the same place as all the rest of us—all the people who wish they had done something different once it's too late."

"Right. Only now I'm chasing after Sally, afraid of doing what I did before. Afraid something will happen to her. I know it's foolish, but I can't help it."

He squeezed her hand. "I wonder if Sally knows what a good sister she has."

Anna managed to smile at that. "Not right now, she doesn't. Maybe someday."

"Someday for sure." He moved slightly, and he seemed to stiffen. "I guess you had a point, Anna. It looks as if we've found the runaways."

Ahead of them, barely visible in the gloom, a buggy lay tilted, its wheel in the ditch. And Sally was climbing out of it.

Matt drew up as far off the road as he could. Fortunately Anna had battery flashers on her buggy, so if all went well, no one would hit them, always a danger when out after dark with a buggy.

Anna jumped down even before he set the brake, running toward her sister. He followed more slowly, suspecting that he was the one who'd have to talk to Joseph and make him see reason.

He could see the look of astonishment on Sally's face as she recognized her sister. She flung herself in Anna's arms. "Thank goodness you're here. You have to help us."

Matt decided he didn't want to be watching when Sally realized why they had come. He stepped around the buggy and went to help Joseph, who was crawling up the muddy bank.

"I don't know how it happened. I don't. I wasn't anywhere near the edge, and all of a sudden we were in the ditch." Joseph was babbling, for all the world like a kid caught with his hand in the cookie jar.

"You sure about that?" Matt asked. "Sure you

weren't snuggling with Sally and forgot to watch where you were going?"

"I didn't . . . I wouldn't . . ."

Matt let out an exasperated breath. "Come on, Joseph. I was your age once. Don't try to tell me you were out with a pretty girl and didn't cuddle."

In the blinking red flasher, Joseph's face looked appropriately red. Matt took pity on him and turned to the horse. "Let's get that gelding unharnessed before we do anything, okay?"

They'd made it two steps toward the horse when there was a shriek behind him. Matt turned, expecting another accident, to see Sally was furious. She must have realized they'd come to take her back.

"Sally, stop that." Anna caught her arm. "Don't you see? You have to get home before anyone sees you. You don't want half the community talking about you by morning, do you?"

The frustration in Anna's voice was justified as far as he was concerned.

"No! I won't do it. I won't go back. I'm going with Joseph. He loves me and I love him."

He glanced at the boy to see his reaction. It was too bad Sally wasn't watching him at that moment. Joseph's face was a compound of shock, surprise, and dismay. Hadn't he ever seen this side of Sally? If not, this might turn out for the best.

"Joseph!" Sally struggled against Anna's hands. "Joseph!"

Matt strode over to her. Clearly Anna's love wasn't working to calm her down. They'd best try something else.

"Stop it," he roared in a voice he'd use on a construction site when someone did something dangerous or stupid. "You're screeching like a hen being chased by a fox. If you were my sister, I'd empty a pail of water over you, but Anna is too kind to do that." He paused. "I'm not."

Sally stared at him, open-mouthed, for several seconds. Then she closed her mouth and looked from Anna to Joseph, probably hoping for sympathy.

"You aren't going to let him talk like that, are you?"

It wasn't clear which one she was talking to, but Joseph seemed to be studying his feet, and Anna was shaking her head.

"Joseph?" She tried again. "You don't want me to go home, do you? You want me to go with you, don't you?"

"Let's get this straight," Anna said, sounding like the schoolmistress she was. "Joseph, did your brother and his wife invite Sally for tonight?"

Joseph stared even more intently at his shoe. The toe of it seemed to be digging a hole in the mud.

"Well?" Matt snapped, getting tired of this young pair of lovebirds.

"No, not exactly." He rushed on. "I mean,

they wouldn't, would they? But Sally said they wouldn't mind. And . . . and I don't think they would," he finished with a flare of defiance.

"Did you give any thought to what would happen when word got around about this exploit?" He decided to drive the point home. "If you're not careful, you'll find yourself married to her before you even have a regular job. Not smart, is it?"

Joseph paled. "I . . . I didn't think of it that way."

"You didn't think at all," Matt said. He let the horse step forward free of the buggy. "Here. Tie him to one of those trees for the moment while we see what the damage is to the buggy."

Nodding, Joseph pulled a flashlight from under the seat and turned it on the buggy. He groaned. "Look at that. The wheel's bent. My daad's going to kill me."

Whatever tension Matt felt relaxed then. Clearly Joseph was more disturbed by the damage to the buggy than to having his evening ruined.

"I wouldn't be surprised," he said, moving around the buggy in a search for more damage, but keeping his ears open for what Anna was saying to her sister.

"There, you see?" Anna took Sally's arm and propelled her toward her buggy. "You've gotten Joseph in trouble with his daad, besides getting yourself in a jam. And if we don't get you home soon, you'll have ruined Easter for everyone."

Sally sniffled. She was apparently moving from shouting to tears. "I didn't mean anything. But I just love him so much and I wanted to be with him. Don't you understand?"

"I understand wanting to be with him." Anna's voice softened. "But you're making too many other people unhappy just to spend an hour or two with Joseph, besides making Daad and Mammi not be able to trust you. Is it worth that?"

Sally didn't answer. She just choked back a sob.

Matt moved toward Anna, catching her eye. "You get Juliet into the buggy. I'll take care of Romeo and then join you."

She didn't quite smile, but her lips twitched. "What are you going to do?"

"Send him along to his brother's," he said promptly. "He'll have some explaining to do, but maybe it'll teach him a lesson."

She nodded. "Yah, you're right. This mess isn't over yet."

He didn't want to watch her get Sally into the buggy. As far as he was concerned, either she'd climb in or he'd pick her up and put her there. He went back to Joseph.

"Look, there's nothing we can do about the buggy tonight. You'd better hope the wheelwright can straighten that wheel or you'll be paying for a new one. You'd best take the horse and go on to your brother's before they get worried. We'll take Sally home."

Joseph glanced uneasily in Sally's direction. "You think she's mad at me?"

"I don't know, but if I were you, I'd steer clear for a couple of days."

"Yah, I'll do that." He looked relieved.

"And take a word of advice from someone older. Don't start courting just because a girl wants you to. You have to both want it, ain't so?"

He nodded, his head hanging. "I guess so."

Leaving him to his just deserts, Matt went back to the other buggy. Sally sat in the back, weeping into a tissue, and Anna waited for him on the front seat.

He felt a momentary desire to make an excuse and walk home, but that lasted only a few seconds. He and Anna were in this together, and that was how it should be.

Fortunately, they reached home with no sign of Mamm and Daad's buggy. Anna breathed a sigh of relief. At least they were here. Given how mournful Sally was, she'd undoubtedly confess to Mamm and Daad the minute she saw them, but at least they hadn't had the worry of going out trying to find her.

Matthew pulled up at the back door. "You go ahead and settle Sally. I'll put Daisy away and check the heifer before I go home." He glanced up at the dark sky. Not a star was showing. "At least we didn't get caught in the rain."

"I don't know how I could have done it without you." Anna put her hand on his arm. "Denke isn't enough."

"Sure it is." He patted her hand. Obviously he was ready to leave. Probably eager. She didn't want to let him go, but she had to. He certainly wouldn't want to get involved in the discussion with her parents.

"Matt . . ." She hesitated, not sure how to say what she wanted to say.

He seemed to understand what she didn't say. "I'll come back to the house and check with you before I leave. Okay?"

"Okay," she murmured, and hurried into the house.

Betsy was waiting for her in the kitchen. "Everything's fine here." She sounded a little surprised at herself. "I cleaned up and got Micah and Grace to bed. Sally just ran upstairs."

Anna nodded, suddenly very tired. "She'll have a lot of explaining to do tomorrow, but everything's all right for now."

Betsy looked as if she wanted to ask at least a dozen questions, but after another look she must have decided not to. "I'll go up to bed, then."

Anna sank down on the nearest chair. "Denke, Betsy. You did a gut job. You won't say anything?"

Betsy smiled. She looked more grown-up

suddenly. "Not a word." She headed for the stairs.

She ought to be doing something, Anna supposed, but instead she waited, wondering how soon Matt would come. Wondering if she had the courage to say what she wanted to say to him.

Mamm and Daad would surely be back soon, and the opportunity would be gone for tonight. She rose, determined to speak before it was too late. Even as she turned, there was a gentle tap at the door.

She hurried to open it, then caught Matt's hand and led him outside. "If I don't say this now, I think I might burst. But not in there, where anyone might hear."

Matt led her a few steps farther from the house, glancing back at it. "I'm beginning to see the drawbacks of a big family. You think we're safe here?"

He was teasing again. In the yellow glow of the outside lamp, she couldn't really see his eyes, but she knew what his amusement would look like.

Ignoring his question, she hurried into speech. "I want to . . . I have to say how sorry I am. All this time you were trying to make amends for something you couldn't have stopped, and I've made it harder for you. I'm so ashamed—"

Matt put his hand over her lips, stopping her with his gentle touch. "Don't. We both lost our way for a time after we lost James. But that's over with. James would be telling us to get on with things, ain't so? That was who he was."

"Yah, that's so." She spoke against his palm. "I love you, Matthew." She used his own words. "I want a life with you."

There was no mistaking the love that seemed to shimmer between them. It was as if she was wrapped in that love, protected, warmed, and cherished.

Matt cupped her face in his hands, looking intently into her eyes. "You're sure?"

"I'm sure," she whispered. He smiled, and his lips met hers in a kiss that was stronger, surer, proclaiming that they belonged together. She wrapped her arms around him, holding him close, loving him so much that anyone who looked at them could see it. Not that anyone could. They were safe from prying eyes here in the dark.

Matt pulled back just a little, looking up. "It's starting to rain."

Joy bubbled up in her. "I don't care," she said, holding him so close that he kissed her again.

This time it was a noise that caused them to pull back. A window shrieked as it was pushed up. Anna gasped, staring at the grossdaadi haus. Her grandfather was framed in the window. His voice was husky but loud enough for anyone in the house to hear.

"If you're going to marry the girl, you'd best come inside and kiss her where it's dry."

"Isaac, stop that!" Grossmammi appeared beside

him, tugging at his arm. She sounded scandalized. "Leave those young people alone and get back in bed."

Somebody slammed the window down.

Anna could feel Matt shaking. For an instant she was alarmed, but then she realized he was laughing . . . laughing with rain streaking down his face.

"You heard what your grandfather said. Let's go inside." He caught her hand. "I think I'm going to like being part of your big family, my Anna."

"You always were," she said. "Didn't you know?"

Wet and laughing, they ran together toward the house. Toward their future, together.

EPILOGUE

Easter Sunday had dawned. Anna stood at her bedroom window, feeling as if the sunshine that slipped down the hillsides and made sparkling gems on the wet grass was making her sparkle as well. A glow of happiness suffused her until she thought that she could almost light up a darkened room. Easter had come, and in its light, the guilt and unhappiness that had darkened her soul slid away and vanished.

She'd hurried downstairs as soon as possible, eager for every moment of the day, but especially for the guests who would come to share supper with them, and one guest in particular. Her heart expanded at the thought of Matthew and what they meant to each other.

The day moved through all of the traditional features of an Amish Easter celebration, from the colored eggs decorating the breakfast table to the family devotions to the walk in the woods Mammi always insisted they take. They came back flushed and laughing, with hands full of wildflowers, to find it was time to prepare for their guests.

Everyone decided to help . . . laughing and scolding and getting in each other's way as they always did. Across the width of the kitchen,

Anna's gaze caught her mother's, and a gentle joy seemed to flow between them. In spite of every trial, the family was still together to celebrate.

Anna's heart leaped at the sound of a buggy coming down the lane. She had to struggle to control the longing to race out the door, instead walking in what she hoped was a calm, dignified manner to greet their Easter guests.

The Burkhardt children hopped down first. Rebecca threw herself at Anna for a hug, while her brother contented himself with a smile. Still, a smile from him was an achievement. The news from the hospital must be good. Hopefully their mother would be home soon.

Carl and Aunt Ella joined them then, and Ella swept Anna into such a warm hug that she knew Matt had told her their news. She just hoped he hadn't gotten his aunt out of bed last night to hear.

By this time Mamm and Daad had come out to welcome everyone. The chatter of many voices gave Anna a moment to catch Matt's gaze. He stood back a step from the hubbub, watching her with a small, private smile. The warmth in his eyes was enough to set her heart beating faster.

Everyone began moving into the house. Mindful of meal preparations, Anna started after them, but Matt caught her hand and held her back.

"You have a moment for me, ain't so?" He could hardly embrace her in front of everyone, but his firm, warm handclasp was enough to tell her what he felt.

"Always," she said. "But the meal . . ."

"Let Sally help your mother for once." He moved so that the horse screened them a little from the windows, and he pulled her closer. The heady scent of hyacinths from the bed along the house seemed to be making her dizzy. Or perhaps it was the way he looked at her.

"How did everything go after I left last night? Nobody had any concerns about my intentions?"

"You know better than that," Anna said, her lips curving in the smile that had been so frequent all day. "Mamm and Daad couldn't be happier about us. Daad didn't even spend much time on Sally's misdeeds."

After a cautious glance to be sure they weren't observed, Matt touched her cheek in a gentle caress. "She was fortunate that our news distracted him. I hope she appreciates it."

"I'm not sure about that, but she's being very quiet and humble today. I think she finally realized she'd gone too far." Anna put her hand over his, pressing it against her cheek. The clouds on her heart had vanished, leaving a quiet serenity in their wake.

She wasn't sure how long they'd have stood there looking at each other if her impatient young brother hadn't called from the door. "Matt, aren't you coming in? I saved a colored egg for you."

322

Matt grinned. "He's as tactful as your grand-father. I guess we'd better go in, or he'll come after us."

Her heart singing, Anna led the way inside, where they were swept up into the chaos of too many people trying to help and getting in each other's way. Despite the confusion, it took only a few minutes to get the food on the table and find places for everyone to sit.

As she looked around the table, it seemed to Anna that she saw everyone in a different, sharper focus. Maybe happiness was contagious, because everyone seemed contented . . . even Sally, who gave her a shy smile when their eyes met.

The family was changing, Anna realized. Growing up, growing old, moving in new direc-tions, expanding with new friends and new family members. Matt, sitting next to her, was responding to something Grossdaadi said even as his fingers touched hers under the table.

The place James had held would always be there, of course, but it had begun to fill up with happy memories of the laughing, generous young man he'd been. The family bonds had not been broken by his loss, she realized. They would go on strengthening through the years. And she and Matt would be part of it, together.

GLOSSARY OF PENNSYLVANIA DUTCH WORDS AND PHRASES

ach. oh; used as an exclamation

agasinish. stubborn; self-willed

ain't so? A phrase commonly used at the end of a sentence to invite agreement.

alter. old man

anymore. Used as a substitute for "nowadays."

Ausbund. Amish hymnal. Used in the worship services, it contains traditional hymns, words only, to be sung without accompaniment. Many of the hymns date from the sixteenth century.

befuddled. mixed up

blabbermaul. talkative one

blaid. bashful

boppli. baby

bruder. brother

bu. boy

buwe. boys

daadi. daddy

Da Herr sei mit du. The Lord be with you.

denke (*or* danki). thanks

Englischer. one who is not Plain

ferhoodled. upset; distracted

ferleicht. perhaps

frau. wife

fress. eat

gross. big

grossdaadi. grandfather

grossdaadi haus. An addition to the farmhouse, built for the grandparents to live in once they've "retired" from actively running the farm.

grossmammi. grandmother

gut. good

hatt. hard; difficult

haus. house

hinnersich. backward

ich. I

kapp. Prayer covering, worn in obedience to the biblical injunction that women should pray with their heads covered. Kapps are made of Swiss organdy and are white. (In some Amish communities, unmarried girls thirteen and older wear black kapps during worship service.)

kinder (*or* kinner). kids

komm. come

komm schnell. come quick

Leit. the people; the Amish

lippy. sassy

maidal. old maid; spinster

mamm. mother

middaagesse. lunch

mind. remember

onkel. uncle

Ordnung. The agreed-upon rules by which the Amish community lives. When new practices become an issue, they are discussed at length among the leadership. The decision for or against innovation is generally made on the basis of maintaining the home and family as separate from the world. For instance, a telephone might be necessary in a shop in order to conduct business but would be banned from the home because it would intrude on family time.

Pennsylvania Dutch. The language is actually German in origin and is primarily a spoken language. Most Amish write in English, which results in many variations in spelling when the dialect is put into writing! The language probably originated in the south of Germany but is common also among the Swiss Mennonite and French Huguenot immigrants to Pennsylvania. The language was brought to America prior to the Revolution and is still in use today. High German is used for Scripture and church documents, while English is the language of commerce.

rumspringa. running-around time; the late teen years when Amish youth taste some aspects of the outside world before deciding to be baptized into the church.

schnickelfritz. mischievous child
ser gut. very good
tastes like more. delicious
Was ist letz? What's the matter?
Wie bist du heit? How are you?; said in greeting
wilkom. welcome
Wo bist du? Where are you?
yah. yes

RECIPES

GERMAN EASTER BREAD
OSTERBROT

Ingredients
1 cup raisins or currants
¼ cup slivered or chopped almonds
Small amount of water
½ cup milk

Soak the raisins in water and soak the almonds in milk. After they are thoroughly saturated, remove and let them drain on paper towels.

Sponge
1½ scant cups flour
⅔ cup milk
¼ teaspoon instant yeast

Combine the sponge ingredients and mix until they form a ball. Knead for a few minutes. Let it sit at room temperature for 1 to 2 hours.

Dough
1½ cups flour
3 Tablespoons sugar
1 small egg, and 1 egg yolk, separated

1 teaspoon instant yeast
½ teaspoon salt
3½ Tablespoons butter
1 teaspoon lemon zest
Apricot jam
Optional: powdered sugar and milk (for glazing)

Place the sponge, flour, sugar, egg, yeast, and salt in a bowl and mix. Knead for several minutes. Add the butter and lemon zest and knead for several minutes, then add the raisins and almonds, turn out on a floured board, and knead until the dough is smooth and slightly sticky. Form in a mound and let rest for 30 minutes.

Preheat the oven to 390°F and prepare a baking sheet with parchment paper while the dough is resting.

Form the dough into a round loaf and place on the prepared baking sheet. Cover loosely with plastic wrap and let rise for about 45 minutes.

Lightly brush the loaf with beaten egg yolk and score a cross into the top with a sharp knife.

Place a pan with steaming water on the bottom rack of the oven. Place the baking sheet on the next rack. Bake for 30 to 40 minutes, checking several times. When the top starts to become dark, tent with aluminum foil and reduce heart to 350°F for remainder of the bake time. Remove from oven.

Brush the hot loaf with apricot jam and sprinkle with additional slivered almonds. Or cool and glaze with a mix of powdered sugar and milk.

This sweet bread is traditionally eaten on Easter morning.

BAKED FRENCH TOAST

Ingredients
1 loaf French bread
8 eggs
2 ½ cups milk
¼ cup sugar
1 teaspoon cinnamon
1 teaspoon vanilla
Dash of salt

Topping
12 Tablespoons butter or margarine, melted
1 cup brown sugar
1 teaspoon cinnamon
Syrup (optional)

Spray the sides and bottom of a 9 x 13-inch pan with cooking spray. Slice the bread into 1-inch slices and arrange in the pan, overlapping if necessary.

Whisk the eggs thoroughly in a large bowl. Add the milk, sugar, cinnamon, vanilla, and salt and whisk until thoroughly combined.

Pour the egg mixture over the slices and refrigerate overnight.

In the morning, preheat the oven to 350°F. Turn each slice of bread to make sure it is coated with the egg mixture.

Combine the topping ingredients and spoon over the bread, making sure to cover all the slices.

Bake uncovered at 350°F for 30 minutes or until it is puffy and golden brown. Serve while hot with syrup as desired. This makes 8 servings.

Dear Reader,

I hope you'll let me know if you enjoyed my book. You can reach me at marta@martaperry.com, and I'd be happy to send you a bookmark and my brochure of Pennsylvania Dutch recipes. You'll also find me at martaperry.com and on Facebook at Marta Perry Books.

Happy reading,
Marta

Center Point Large Print
600 Brooks Road / PO Box 1
Thorndike, ME 04986-0001 USA

(207) 568-3717

US & Canada:
1 800 929-9108
www.centerpointlargeprint.com